Professor Pfi
and his strange co
and other Portugu̵ese stories
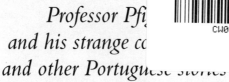

From the Portuguese series

MIGUEL TORGA
Tales and More Tales from the Mountain

JOSÉ RODRIGUES MIGUÉIS
Happy Easter

JOSÉ SARAMAGO
Manual of Painting and Calligraphy

MIGUEL TORGA
*The Creation of the World:
The First Day and the Second Day*

EUGÉNIO LISBOA (editor)
*The Anarchist Banker
and other Portuguese stories*

Professor Pfiglzz
and his strange companion

AND OTHER PORTUGUESE STORIES

Edited by
EUGÉNIO LISBOA

CARCANET

in association with
CALOUSTE GULBENKIAN FOUNDATION
INSTITUTO DA BIBLIOTECA NACIONAL E DO LIVRO
INSTITUTO CAMÕES

This selection first published in 1997 by
Carcanet Press Limited
Conavon Court, 12–16 Blackfriars Street
Manchester M3 5BQ

Preface and selection
Copyright © Eugénio Lisboa 1997
The acknowledgements on p. vii constitute an extension
of this copyright page
The moral right of the authors has been asserted in accordance with the
Copyright, Designs and Patents Act of 1988
All rights reserved

This book belongs to the series *From the Portuguese*,
published in Great Britain by Carcanet Press
in association with the Calouste Gulbenkian Foundation,
and with the collaboration of the Anglo-Portuguese Foundation.
Series Editors: Eugénio Lisboa, Michael Schmidt, L.C. Taylor

A CIP catalogue record for this book is available from the British Library
ISBN 1 85754 241 X

The publisher acknowledges financial assistance
from the Arts Council of England

Set in 11/12pt Bembo by Posthouse Printing and Publishing Ltd, Findhorn
Printed and bound by SRP Ltd, Exeter

CONTENTS

This is the second volume of Portuguese stories. Volume one included stories by Eça de Queirós, Fialho de Almeida, António Patrício, Fernando Pessoa, Irene Lisboa, José Régio and José Rodrigues Miguéis.

ACKNOWLEDGEMENTS

The publishers acknowledge with thanks permission to publish these translations from the following copyright owners:

Domingos Monteiro 'Paternity' from *Contos do Dia e da Noite,* © Domingos Monteiro – Sociedade Portuguesa de Autores, 1997

Branquinho da Fonseca 'O Barão' from *O Barão* © Branquinho da Fonseca - Sociedade Portuguesa de Autores, 1997

Miguel Torga 'Alma-Grande' translated by Ivana Rangel-Carlsen from 'O Alma-Grande' in *Novos Contos da Montanha* thirteenth edition, 1986, © the estate of Miguel Torga. This translation was first published in *More Tales from the Mountain* by Carcanet in 1995 and © Ivana Rangel-Carlsen

Joaquim Paço d'Arcos 'A História de Venâncio, Segundo Oficial' in *Carnaval e Outros Contos,* © Joaquim Paço d'Arcos – Sociedade Portuguesa de Autores, 1997

Manuel da Fonseca 'Maria Altinha' from 'Aldeia Nova', © Editorial Caminho, 1997

José Marmelo e Silva 'Despoimento' from *O Sonho e a Aventura,* © José Marmelo e Silva – Sociedade Portuguesa de Autores, 1997

Maria Judite de Carvalho 'Tanta Gente Mariana' from *Tanta Gente Mariana,* © Maria Judite de Carvalho – Sociedade Portuguesa de Autores, 1997

David Mourão-Ferreira 'E aos Costumes Disse Nada' from *Gaivotas em Terra,* © David Mourão-Ferreira – Sociedade Portuguesa de Autores, 1997

Herberto Helder 'Polícia' from *Os Passos em Volta,* © Herberto Helder – Sociedade Portuguesa de Autores, 1997

Mário de Carvalho 'Definitiva História do Professor Pfiglzz e Seu Estranho Companheiro' from *Contos da Sétima Esfera,* © Edições Rolim, Lisbon, 1981

PREFACE

Portugal, as critics of the stature of Gaspar Simões and Guilherme de Castilho have noted, has been more prolific in authors of short fictions than in full-scale novelists. Castilho, indeed, went so far as to say that there had been only one great Portuguese novelist – inevitably, Eça de Queirós. True, he said this fifty years ago, but even then Teixeira Gomes, Almada Negreiros, José Régio, Aquilino Ribeiro and Camilo Castelo Branco gave him the lie. What no one would dispute, though, is Castilho's reciprocal proposition: that for some reason Portuguese authors have excelled in novellas and 'contos', tales of lyric dimensions. When Castilho made his own excellent anthology of *Os Melhores Contos Portugueses* he speculated in an Introduction that the predilection for shorter works reflected a Portuguese tendency to be hasty, undisciplined, impulsive. Ascribing such characteristics to a whole nation entails, of course, the widest generalisation: Castilho's sits oddly on Portugal's stoic peasants and soldiers, her far-ranging seamen and settlers. However, sticking to literature, I was once struck by a passage in a study by H.E. Bates in which he said of the short story, as a form, that it

> is at once restricted yet free; its range of time and place and movement is necessarily limited, and like drama it is forced back to the use of suggestion, implied action, indirect narration, and symbolism to convey what might otherwise be conveyed by a plain catalogue of solid words.

Now, the Portuguese art, *par excellence*, has been poetry and it is fair to speculate (at the level of literary conversation) that whatever-it-is that has led so many Portuguese authors to embrace the formal constraints and necessary allusiveness of verse has also made them prefer short to long forms of prose; but searching out possible reasons for this preference would require arcane debate and had better detain us no longer.

When making this selection I had first to decide whether to confine it to stories reasonably described as 'short' or to include longer pieces, even one or two verging on the novella. The plain merit of pieces like 'Paternity', 'The Baron', 'And she said nothing' and 'They used to go for long walks on Sunday' settled the matter: the collection would have to run to a wide assortment in length.

Given the overall ration of pages, the inclusion of such longer pieces meant the omission of several shorter ones; selection became yet more difficult. My original 'long-short' list of authors had run to 38: publishing realities meant reducing that number by half. In a few cases I could scrape up some rather arbitrary reason for exclusion: something by the same author was currently available in English (José Cardoso Pires, Fernando Namora), or the obvious story to choose presented particular problems for a translator (Aquilino Ribeiro): but I could not find even such specious arguments for excluding, say, Almada Negreiros, Virgílio Ferreira, Ramalho Ortigão, Trindade Coelho, Sophia de Mello Breyner Andresen, Urbano Tavares Rodrigues, Vitorino Nemésio, Ernesto Leal, Mário Dionísio, Faure de Rosa, Luís de Stau Monteiro, João Palma-Ferreira, João de Melo, Almeida Faria, and so on and on. Since few such riches could be crammed into so tight a space, choice was bound to seem not merely subjective but wilful; all the same, drastic decisions had to be made and, after many vacillations, I was the person condemned to make them. However, I sought consolation in wondering if public demand would induce the publisher to follow these two volumes with a third.

EUGÉNIO LISBOA
London, May 1996

BRIEF LITERARY BIOGRAPHIES

DOMINGOS MONTEIRO (1903–1980) Read Law at university but devoted his life to literature – novels, poetry and above all short stories. His range of subject matter was wide, and included a talent for fantasy.

Main works: Novel: *O Mal e o Bem* (1945). Short stories: *Enfermaria* (1943); *Prisão e Casa Mortuária* (1943); *Contos do Dia e da Noite* (1952); *Histórias Castelhanas* (1955); *Histórias deste Mundo e do Outro* (1961); *O Destino e a Aventura* (1971); *Letícia e o Lobo Júpiter* (1972).

BRANQUINHO DA FONSECA (1905–1974) One of the founding editors of *Presença*, he wrote poetry, novels, plays and, notably, short stories. In his work a basic realism can sometimes strike overtones of the metaphoric, symbolic and mythic as in the powerful and unforgettable long short story, *The Baron*, included in this anthology.

Main works: Novel: *Porta de Minerva* (1947). Short stories: *Caminhos Magnéticos* (1938); *Rio Turvo* (1945); *Bandeira Preta* (1956). Novella: *O Barão* (1943).

MIGUEL TORGA (1907–1995) Wrote movingly of his childhood in a peasant family in remote Trás-os-Montes and of his boyhood on his uncle's plantation in Brazil. Returning to Portugal, he qualified as a doctor at Coimbra and began his practice in his native region. His outspoken description of local conditions led to his imprisonment and the banning of his writing: this was published abroad, in unrelenting opposition, until Salazar's death. He lived to become the doyen of contemporary Portuguese letters, three times nominated by judges for the Nobel Prize.

Main works: Autobiography: *The Creation of the World, Days One to Six* (1937–81); *Diário* (16 volumes 1941–1993). Poetry: *O outro livro de Job* (1936); *Lamentação* (1943); *Penas do Purgatório* (1954); *Poemas Ibéricos* (1965); Short stories: *Contos* (1941) and *Novos Contos da Montanha* (1944); *Bichos* (1940); *Pedras Lavradas* (1951).

JOAQUIM PAÇO D'ARCOS (1908–1979) His early life was spent in Africa and Asia – Angola, Macao and Mozambique, an experience reflected into his fiction. However, it was a cycle of novels depicting different strata of social and political life in Lisbon that brought him fame. He excelled as a short story writer.

Main works: Novel: *Crónica da Vida Lisboeta* (1933–52). Short stories: *O Navio dos Mortos e Outras Novelas* (1952); *Carnaval e Outros Contos* (1958).

MANUEL DA FONSECA (1911–1993) Poet, novelist and short story teller, he vividly depicted scenes of life in the Alentejo.

Main works: Poetry: *Rosa dos Ventos* (1940); *Planície* (1941). Novels: *Cerromaior* (1945); *Seara de Vento* (1958). Short stories: *Aldeia Nova* (1942); *O Fogo e as Cinzas* (1951).

JOSÉ MARMELO E SILVA (1913–1991) A teacher by profession, he dealt with sexual themes in a way unusual at a time of dictatorship in Portugal and managed, in no less daring and subtle a fashion, to edge away from the art-stories of *Presença* towards a neo-realistic, marxist-tinted fiction. Somehow he eluded censorship.

Main works: Novellas and short stories: *Sedução* (1937); *O Sonho e a Aventura* (1943); *Adolescente* (1948).

MARIA JUDITE DE CARVALHO (1921–) A talented writer of short stories, she chiefly portrays a grey and often hopeless world of meanness and frustration, in which the principal victims are women.

Main works: Novellas and short stories: *Tanta Gente Mariana* (1959); *As Palavras Poupadas* (1961 – winner of the Camilo Castelo Branco prize); *Paisagem sem Barcos* (1963); *Os Armários Vazios* (1966); *Flores ao Telefone* (1968).

DAVID MOURÃO-FERREIRA (1927–1996) Outstanding poet, novelist, short story teller, playwright, translator and scholar. A remarkable university professor and one of Portugal's greatest modern essayists and literary critics. From 1976–9 he was Minister of Culture. A key and charismatic figure among Portuguese writers.

Main works: Poetry: *A Secreta Viagem* (1950); *Tempestade de Verão* (1954); *Os Quatro Cantos do Tempo* (1958); *Infinito Pessoal* (1962); *In Memoriam Memoriae* (1962); *Órfico Ofício* (1978). Novels: *Gaivotas em Terra* (1959); *Um Amor Feliz* (1986); Essays and criticism: *Vinte Poetas Contemporâneos* (1960); *Motim Literário* (1962); *Hospital das Letras* (1966); *Tópicos de Crítica e História Literária* (1969); *Sobre Viventes* (1976); *Lâmpadas no Escuro* (1979).

HERBERTO HELDER (1930–) Perhaps Portugal's greatest living poet, and a writer of short stories as well. He blends romanticism with modernism, and uses metaphor to create a strange, fantastic universe.

Main works: Poetry: *Poesia Toda* (1973); *A Cabeça Entre as Mãos* (1982); *Do Mundo* (1994). Short stories: *Os Passos em Volta* (1963).

MÁRIO DE CARVALHO (1944–) One of the most talented and original among contemporary writers, he mixes the most ordinary with the fantastic and surreal to achieve a distinctive atmosphere full of surprise and humour.

Main works: Short stories: *Contos da Sétima Esfera* (1981); *Casos do Beco das Sardinheiras* (1982). Novels: *Era uma Vez um Alferes* (1985); *A Paixão do Conde de Fróis* (1986); *Un Deus Passeando pela Brisa da Tarde* (1994 – winner of the Portuguese Writers' Association Grand Prize for Fiction and the 1996 Pegasus Prize for Literature).

Professor Pfiglzz
and his strange companion
and other Portuguese stories

Domingos Monteiro

PATERNITY

translated by Roberta Fox

I

I had known Dr Silveira for a long time. A small man, thin, communicative; many were the times I'd laughed to myself, remembering the jokes he used to tell his numerous friends, sitting at the table next to mine. Dr Silveira always had a joke or a comment. To some extent, we were already on intimate terms by the time we met, brought about by long frequenting of the same café.

When, much later, on holiday in Ericeira, without any formal introduction, he addressed me, by my name – 'Antunes, how are you?' – and immediately after acquainted me with his wife, Dona Lucília, I wasn't surprised.

He knew my name, what I did for a living, and even that I had just qualified with a rather high grade.

With the greatest of ease, and almost as if he had been present, he explained to his wife that I had written a brilliant exam and that it would naturally follow that the University would encourage me to read for a doctorate and take up a lectureship.

'Don't say that, Dr Silveira,' I protested self-consciously, embarrassed by his having guessed my innermost heart's desires. 'Don't say that…'

But he cut short my protests. With an unquestionable logic, he proved, from A to B, that it could not be otherwise, and that in the wink of an eye, after having revealed what my teachers thought of me – it seemed he was on familiar terms with the majority of them – he masterminded a plan for my future, so joyous and pleasant that I could only feel flattered and grateful.

'Thank you, Dr Silveira, thank you very much…'

'And now, Antunes, after my holiday, hands to the task… With your personality, what you must go for is theory. You're more inclined towards dialectical discourse than to the mean little argumentations involved in court cases. Your strength lies in visualising, not observing. What's more, your whole family has never done otherwise. And you're all alike.'

My amazement grew. Dr Silveira, with whom I had never spoken and whose only relationship with me was based on us being frequenters of the same café, knew everything about me: not only the most hidden aspects of my personality, but even the ways of my family – who rarely came up to Lisbon – and who went about their peaceful, almost vegetable like existence, in a lost village in the faraway Trás-os-Montes plateau.

For three quarters of an hour, he spoke in that frenetic style of his, so characteristic of him – and with which I was only too familiar from hearing his high pitched voice, from the corner of the café where I used to isolate myself to write or study – carving out my personal future, in all its minutiae, without forgetting – God forbid – to arrange a wife for me, a suitable girl, full of virtues and endowed also, not least appetisingly, with worldly goods…

'Lucília, what do you think of Rosita?'

Dona Lucília didn't agree. Rosita was too lively, too fanciful, with a difficult temperament. Maria de Guadalupe seemed to her a better choice: a more solid fortune and a more even temperament.

Now Dona Lucília was also concerning herself with me and my fate. While she spoke, she would look at me with that fond rapture, reserved for young men, very peculiar to comfortable, fleshy, middle-aged ladies.

Undaunted, Dr Silveira adopted the second hypothesis:

'You are right, Lucília, you are absolutely right…'

You could see that Dona Lucília occupied a prime position in Dr Silveira's life. Even more: Dona Lucília was one of those women who always occupy pride of place no matter where they are – one of those people who when faced with her own small worries, by comparison render insignificant the great tragedies in life.

Without regard for my enforced silence, it was immediately arranged – or better still, the two of them arranged – the manner of introduction and almost the date for the wedding. Since my stay in Ericeira, I and Dr Silveira had become inseparable friends.

It is almost needless for me to say that I never applied for the lecture-ship, or married Guadalupe. Her sad and earnest eyes coupled with her substantial fortune, were not enough to make me overcome my unconquerable aversion to marriage. I think the girl suffered as a result, because Dona Lucília and mainly Dr Silveira, had painted such a bright picture of me, in such flattering colours, well before I was introduced to her, that she was expecting me to be her sort of Prince Charming, right out of a love story.

The 'flirtation', started as a result of the imperious suggestion and powerful input of the Silveiras, became lost in the shadows and fog of Sintra – where Guadalupe had spent the summer and where Silveira had a home – cushioned by the indecision of vague words and loose promises, right at the beginning of October, and as if shrouded by the dry leaves of fruitless trees…

II

For a few months I kept away from Dr Silveira. A sort of remorse – I was convinced they were feeling, he and Dona Lucília, a huge disappointment – made me avoid their company, and I even abandoned the café we both frequented.

But it was written that between myself and Dr Silveira would be established the greatest and strongest intimacy, and one spring afternoon as I was walking up the Avenue ruminating, with the despair of a neophyte, a legal issue which I had been called upon to resolve, the end of a walking stick punctured my ribs and an avalanche of hugs and words fell upon me before I could overcome my surprise.

Dr Silveira was standing in front of me, dressed in light-coloured clothes, with a red carnation in his lapel, small and full of trepidation as always.

'My dear friend…' I mumbled. But, before I could completely articulate the excuse which I was frantically trying to fabricate, Dr Silveira interrupted me:

'My man, what's become of you?' – and without waiting for an answer he continued: 'No, don't say anything… I know… So, you have a practice and brilliant cases! What one would call an auspicious start to a career!… I always said you would be a star… That remark you made in the defence of the man who ran over and fatally wounded the traffic policeman, was astounding! "Sic transit gloria mundi!" Bravo!'

I went red with embarrassment. The phrase, apart from being out of proportion and cruel, was, in that instance, in unbelievably bad taste. What was right, though, was that I had shone in court and it had even reached my friend's ears. He continued to know everything about my life: where my office was and what it looked like, who my colleagues were, and that I'd already abandoned the idea of a doctorate.

'There I think you've made a mistake. And I don't mean just because of you. The Faculty needed somebody to introduce some fresh air into its spirit. It's more and more academic. And you were just the right person for the job...'

I was about to protest when Dr Silveira, in a serious voice and holding my arm, continued:

'I'll tell you who is very angry with you. Lucília! And she has some reason to be...'

I thought he was talking about Guadalupe and I started apologising.

'You know, Doctor, Guadalupe and I had very different personalities. I thought it better and more loyal...'

But Dr Silveira didn't allow me to continue:

'Oh my friend, it has nothing to do with Guadalupe! Both Lucília and I thought you did the right thing. Just between you and me, as no one else is listening: Guadalupe is a nice girl, but she's nothing more than a tiny insect. She wasn't right for you. You hardly need a woman who makes quince jam, embroiders tiny pillows with peasant motifs, gets your slippers for you in winter... What you need is a woman, a real woman...' Dr Silveira did not explain what he meant by the term 'real woman', and continued: 'No. That's not why Lucília feels hurt. Lucília never gets angry because of the things we do to others, but because of the things done to her. You promised to give her news... and you didn't. You promised to come for dinner with us every Saturday... and you haven't. And you haven't even phoned.'

'You are absolutely right,' I mumbled, 'but...'

'There are no ifs and buts,' interrupted Dr Silveira. 'Just phone her and don't fail to turn up next Saturday...'

We had got to the top of the Avenue. Night had fallen and there was a little fresh wind beginning to blow in from the North. Here and there lights were going on. And I was beginning to get an urge to have dinner and was looking for a pretext to say goodbye:

'Right, Saturday...' I repeated. His face became serious and it was with a deep and cavernous voice that he said:

'You know, Luís, I am very worried, very worried...'

I was used to Dr Silveira's verbosity and the speed with which he would jump from serious matters to light hearted ones, or vice versa.

But, this time, his dramatic tone touched me. What's more as it was the first time he had called me by my first name, it gave his words a tone of shocking intimacy, almost poignant.

'Very worried, why!' I asked, seriously interested.

'Can't you see the tragedy looming? Can't you see?'

I looked at him, truly amazed.

'What tragedy, Dr Silveira?'

My tone was lightly ironic, and the revelation of this imaginary and unknown danger didn't impress me.

My friend was aware of this underlying irony:

'Ah, the irresponsibility of youth!'

His hissing words, as on previous occasions, began to amuse me but also to intrigue me:

'Better say children, Doctor!'

Ignoring my interruption, Dr Silveira went on speaking for some time, in that vague and allegoric tone peculiar to him. Little by little, I began to grasp his thinking but I decided to let the rhetorical storm blow over in order to insist:

'What Apocalypse, is it that you fear?'

'The war, man!... The war!'

We were in the spring immediately preceding the last conflict. The clouds thickened over the horizon. The signs of an impending war were more than obvious, but the truth is that I had never taken them seriously, nor weighted up their significance.

'Let's presume there will be a war,' I replied in a doubtful tone, 'so what?'

'So what? That's rich! Can't you see the risk Mankind will run? Just think for a moment if Hitler wins, which if it isn't probable, is at least possible... Do you realise what it means?'

I shook my head as a sign of ignorance.

'You don't know? Another Middle Ages. An 800 year regression. The Latins enslaved, even the Anglo-Saxons, despite their germanic blood – even they – relegated to second class... But, even if he loses, that will not mean we will escape mass destruction, the loss of millions of lives, our civilisation shaken. In brief, misfortune, suffering and death!...'

As I noticed later, there was something prophetic in my friend's words, but at the time I did not sense it. Being young, his doom-like and abstract predictions did not mean anything to me, and I still did not understand why he was so distressed by a remote theory.

'Oh Doctor, I don't understand,' I ventured. 'Fine that you should be upset by this rather speculative prospect... but to this extent! Amongst the dead and the injured, some will manage to get away. And one of them,' I joked, 'will be you, Dr Silveira, as you're beyond conscription age.'

'So you think that's what bothers me?' he answered in a solemn tone and slightly shaky. 'I have already given what I had to give. It is not for my sake, but for everything it represents for my universe. For all of you. And, what's more, I have a reason to worry, do you understand?'

Surprised, I asked:

'A reason, a personal reason?'

'Very personal...' He lowered his voice, and took on a confidential tone. 'As you know, England will be the first to be targeted in the conflict. She will be the one to have to make the greatest sacrifices... and that is what bothers me in particular.'

My degree of surprise went up a notch.

'But Doctor, you are Portuguese,' I objected.

'I know. But John is English and he's going to be twenty... Do you understand now?'

I understood even less. I had known Dr Silveira for a long time, and had communed with him privately over two years and I had never heard him speak of John. Not Dr Silveira, nor Dr Silveira's wife, nor any of his close friends. Truly surprised, I asked:

'John? But who is this John, Doctor? I think that in England, if we just start with John Bull, there are millions of Johns...'

'I know. But only one is my son...'

I fell from the clouds. That to me, was the greatest of all surprises. I had always heard that Dr Silveira had no children. Even more, that it was one of his greatest regrets. He had said so, Dona Lucília had said it herself, sadly: 'Ricardo never forgave me for not giving him a child. But the Lord did not will it.' And now, suddenly, Dr Silveira appeared to be a father and with all the anxious worries of a loving parent. My astonishment knew no bounds:

'And you never said a thing, Doctor! A son! That's a good one!...'

Dr Silveira had taken my arm and almost whispered into my ear, in a broken voice:

'Yes, my friend... A son! A big boy! Tall and blond like you! With blue eyes just like yours! And no one knows this in Portugal. Not even Lucília, not Rocha' (Rocha was their physician and his closest friend) 'no one... We all have one secret in life, and this is my secret. You are the first I have told and maybe you will be the only one. I have the greatest trust in you.'

I felt flattered, but at the same time perturbed. Dr Silveira had lost for me, that anecdotal characteristic which despite his true intelligence and the real affection linking us, made me think of him as a spinner of tales. This newly shared secret, created between us a new kind of intimacy, and in my eyes Dr Silveira had become a greater and more humane figure.

In a solemn and moved tone, assumed when undertaking promises one later breaks, I reiterated:

'And you can, Doctor. I certainly will not be the one to tell anyone.'

III

From that day onwards John, like a hidden divinity, came to dominate all our meetings, which served to confirm all of Dr Silveira's predictions, turning each time more intense.

The war broke out in September, and Dr Silveira's story, which was only revealed in a rather long circuitous route, and over a period of days, gradually lost its romantic aura to assume a dramatic dimension.

Dr Silveira had met Kitty, John's mother, in Coimbra, twenty-one years before. Kitty was an idealist who had fallen in love with the poetry of Browning and had decided to attend a summer school in Coimbra to learn Portuguese, and read Camões in the original.

At the beginning she was a nebulous figure but later, as evoked by Dr Silveira, she acquired such clarity and precision that I could see her with her golden tresses, periwinkle eyes, a white lily in her slender hands, walking in the moonlight through the medieval streets of Coimbra. I could hear her mumble poetry in her Portuguese spoken with mixed up genders and numbers – verses Dr Silveira repeated, in earnest mimicry, sticking to the distortions – and which in this way, heard from a distance of twenty years, were like dried leaves stuck between the ancient pages of a book of memoirs. There was something both ridiculous and poignant in that recollection, to such an extent that he remained caught between a glimmer of a smile and a tear, without knowing which to opt for. During the long winter nights, and on Saturdays when I went there for dinner, after Lucília had gone to bed and retired to her rooms, a peculiar kind of dialogue would start up between us during which

I was more than just someone to speak to, rather an interested and keen listener. It was as if Dr Silveira was taking a walk along a long memory lane, leaning on my arm, picking now and again, so as to be reminded of an old scent, an old wilting flower. And it all resembled the embodiment of ghosts to such an extent, that I secretely classified those meetings of ours in the library, near the open fire and facing the small table on which, like a friendly genie, rested the old whisky bottle, as our 'seances'.

From our first chance encounter in the Botanical Gardens to the long nocturnal walks along the winding streets of Old Coimbra, along the Beira Road and the Choupal, I witnessed the unfolding of the unlikely alliance between the nordic sylph and the southern Don Juan. Little by little the wintry Saxon resistance gave way and finally succumbed, like a spring frost, to the burning rapture of Italian enthusiasm. During Dr Silveira's passionate and simultaneously bellicose recollection, there existed a paradoxical mixture of amorous amazement and a racial struggle. His attitude veered between the romantic lover and the conqueror of a city, but I was neither aware of the contradictions nor of the excesses. Faced with the enchantment of his eloquence, it all seemed natural to me and I didn't even question how he, so small and fragile, had managed to carry for quite a few kilometres in his nervous and delicate arms the athletic and robust virgin he had described, until they had reached the small hidden house among the shady fronds, in the outskirts of Coimbra, where the first amorous sacrifice had been consummated…

At first just a whisper, Dr Silveira's confidences reached at times a dangerous intensity and pitch ill suited to the cautiousness appropriate to an intimate secret. That is why at intervals I found myself forced to remind him:

'Careful my friend. Lucília could be listening.'

Lucília was however used to her husband's loud voice accompanying the rhetorical whirlwind lasting the entire night. That was the manifestation of his presence at home, and it almost became like a narcotic, not unlike the sound machines make, heard at night by watchmen in factories.

'Don't worry,' he replied. 'She can't hear. Lucília does everything with conviction. Even sleeping.'

Our conversation would sometimes last until three or four in the morning, and it wasn't unusual for Dr Silveira to insist on accompanying me home, filling the silence of the streets, to the amazement of passersby, with the echo of his tirades, be they lyrical, or point-edly dramatic. It was one night in December under the light of a streetlamp – those gas lights, then still so numerous, and which today are but a romantic reminder in the city streets – that Dr Silveira told me the tale of their separation.

It was a cloudy night, full of crosswinds, punctuated by a falling star here and there, with a nasty frosty breeze, penetrating and sharp which made for fast walking. I had already understood his need to go out, that same impatience which always preceded his serious confessions. Several times he had walked up to the window and praised, quite disproportionately, in his flowery style, the salutary and virile charm of winter evenings. As for me who was already dreaming of the pleasures of leaving the warm corner of the room in the comfort of a taxi which would carry me to the cosiness of my bed, I was abruptly pulled out of my daydreaming by his sudden decision:

'What if we went for a walk? Isn't it just asking for it?'

It was already well after two in the morning, and although I knew what it would entail, a sort of long distance running, like two delayed messengers, through the deserted streets, suddenly coming to an abrupt half in front of some doorway, I dared not refuse him and accepted passively:

'How right you are Doctor. Let's go.'

After wandering the streets in silence, during a good half hour, Dr Silveira suddenly came to a stop:

'It was on a night like this,' he started. And without sparing me the description of the night itself, which to make matters more colourful, would be zigzagged by distant lightning, he continued: 'I already knew she had to leave, summoned by a command of her father's and that we had exhausted to the very end, the permissible deadline. It was only then I discovered Kitty was pregnant. At the age of twenty-five' – by my reckoning, Dr Silveira at the time must have been slightly older – 'I did not anticipate the tragedy implied, nor did I feel the joy I would feel today: now that I know father-hood to be the best and noblest prolonging of Life. A mother gives birth to a child and loves it physiologically, a little like an animal does. A father loves it with his intellect. The mother conceives it, the father dreams and idealizes it. Maternal love is a consequence of instinct. Fatherly love is a state of mind…' My friend's face had trans-formed itself. And I, despite the cold and the discomfort of the hour, felt moved and duty bound to console him, not that I knew why.

'Poor Dr Silveira!' I murmured.

My friend agreed:

'Yes, you can say poor again, but for another reason. At the time I behaved like a bastard and a coward. I was not aware of the transcendence and solemnity of the occasion. I was also not conscious that I had created an inescapable and sacred duty, I only thought selfishly of escaping complications. She had confessed it to me, simply and without making a single demand. But like any other woman, be she Portuguese, English or Chinese – she expected something from me. She surely expected from me a promise of marriage which any truly self-respecting man would not hesitate to have made... But I wasn't able to make it. I was already committed to Lucília, my heart divided – just between you and me since no one can hear us now – unequally and unfairly. It didn't occur to me that she had a greater claim, I could only see the commitment I'd made which stood between us like an insurmountable wall. Lucília represented for me the calm and reasonable tenderness which leads to propriety and stability. Kitty, although I cared for her sincerely, was synonymous with adventures and dreams without a tomorrow. Like a lot of other people, I divided women into two categories, without remembering that they too have the same joys and sadnesses, and for that very reason should have the same privileges. I suggested to her then the customary solution amongst so-called well-to-do people, applicable to problems of this nature. She did not immediately understand and I repeated: "You could..." and I repeated slowly the repulsive suggestion. She understood, livid. She stood up, from the bench in the little garden, on which we were seated. She protected her womb with her two hands and looked at me as if I was a murderer. Suddenly, she broke into a run towards the road as if she were an animal being pursued. With a great deal of difficulty I managed to catch her. I then knelt, wept, begged. I had no idea of the seriousness of what I had said, only the effect my words had had. Little by little she calmed down and as she was in love with me, she forgave me in the end. But as far as the child was concerned, she remained unshakeable: "You have lost the right to this child, do you understand?... It will just be my child... just mine." I agreed without any difficulty: "Fine. It will just be yours". The truth is that at the time – pathetic and unaware as I was! – the child meant little or nothing to me. What mattered to me were the consequences for her. "And what are you going to tell your parents? Your family? Your father?" Full of the Latin prejudice governing sexual honour, it was above all her position vis-à-vis her father that distressed me: "Yes, your father?"

'She remained silent for a moment, and then she smiled, with that inimitable smile, discreet and subtle like perfume... "I will say... yes... I will say the father was a ray of sun..."'

Dr Silveira's face had changed and there was in him a mixture of pride, anxiety and at the same time something which I can only qualify as a sort of transcendent humility.

IV

That night Dr Silveira didn't say another word on this matter, and I didn't dare ask him anything else. But if the truth be known I was dying to know what had happened, with that hungry curiosity which is both my best quality and my worst fault. As was his wont, he quite unexpectedly raised the subject again a few days later:

'Don't you want to know the rest?'

'Of course I do.'

We were seated in his office, near the fire and the mood was completely different to what it had been the night of his first revelation. However, Dr Silveira continued with the greatest of ease as if the fortnight between the beginning of the confession and the present moment hadn't passed.

'In the few months after her departure, I wrote to her several times but received no answer. Finally, my letters were returned with a message informing me that no person of that name resided at that address. I lost interest, and my engagement followed by my marriage to Lucília contributed largely to my distress. For four years – four years of incomprehensible selfishness – I did not give the matter a thought. I did not know whether she was alive or dead or if a child had been born or not. And the truth is that I was almost indifferent to it. But one day I started worrying about Lucília's infertility. Discreetly I would ask if there was "anything the matter", and faced with her melancholic denial, I felt possessed of a feeling of bitterness and anxiety difficult to describe. And one final day...' My friend remained silent for a few moments, and in his lively and dry eyes suddenly the beginning of a tear could be seen.

'Oh Doctor!' I said moved. And despite my sharp curiosity, I suggested generously: 'Leave it for now...'

'No. It's good for me to get it off my chest...'

I didn't insist and Dr Silveira continued:

'... And one fine day, something happened which didn't look as if it was connected with this in any way, which goes to prove that God does write in crooked lines. Lucília fired the maid and found another one. I, who never meddle in these household matters, found it quite normal that she didn't consult me. So, when at dinner time I saw a pale girl serve at table, I limited myself to raising my eyebrows inquiringly. Lucília seized the moment she left the room to explain: "I couldn't stand the other one another minute. This one knows her job and she seems to be a good girl. But there is a problem here that only you can solve..." I protested: "Me? It's your business." The maid came in again and she whispered: "No, no. I'll tell you later". When we finished our dinner she said: "This girl has a child, a four year old, and I don't know whether you want children here in the house..." I made an evasive gesture as if I didn't care one way or the other and said: "It's your decision." I don't know why but although I felt upset I didn't dare oppose her. Our home is her domain and I never interfere. Still, she must have been aware of my unease, and with the shame typical of a childless woman, added: "I'm also not very happy about it. It reminds me..." She didn't finish her sentence but went on to justify herself: "Well... I felt sorry for her. She doesn't want to be apart from the child and that makes it very difficult to find a job. On top of that she's not even married. The man left her before the birth and married someone else. He never even saw the child. He doesn't even know whether it was ever born, if it's a boy or a girl." "Unbelievable! Such villains in this world," I shouted, truly outraged. Hardly had I uttered the words, that I went pale. My wife mistook my outrage and said tenderly: "Not everyone is like you, Richard..." It was like rubbing salt in the wound. I agreed meekly: "Yes; they're not all like me..." I felt myself to be the lowliest and most cowardly creature in the Universe. With that sentence, from the depth of my conscience, I had defined myself... I, a man with the reputation of being good and honourable, a role model – at least in Lucília's eyes – was nothing more than the worst kind of scoundrel... Yes, I too had abandoned a pregnant woman and married another. I also didn't know whether my child had been born or not, boy or girl. Like the maid's child, mine had never known its father... It is true to say that Kitty was rich – or I presumed she was – and that the maid was poor, but morally speaking, the dilemma was the same. Those four years of peaceful happiness, were nothing more than four years of unconsciousness, four years of utter disgrace. Added to my remorse, I felt this absurd longing for my child, this child of mine who for four years had grown up invisibly, both inside and outside myself. I had this urge to tell Lucília everything, come what may. Like a Dostoievsky character, my deepest desire was to own up and be publicly humiliated. But I didn't have the guts. My eyes were brimming with tears of despair and rage – tears which Lucília interpreted favourably, in her own way: "Don't worry, Richard. You're too good…" At that moment – God forgive me – I almost hated her, and my drama, my real drama on that day…' The very next week, he continued, he started inventing a pretext to go to England. 'It was the first time I had travelled without my wife, and I had some difficulty convincing her. But Lucília believes everything I tell her and in the end she agreed to it. And so I went, to no avail. She no longer lived in her old house which was a private home and had been sold shortly after Kitty had returned to England. From the surname of the vendor, I gathered it must have belonged to her father, and I came to a typically Portuguese conclusion, that they had gone into hiding to cover up their "shame" in some isolated corner in the provinces. For ten years – I who had to appear happy and carefree so as not to have to confess to Lucília my secret – went to England countless times, but always in vain. They were ten years of sheer anxiety, until one day…'

Dr Silveira stopped, and over his face marked with vertical lines, passed a sort of shadow, all the drama of his past. He remained staring with a vacant, absent look while I, full of curiosity, insisted:

'Until one day Doctor… Until one day…'

His eyes suddenly shining and his face alive again, as if all the tiredness had disappeared in an instant, Dr Silveira took up the thread of the story again:

'Until one day chance favoured me. I went into a museum in London to look at an exhibition of Egyptian pottery (as you know pottery has always been one of my passions) when I saw her walking in front of me with that walk like the floating sylph she had always seemed to me, as if walking on clouds. I saw her from the back, but there was no mistaking her. She, with the same youth of before, as if those ten years hadn't gone by, only her eyes were more serious, less humorous. "Kitty," I whispered. "I beg your pardon." She looked at me with total indifference, as if she had never seen me before. There was so much coldness, so much disinterest in those eyes that someone else would have hesitated. But I couldn't allow myself that and was determined to use the opportunity. "Kitty, forgive me, but I want to see my child." She pretended not to understand: "I don't understand." And she tried to move away. I, however cut her exit and grabbed her by the wrists. Some of the visitors looked at us with that cold curiosity of the English, and a museum guard, suspecting something odd, came closer ready to intervene. "Look, Kitty, I am ready for anything even a scandal, to go to the police and be arrested if necessary, but I want to see my child." She had a moment's indecision which I used to tell her: "I have rights under British Law, and if you oppose me I will go to court..." I had no idea whether this was true or not, but it is fair to say that my words had made an impression. I felt wretched, but in order to see my child, I was ready to commit any unspeakable act, including threatening my own victim. Furthermore a great joy filled my soul. My child existed! My child was alive! I was a father! I felt very proud. My child! "Come," she said, "but on one condition: you are going to see *my* child not *yours*. Do you hold to this?" "I swear," I said ready to accept anything.'

Dr Silveira's face transformed itself. The real man, the eternal man, who hides his permanent desire for continuity and infinity, I saw for the first time. The Dr Silveira I had known, the frivolous story-teller, had vanished and been replaced by another being with neater and more expressive traits. Paternal love, the authenticity and depth of which I had always questioned, because of a thousand year tradition giving maternal love an essential and almost exclusive pre-eminence, was obvious at that moment. Moved, but also proud, of what I am not quite sure, I hugged Dr Silveira. The existence of that hidden life, endowed him in my eyes, with some sort of superiority.

In the meantime, Dr Silveira continued to unravel his secret:

'During all this time I have been "a friend of his father's", a father of whom I painted a rather flattering portrait. Almost every year I go to London, and Lucília has already become used to this annual pilgrimage of mine which I justify under various pretexts. And don't think Kitty is the attraction! The only thing binding us, but which also separates us, is the existence of the child we had together. I have managed to make friends with him, because there isn't between us that sort of wariness, inhibition, which usually distances a son from his father, during the period of adolescence. The time we spend together is for me a joy tinged with bitterness, and despite everything, I have already read in his eyes, a vague suspicion. But as much as that might be my heart's deepest desire, I would never be the one to confirm it. Apart from being an act of betrayal, I would risk destroying the image of the father I created. He is my son, and I don't want to lose him in any way because one can lose a child. Do you understand now why I fear the war? Do you understand, my friend?'

'I understand,' I nodded solemnly. 'I understand very well.'

In fact I was beginning to understand, and for the first time the image of the war assumed in my eyes – via John whom I didn't even know – its true and tragic expression.

V

The war continued with alternative periods of discouragement and hope, but the outcome appeared more hopeful now for England and its allies.

Dr Silveira had filled his house with maps and on Saturdays gave me lessons in fictitious strategy based mainly on a summary knowledge of military positions and technical reasons, which either made me smile with sceptical irony, or made me stand with my mouth agape faced with such erudition. The house had been filling up with books on the subject including Foch's *Memoirs* and Napoleon's soporific *Memoirs in Saint Helena*, both books I did not believe anyone except Dr Silveira – whom I with affectionate malice had nicknamed General Silveira – capable of reading. Both books he seemed to know by heart, when he needed to find a quotation to justify his arguments.

It was rare for a week to go by during which he was not responsible for a landing or the annihilation of an army corps, in short, either the total destruction of enemy fortifications or, by devising unassailable tactics, winning a resounding victory.

He used miniature flags to illustrate his strategic thinking, moving their position constantly and rapidly across the map, and I followed with interested eyes those giddy military manoeuvres which Dr Silveira would justify with irrefutable evidence.

'Do you see this light artillery battalion, here on number 82? Well, my dear, with this bayonet charge positioned on the right' – Dr Silveira still believed in bayonet charges and couldn't do without them – 'the enemy troops face a fatal dilemma.' Dr Silveira's dilemmas usually had three solutions, either to be knifed in the back, shot with a machine gun, or give up in total disgrace…

And he would use his influence, advance in three rows or tactically withdraw, a measure he would only resort to after serious consideration and most reluctantly as it just wasn't his personality.

'Do you know what all these generals are lacking, in spite of their competence? Audacity, my friend, and above all imagination.'

I would agree with him enthusiastically. And although this make believe war of his, far removed from the battlefields, without mutilated bodies and destroyed cities, was similar to a chess game, I felt it had something dramatic about it, a sort of childish cover-up of a deep-seated anxiety. Deep down the cause of all this agitation was the thought of John, the fear of the dangers John, almost of conscription age, would definitely face. Dr Silveira wanted to end this war before then, and availing himself of a thousand year old and traditional process of magic, gradually, for lack of anything better, destroyed the enemy on paper in the comfort of his office. This is why Dr Silveira's war moved me, even before it would take on its tragic human aspect later.

One Saturday evening upon my return from a holiday in the north, I came to find Dr Silveira's library completely altered.

On top of the tables, in the deepest recesses of his shelves, and even hanging from the ceiling, there were aeroplane models of all shapes and sizes, from the daring 'Hunters' to fat bombers. Even the paper weight on his desk, was a small metallic plane perched on a globe – a symbol of the aviation dominating the world.

I had already noticed during dinner, that Dr Silveira's strategic plans had changed radically. The infantry which until then, in his opinion, would be the decisive victory factor, had been relegated to a secondary position, and now only aerial superiority would decide the winner. Judging from the impatience with which Dr Silveira was anticipating Dona Lucília's exit – who on that day out of kindness towards me had stayed a little longer to chat – he had already foreseen a 'stab in the back'. In the eyes of the increasingly larger Dona Lucília, the war did not have great significance. She was much more interested in life's small everyday details than in anything related to that monstrous and distant war. Several times she had interrupted her husband's enthusiastic suggestions, with enquiries about my personal life: how I'd spent my holidays, the health of my relatives, and the ups and downs of my love life (Dona Lucília had not given up on the idea of finding me a wife) to the point of scolding him:

'All you talk about from morning to night is the war! And the hatred you feel for the Germans! It hasn't even occurred to you that they too are mortal… and you don't care about anything else!… Nothing else…'

One could see that Dona Lucília considered the war to be some sort of rival and she wasn't able to hide her resentment.

When well after eleven o'clock Dona Lucília finally went up to bed, my friend's impatience reached its limit. He abruptly leapt up from the sofa, came at me and whispered in my ear.

'Lucília doesn't understand anything about the anxiety I feel, and I can't explain it to her. It's horrible to have to hide my secret like this!... I couldn't wait for you to get here...'

From the exalted way Dr Silveira was speaking I sensed immediately that something had transpired while I had been on holiday. Apprehensively I asked him:

'What has happened, Doctor?'

'What has happened?' He stuttered which was always a sign of violent emotions. 'What has happened? Something terrible! What I feared most, John has enlisted in the Royal Air Force.'

From that moment on, John's military career was truly spectacular. After three months, he went into combat for the first time and shot down two enemy aircraft. In his fourth month he was promoted to lieutenant. In the fifth awarded the Military Cross.

Dr Silveira's excitement had reached such exalted heights that, if it had not been grounded on such stirring motives, it would have assumed in the eyes of any sensible person profoundly ridiculous proportions. Dr Silveira's library had been changed into something beyond description, with cardboard sheets used as landing fields, traffic lights, hangars, little wooden blocks became aeroplane bombs, and sometimes even a bombarded city, with red lights simulating a fire following an air raid. When he described John's battles, it was as if he had been there and he, Dr Silveira, would be flying, going to such pathetic acrobatic lengths, that I worried about him. Dr Silveira would go up in the air into a 'vrille', drop like a falling leaf into 'loopings', and simultaneously imitate the battles with the accompanying furious sound effects of engines, machine gun firing, the roaring of anti-aircraft grenades and many a time the sound of the crash made by an enemy plane's impact on hitting the ground.

And all this was guided by a running commentary and a precise and detailed report as if he had seen, truly witnessed, what had happened.

The quieter days were reserved for solemn occasions. We saw John praised in front of the regiment in formation, John leaving an aeroplane after a heroic battle, the captain awaiting him, or even John being decorated by the younger Princess, dressed like a 'hussar', and receiving from her virginal lips, on his cheeks flushed with emotion, the honourable and sweet 'accolade' to the sounds of 'God Save the King', which Dr Silveira would hum.

At the beginning of the summer, John was promoted to Wing Commander, and Dona Lucília, who sometimes was awakened by the above mentioned bizarre sounds, started getting worried. One Saturday, when I arrived at their home a little bit earlier than usual, and Dr Silveira had been delayed, distracted by all the Rossio billboards; Dona Lucília took advantage of the moment to share her unease with me.

'I don't know what's wrong with Ricardo. He's really possessed at the moment: he can't sleep, he won't let me sleep. Aviation has gone to his head, he even dreams about it aloud. I'm really getting quite worried.'

I tried to comfort her:

'Dona Lucília, you know what your husband is like, full of passion and enthusiasm. You know how worked up he gets. Don't worry, it will blow over. It isn't too serious.'

But Dona Lucília was not convinced.

'No, my friend. I've known Ricardo for many years and I have never seen him like this. He is out of control, and there is something here I don't get.'

Despite her innocence, Dona Lucília was beginning to suspect something and I felt it my duty to communicate to the husband the wife's suspicions.

'You should be careful, Doctor,' I concluded.

He heard me in silence – which in his case was a sign of deep concern – and agreed:

'You are right my friend, this cannot go on like this.'

I thought his reaction was perfectly normal and I did not understand the profound, almost prophetic significance his words would assume later.

VI

As usual, the holidays interrupted our time together, and for two months – since neither he nor I were letter writers – I had no news of Dr Silveira. I would only get those later – and in the most unusual and unexpected way – via a telephone call from Dona Lucília. From her sombre and low tones, I immediately understood that something serious and deeply personal had happened. I must confess that I thought of everything, except the obvious.

'Come, my friend, come as soon as possible,' she pleaded almost begging. 'Only you can distract Ricardo. You are the only person he speaks about constantly…'

'But is he ill?' I asked carefully.

'No. Not exactly. He has had very bad news.'

Like a flash it came to me, and the thought of John struck me like lightning. Something has happened to him, I thought. But in that case Dona Lucília must already know about John…

In the meantime, I decided cautiously not to give away anything and only asked:

'What bad news, Dona Lucília?'

'I will tell you later… Come early so you can speak to me first.'

'All right, Dona Lucília. I will come early.'

And I did.

Dona Lucília received me in her small sitting room, her 'sanctuary' as she called it, reserved especially for her close relatives and family secrets. She got up when I came in, but remained in darkness, so that I could hardly make out her face or what she was wearing.

'Oh, my friend, how grateful I am to you.'

I now began to trace her pale features and the black clothing and I felt a pang in my heart, a feeling of doom which made my mouth dry. But I did not dare ask anything.

'John,' she started hesitantly. 'John died…'

My fears and my suspicions had been confirmed: John had died and Dona Lucília knew everything. Prompted by a ridiculous impulse, I bent down, took hold of her hands, kissed them, while my eyes filled with tears.

'Poor boy!' I mumbled.

'So young!' she whispered. 'I did not know him, but it's as if he had been a son of mine! And for twenty years not a word! Ah, men! I should have been angry with Ricardo but I didn't have the courage. Who knows what he has suffered!'

Only then did I remember the main character in this drama and cautiously I enquired:

'Where is your husband?'

'He went to Sintra but he must be on his way back. Since John's death, he goes there every day. The farm manager tells me he roams alone amongst the trees. I am always anxious until he gets back.'

A painful curiosity spurred me on:

'And when did John die? How did he find out?'

'A month ago. He read it in the Portuguese press.' She got up, walked to the desk and handed me a newspaper cutting. 'Have a look…'

ENGLISH PILOT'S GLORIOUS DEATH

Squadron Leader John Colley's aircraft, following a serious battle during which he downed five enemy fighter planes, crash landed in the vicinity of Newcastle. The heroic pilot died instantly.

I read and re-read the article, and in my distress, I did not even notice the door opening, and Dr Silveira coming in. It was Dona Lucília who brought it to my attention.

'Ricardo…' I whispered.

Only then did I make out the tragic dark figure in the doorway. Still holding the article in my hand I walked up to him. Without a word, Doctor Silveira fell into my arms and sobbed convulsively on my shoulder.

VII

Little by little Dr Silveira was resigning himself to the situation, at least superficially. The initial despondency had been followed by an eloquent exaltation, more true to his nature. The mood of heavy sadness had been dispelled and it felt at times as if John had been brought back to life. From one day to the next, my friend had exchanged his heavy mourning clothes for his usual light coloured suits and colourful ties.

'It's in honour of my friends,' he had explained.

He and Dona Lucília had decided on an explanation between them, saying a nephew of theirs had died and only she stuck to a discreet touch of mourning and a melancholic reserve; I did not know whether it was due to John's death or her marital circumstances.

'I do not want to add to the world's slanderous customs,' she had said to me.

'You're right, Dona Lucília,' I agreed. And, as a faithful friend of the household, I loyally kept the family secret.

Dona Lucília also felt a particular kind of jealousy, not out of place given the situation, which from time to time came to the surface.

'Ricardo has really hurt me… We were already engaged when he met Kitty. But I forgave him. The truth is I could not have given him what she did, and what fate took away…'

But, if the truth be told, fate had not taken away everything. If you really thought about it, John continued to be present, and his image filled the whole house like never before. The photographs, hidden for years, could now be displayed on top of every available space. John at three months, John at two years, John at school, John at Oxford, John playing polo and cricket – apparently he had been excellent at the latter – in short, John in every conceivable position. Crowning this collection, a large framed photograph, a light piece of black crepe ribbon resting over the crest, of John in his Air Force Lieutenant-Colonel's uniform, his chest gloriously covered in medals. He had been a handsome boy, a bright look in his eyes, who had stirred in me a vague memory – the sensation of having seen that face somewhere before.

In fact, that collection of photographs betrayed a striking dissimilarity from one to the other, which could only be justified by the different clothes, poses and ages. I remarked on this fact to Dr Silveira who explained:

'I had never met anyone who could change so much… Every time I went to London he looked like someone else.'

Dr Silveira had become happy again, but there was something not quite right about this joy of his. He often spoke of John, as if he was alive, which made me feel ill at ease. I mentioned this to Dona Lucília and she agreed:

'I have also noticed this, and it worries me. Ricardo has not accepted John's death, not even admitted it. He is trying to fool himself; nothing else. Because deep down – and I know him – he is suffering immensely.'

Dona Lucília must have been right and for that reason all that ill-placed exuberance touched me.

During the year following John's death, I must have heard more than a hundred times the description of his last battle. Dr Silveira spoke as if he had been there and every time he would add another detail. In the end the number of aircraft shot down by John had increased to such an extent, as if the number of planes had gathered interest. Having started as five in the newspaper report, they had now become eleven.

Without noticing, my friend was gradually introducing changes in that final act which in the end had given it an epic and dramatic slant, but still keeping its moving quality. In his last version, John had not died immediately and despite being mortally wounded, had had enough strength to utter a few words. I cannot remember exactly what they were, but I know they had the hallmarks of a memorable historic phrase. I knew that in reality there was only his courageous death to speak of, but Dr Silveira's attempts to make this more impressive, moved me profoundly. Still, when he whispered to me that the English Royal Family had worn black for three days, I couldn't help smiling.

When the war was over, after an outbreak of extraordinary joy to mark the victory of the English over the Germans, Dr Silveira once more succumbed to a sort of melancholy, albeit a more discreet version thereof. The wound still bled, but was mitigated by the pride felt at being the father of a hero. More than ever, John's presence was sensed all over the house, and the cult to his memory – in which Dona Lucília was a participant – was beginning to assume quasi-religious aspects.

Since the library was now not large enough, there was also a room belonging to John (which needless to say he would never occupy), a sort of sanctuary in which were kept all the relics that Dr Silveira, bearing a solemn officious attitude, had dug up in a box from England; which he himself, in a taxi, had gone to collect from the docks. It was a motley collection of objects, a bit of everything, from broken mechanical toys to old school books, football boots and university clothes, all the necessary to quickly conjure up the open curriculum vitae of a young Englishman taken in the flower of youth. Present also were a collection of souvenirs from his short and brilliant military career, kept in an ebony box, the most spectacular being a grenade fragment, a piece belonging to the propeller of his last plane but to cap it all, the glorious Military Cross which, out of extraordinary sensitivity, Kitty, the distraught mother, had sent to Portugal. Dona Lucília had been moved to tears by this gift especially because accompanying it was an odd little note in which was stated that the precious relic was dedicated by Kitty to 'John's other mother'...

All this was absurd but I, the only confidant in all this drama, had also to some extent made of John a bosom friend and in the end I found all this quite natural.

Dr Silveira's home had now become an English home, with

English food, huge breakfasts which my friend swallowed with endless gusto, all done according to John's tastes. I, myself, when I had to take some major decision, could not escape – strange as it might seem – imagining what John, had he been alive, might have thought about it.

VIII

When two years after the war I went to England to make a claim in a bankruptcy case on which I was working for a client of mine, an idea suddenly came into my head – to visit John's grave. Having managed to retrieve one pound out of the two thousand owed, lost forever now, in order to compensate for my professional failure I covered it up by giving it a more profound dimension. In that state of mind, and compelled by 'a longing for an unknown person' of which the poet speaks, on a radiantly sunny day, in radical contrast to the traditionally overcast London and my grey mood, I made for the War Ministry. I wished to know where lay the last remains of my hero, but all they could tell me was his last address when still alive, in a London suburb, since his family had taken care of the funeral. This somewhat went against the description of the funeral cortège given by Dr Silveira, in which participated lancers whose lances were covered with funeral ribbons, funereal marches played by the royal band and a long procession made up of the Empire's military dignitaries. In addition this presented me with a serious problem, having to face the silent pain of his grief-stricken mother and justify my presence. But as it was on a sentimental whim and out of a sense of obligation, born out of my duty towards a dear friend, I did not hesitate for a moment. And the next day, armed with a bunch of red carnations, which cost me the earth (but I knew them to be her favourite flowers) I made my way to John's house, attempting to work out in my poor English, some sentences both dignified and moving.

But everything would turn out very differently from what I anticipated and still today, when I remember it, I feel my face flushed with justified embarrassment.

Received by a dishevelled girl of about eighteen years of age, it was immediately very difficult for me to attempt to explain my intent and when she, without having completely understood what I wanted, introduced me to a lady whom I realized was the typical

English middle-aged matron – all bones and red faced – my unease grew. No matter how much the passing of time and life's misfortunes had taken their toll on those features, in no way could they have, even in times long gone by, belonged to the idealised picture as painted by Dr Silveira. My surprise grew when I realised that she was not John's mother, but his wife. I felt, suddenly, that here I was in the presence of one of those romantic impulses, very frequent in times of war, which lead young men faced with danger and death to marry women old enough to be their mothers, who had nursed them or been their war godmothers. But even those thoughts I had to cast aside when I was shown Lieutenant-Colonel John Colley's photograph and I found myself staring at a huge man well over forty years of age, monocle over his left eye, a large bald patch, a brush moustache over his upper lip.

It was most definitely a soldierly figure but bearing no resemblance whatsoever to the twenty-two year old, almost beardless youth, with delicate and lively features, his hair blond and curly, and whose sanctuary and cult was held in a Lisbon household.

I immediately saw I had been a victim of a misunderstanding, but although intending to clear it, I did not have, in such an emergency, the courage to say so. After having explained, to justify my presence, that I was a spokesperson for a group of Portuguese admirers of the dead man, I went with the girl who had opened the door – and whom in the meantime I had understood to be his youngest daughter – to the small cemetery, a few miles away.

There was something farcical about my situation and I couldn't help feeling completely ridiculous, inside the slow and noisy taxi taking us to the graveyard – she looking at me with a bewildered look, in which could be perceived a sort of sad irony, while I clutched with both hands nervously, the bunch of red carnations. We did not exchange more than a few monosyllabic words, but I had a feeling that – while I felt like the unhappy bridegroom being led to the altar – she, albeit tentatively, did not entirely trust me. What is sure is that we were both anxious to put an end to all this and once the flowers had been laid and the one minute silence upheld, we said goodbye forever with a conventional handshake, since she had rejected my offer of taking her back home.

She, in fact, was the one to leave the cemetery first, and I remained alone in the middle of the bare tombs, not thinking about the meaninglessness of life, but sensing somehow what I today know to have been the beginning of the excruciating nagging doubt which later would come to plague me.

The following day I went to the Ministry of War again, and for the next few days I went from department to department, bothering the civil servants, attempting to undo what I felt was my mistake, and inappropriate behaviour. But there was no mistake or inappropriate behaviour. There was only one John Colley who in the Air Force had achieved the rank of Lieutenant-Colonel and died heroically in combat. As extraordinary as it may sound, there was not in the entire British Army, or in any other military sector, another John Colley, who had achieved a high rank or had been responsible for any act worthy of mention. And only after extensive research, was found in the army in India, a soldier of that name. But he, who had enlisted in 1910, apart from having only one l in his surname, was old enough to be a grandfather.

IX

When I returned to Lisbon, my state of mind was one of utter confusion. I really did not know what to think and firmly rejected the idea that I had been the victim of an incomprehensible hoax. I had been Silveira's confidant, I had witnessed the intimate repercussions of that drama, and in no way could I question his enthusiasm, and far less the sincerity of his tears. Fatherly love reached in him such heights, and coloured his attitude and actions to such an extent, that just in itself, quite independently of the reason for it, it was an honourable sentiment. How to raise the issue, how to convey the facts without them betraying the underlying suspicion which did not yet really exist or to the very least had not taken root in my mind? I controlled therefore my initial urge to find Dr Silveira and tell him what had happened, seeking thus an explanation I was not sure he would be able to give me. My thoughts, as if they had adopted Dr Silveira's rhetoric style, led me to believe this would be to throw *on a wound opened by Fate's scalpel the bitter bile of mistrust*. The desire to speak to Dona Lucília also appealed to me, but this too I postponed after lengthy examination. Potentially such a conversation could also come to represent an improper and gross denunciation.

As a result I spent the first month after my return without knowing what to do, with a growing agitation and without the courage to go to Dr Silveira's house. He had known of my trip to

England and I was expecting therefore, at any time, a call from him. I had not told him of my intention to visit John's grave and pay him my first and last respects because I myself had not been aware of it – but it would have been normal if he had wanted to talk about the country were John, his darling son, was sleeping his eternal sleep.

But Dr Silveira did not phone and his silence, as it went on, was becoming more and more suspect. It looked as if he himself wanted to avoid me which, if it saddened me, also deeply irritate me. There I was stuck in this 'impasse' when a simply physiological incident came to show me the next step. One fine morning I woke up with an insidious pain in my left arm, so severe that towards the end of the afternoon I could not stand it any longer. I needed to consult a doctor, but the truth is that having always been in excellent health, I could not think of any specialist in Lisbon. I had decided to just go to any doctor when suddenly the name of Dr Rocha came to me, someone Dr Silveira had introduced me to and of whom he had spoken highly, possibly exaggerating as usual his high medical reputation.

I knew nothing beyond what he had told me, but my illness could not be so serious that any doctor with some experience could not diagnose and heal. I must confess that at the time I was not thinking of anyone else except myself and my need to relieve the pain plaguing me, but when looking in the telephone directory, to find out where his consulting rooms were, and having found his name, Silvestre Rocha, a flash of inspiration came into my head. Maybe Dr Silvestre Rocha, who had been a contemporary of Silveira in Coimbra, and who apart from being a close friend of his, was also the family doctor, would be able to give me some information that would dispel my doubt. And with this double intention I went to his consulting rooms.

Once the consultation was over and I had been prescribed salicylate (it seems I had some rheumatism) Dr Rocha provided me with the cue by refusing payment and mentioning at the same time our mutual friend:

'Don't even think about it. No charge. Just tell me something. Have you seen Silveira?'

This question did away with my last hesitation, because the truth is that without it, I might never have spoken about the issue. As a matter of fact, in times gone by, when demanding of me utter discretion, Silveira had targeted in particular Dona Lucília and Dr Silvestre Rocha, the first for obvious reasons, and the second because in his own words, 'not only did he not take anything seriously, but was incapable, something to do with his personality, of keeping a secret'. But the reason for such caution, was by now in a manner of speaking redundant: John had died, Dona Lucília knew everything, and therefore it wouldn't matter if Dr Rocha should also come to know…

Still, it was not without some emotion that I answered:

'No, I have not seen him for three months. I spent six weeks in England and since my return I still have not spoken to him… And, since we're on the subject, I would not like to meet with him without speaking to you, Doctor, about something which has to do with Dr Silveira and which is worrying me seriously…'

I had taken my courage in both my hands, and knowing Rocha's disposition for fun, I wanted to give my words the minimum of solemnity, that is, a perfectly normal tone. But I was too upset to manage that. Dr Rocha, noticing my discomfort, interrupted me.

'You do surprise me, man! Is it possible that anything in the world concerning Dr Silveira could worry anyone! It is true I have not seen him for over a year and a half and speak to him on the phone only from time to time, but I have known Silveira for thirty years and he can't have changed that much in so short a space of time.'

'I agree, Doctor,' without giving much thought to his retort. 'It is precisely because you know him well, and are his doctor…'

I was already well into what I was going to say when he again cut my speech:

'Family doctor, that's only in a manner of speaking. Both Silveira and his wife have always been hale and hearty and as far as I can remember in twenty years, I treated Lucília once for a bit of 'flu and Ricardo a sprain…'

'Still, as an old friend of theirs,' I interrupted him again, 'and it is in that capacity that I want to speak to you about a certain private matter… and I ask of you complete confidentiality.'

A spark of curiosity came into Dr Rocha's eyes and he adopted quite a different tone:

'Friend, yes. But I don't quite get…'

'You soon will, Doctor…'

And without further ado, I went straight into it, told him everything, word for word, without leaving out the slightest detail.

Dr Rocha listened to me in silence with a slight smile, but remaining up to a certain moment perfectly composed. Only when I spoke of my trip to England and my visit to the Ministry of War, John Colley's house and the cemetery, did he start laughing. First of all softly and then louder and louder, until he burst into really loud hysterics.

I very suddenly stopped my narrative and both surprised and hurt, I could not help commenting:

'I don't understand what you find so funny!'

Dr Rocha blew his nose and attempting to control his fits of laughter, explained warmly:

'Listen, forgive me, my man. I believe what you're saying, and I did not want to hurt your feelings in any way. I can well understand what you are going through. But I must confess, that no matter how hard I tried, I couldn't control myself. This is of the purest Silveira…'

My irritation had now been replaced by surprise, tinged somewhat by a distant worry that I could not control. It was in a shaky voice that I asked:

'What do you mean by that?'

'I mean that I believe you, not him…'

'So, Doctor, you think this is nothing else but a fantasy?' (I could not quite find the right word). 'A figment of his imagination?…'

Dr Rocha was adamant:

'I don't think: I know for sure.'

I couldn't help commenting:

'But, Doctor, I myself saw the photographs and his tears. I witnessed what he went through when John died… I saw him wear deepest black, both him and his wife…'

'You my friend might have seen all that and more.' answered Dr Rocha, a smile on his lips, 'but I'm sticking to my opinion. All this is nothing but an outright lie.'

I shuddered violently, and raising my voice almost to the point of rudeness, I protested:

'What you are saying demands an explanation.'

'So it does, and I shall give it to you.' And having reassumed his serious tone of voice, ever so professional at the beginning, he added solemnly: 'You, my friend, are very young, and you have known Dr Silveira for a very short while…'

'I'm not as young as all that, and I have already known him for four years,' I interrupted abruptly.

'In terms of Silveira that is not very long. I have known him for thirty, and even then he still surprises me. Silveira is a very good man, but somewhat unusual. His reality is never a so-called sensible reality, nor is it other people's reality. A little while ago I mentioned the word "lie", but perhaps that is not the right word to describe it, although that is the one usually used. It might be better to call it "fantasising" – unintentional fantasising, of course, because the first person to be mystified is he himself.'

'But to be like that, would be terrible morally speaking,' I couldn't help saying, my trust in Dr Silveira somewhat shaken.

'I don't agree with you. He never says anything unless he believes in it. And that to some extent, justifies it, don't you think?'

No, it didn't seem like that to me at all, and I was beginning to feel a deep irritation against Silveira, Dr Rocha and even against myself. I was abandoning the case leaving it undefended, which not only was disloyal, but also against my nature. That is why I replied with a certain harshness:

'Listen, Doctor. Everything you're telling me is very subjective, and is no real proof. The facts I witnessed were solid and verifiable, the doubts I now have are as solid. I can only believe – although with some distaste – that Dr Silveira has lied to me, or better still if you prefer, mystified me, given this concrete proof. I do not believe in judging anyone on the basis of an opinion.'

There was a certain rudeness as much in my words as in the tone I spoke them, but Dr Rocha did not show any sign of being offended:

'Fine, my friend. If you want objective proof, I can give it to you. I can even give you an irrefutable motive.'

I started to feel some fear but I could no longer go back and so I encouraged him:

'I'm all ears, Doctor...'

Dr Rocha smiled.

'So listen, and don't go over the top or be angry with Silveira. First of all in Coimbra, there never was such a person as the English woman. I got my degree in Coimbra, as you know, and was in the same year as Silveira. And an English woman like the one you describe, could never have existed unnoticed by anybody, much less by me, who was his colleague and close friend. Furthermore: should an event of that nature (and I can tell you that in Coimbra, in those days, it would have been an event) have taken place, sides would have been taken and there would have been endless arguments and speculation. If that sweet and romantic English woman had really existed, she would forever have become embedded in Coimbra folklore... Don't you think what I'm telling you is, if not concrete proof, at least a very powerful argument?'

'Yes, to some extent, I had to admit, but couldn't that English

woman have lived, maybe, at another time and in another area, and
Dr Silveira in order to create a more interesting atmosphere, have
placed her in Coimbra?'

I clung desperately to my idea and I was hanging on to the last.

'It's not very likely, but could be,' agreed Dr Rocha, in a concil-
iatory manner. 'The worst is that I have a more serious reason, so
serious, that I don't even know if it would be right to mention it…'

'After everything you have said, Doctor,' I answered in an aggressive though solemn tone, 'not only do I think it is right, I feel it is
your duty… Your words, Doctor, without decisive proof, could
almost amount to defamation.'

I had reached such a pitch of irritation and anxiety that I could
no longer behave with any decorum.

Dr Rocha remained looking at me for a while and I even thought
for a moment that he was simply going to ask me to leave. But he
didn't. Inwardly he debated a personal issue, and hadn't even noticed
my lack of courtesy. Without paying any attention to what I had said,
he continued in a halting tone:

'To give you the proof you demand. I have to betray a trade secret,
no less. And I will only dare do this, if you, my friend – and even so
my behaviour will remain questionable – give me your word of
honour that you will keep it exclusively to yourself.'

Without wanting to admit to it, I was impressed, and it was in a
shaky voice that I said:

'I give you my word of honour.'

'Then listen, and remember that if this is a serious betrayal of trust,
it is also partly, the proof that Silveira…'

There was a silence between us and once more I felt prey to a
mysterious anguish. But stronger than this was my need to know. I
remained looking at him inquiringly.

'The thing is, my friend,' Dr Rocha went on making a visible
effort, 'Silveira cannot have children…'

'What?… He can't have children?! I don't understand, Doctor. Dr
Silveira cannot have children, why?'

'I will explain.' Dr Rocha regained his usual composure and
carried on, in the professional tone assumed by those explaining a
medical case: 'Three years after he got married, Silveira came to see
me in my consulting rooms. He was worried about his wife's
presumed infertility, and as was his wont – you know him! – he came
full of biblical quotes. Although it didn't mean anything, because he
deeply loved Lucília, he would speak in terms of special cures,

divorce, and even old fashioned repudiating! In the middle of all this, there was only one serious issue: his true unhappiness at not being able to have children – an unhappiness which was also shared by his wife. As a result I promised that I would question and examine her, if she agreed, although these examinations in themselves were not conclusive. She accepted. Lucília was a young and robust woman, and apart from that, extremely normal which immediately led me to believe that the blame, in this instance, lay with him and not her. It was then I remembered that Ricardo had had one of those illnesses in Coimbra which could result in sterility. I put it to him and advised him to go for an analysis. Although upset, he went through with it and the result left no doubt… It is true that I – out of kindness – did say to Ricardo that the results of these analyses were not always decisive. But the truth is that he is very intelligent and although he never admitted it, he too had misgivings…'

Dr Rocha kept quiet and later I asked him to forgive my impertinence, and added:

'But in that case, Doctor, Dr Silveira's behaviour towards his wife and myself, especially towards her, is, apart from being incomprehensible, truly monstrous…'

'Neither one thing nor the other, my friend,' disagreed Dr Rocha. 'I even believe that given his personality it's understandable and human.' And he concluded: 'What you have told me, strange as it may seem, is nothing more than a simple overcompensation.'

I, at the time, did not entirely understand what Dr Rocha meant by that mysterious sentence, and when I left his rooms, I felt a violent irritation which was waking the desire to avenge myself against my dear friend who had abused my good faith and ridiculed my most personal and delicate feelings.

X

That night I could hardly sleep. There was both in my arm and in my soul a hidden pain I could not overcome. From the disillusionment I felt I was not able to assess what Dr Silveira had meant to me, and my betrayed and vilified friendship demanded some sort of punitive measure. In any case, both out of the need to respect the promise I had made Dr Rocha and to spare Dona Lucília, as much a victim as myself, I needed to unmask Silveira. The truth is that his fantasising had had its desired effect. John had created in my consciousness such a sense of reality, that deep down, it was him I wanted to avenge for whatever diabolic offence.

Dr Silveira seemed to me, and my own idea of justice, to have committed a sort of patricide – a father who after having made a son, brought him up with all the love, had made him die an incredibly tortured death.

There was something totally irrational and contradictory in this reasoning, but the truth is that it went on during my morning sleep and assumed all the nightmarish proportions of a medieval painting by Hieronimus Bosch I had seen in a Lisbon museum.

In the morning when I woke up my mind was made up. On that day, which was a Saturday, I would, having arranged it on the phone, go and have supper at Dr Silveira's house. And when Dona Lucília had gone to bed, as was her custom, I would brutally put the question to him. In spite of all the evidence, and his conduct towards me, I did not wish to condemn him before hearing him out. I also wanted to be loyal and no one more than me – although this seemed impossible – wanted him to find some justification for his attitude.

In my head I pictured the dialogue between us and somehow couldn't bring myself to feel moved by what I imagined would be his total confusion and humiliation – which only went to show the degree of my irritation. I knew that this would signify the end of our companionship and friendship, but nothing at that moment could deviate me from my path. During the afternoon, however, my decision had lost some of its impetus and I probably would have postponed my punitive visit to Dr Silveira's house, if a peculiar coincidence had not forced me to proceed with it. Unexpectedly I received a visit from Dona Lucília which left me completely bemused. Only once had Dona Lucília, accompanied by her husband, honoured me this way and for that reason she must have put down my visible shock on seeing her, to this unexpected visit, a shock which I exaggerated.

She had brought me a bunch of flowers from her garden in Sintra, 'the last of the season', and she herself, with maternal care, placed them in the only available vase.

I found out that she and her husband had prolonged their stay in Sintra and that they had only returned the day before. This would explain Silveira's silence which, contrary to what I had imagined, was not as a result of his frightened or mortified conscience but a perfectly normal act.

It appeared that Silveira was now very interested in meteorology and was building in Sintra a classic observatory with all the up-to-date equipment, was anxious for me to come and would now be furious when he discovered that I had been back a month and had not sought him out.

'But you have been away and I couldn't have known,' I said apologetically.

'Sintra is not that far and it is not difficult to find out our whereabouts,' Dona Lucília jokingly reprimanded me. 'You are simply an ungrateful beast.'

I couldn't tell her the real reason and so I only said:

'I have had so much to do…'

'But there is always time to make a telephone call…'

I kept quiet, ashamed, accepting the reprimand, at which point Dona Lucília assumed a serious face, more earnest than usual:

'Both Ricardo and I are very fond of you. But for him, you are not just a friend, you are someone he needs. You are the only person he opens up to. It's different with me. I am his wife, and although he feels at ease with me, it is not the same. You understand, Luís… to keep quiet hurts him, and it is only when he speaks that he forgets… You have just come from England haven't you? It's very likely that he would like to talk to you, ask you things that only you can answer. Since John died, Ricardo is not the same. I never imagined a father could feel so deeply the death of a son, especially a son he hardly knew.'

'Me neither…' I said with an automatic irony, which fortunately Dona Lucília interpreted as simple agreement.

'You see how we agree…' Dona Lucília got up from her chair and gave me her hand. Moved, I kissed it. I seldom did this, because I have always hated these social practices, but in my case it went beyond protocol and was more a sincere homage to her kindness.

'See you later Luís… And do come, all right?' she insisted.

The marital loyalty of this woman, whom I myself, from the beginning had superficially judged to be a useless human being, had an effect on me totally opposed to what might be imagined. Instead of mitigating the irritation I felt against Dr Silveira, it fuelled the fire and aggravated the anger I felt. No matter from what angle I saw it, his behaviour, which made others suffer as a consequence of an imaginary pain, appeared to me repugnant and could only be justified by a state of madness utterly belied by the apparent tranquil life he led. He was in fact a fantasist, but not in the good sense Dr Rocha meant, but in the most disgraceful moral sense of the word. For that reason, maybe he did not even deserve the loyalty which I had previously thought of according him.

He had played with my deepest feelings, making me go through a series of ridiculous hoops, and at the same time made his wife believe in her own barrenness, without caring how much she might have suffered as a result. And to cap it all – oh heavens – she had even donned mourning on behalf of an imaginary being. It was my turn now. And since I could not publicly unmask him, clearly shout my contempt, because of the esteem and the respect I felt Dona Lucília deserved, I would use his own weapons, fantasy and lies, to torture him slowly. I think at that moment – and I still don't really understand my psychological attitude – I passionately hated Silveira.

It was in that treacherous state of mind, that I crossed the threshold of his home, warmly embraced him and sat at his table.

XI

Dinner proceeded without a hitch and although Dr Silveira tried on several occasions to speak about John, I always changed the subject referring to England and its problems in a very abstract manner, or steering him towards Meteorology, at the time his great passion. This worked well and Silveira launched into an enthusiastic explanation and so original, that someone who might not have known him or knew nothing about the subject, might have believed this to be a new science invented by him. The cyclones, anti-cyclones, head winds, high and low pressures, gained in his explanations quasi-human proportions, and he almost, in his enthusiasm, declared himself the inventor of the barometer…

For whatever reason, that insane eloquence had its effect, and I felt my anger and at the same time the cold and enraged determination to avenge myself to be anaesthetised. It was in that tolerant spirit that I went to the library and I would almost surely have kept quiet if one thing had not wakened in me a new wave of fury. The library was in darkness, and the only thing you could see, lit up by a small projector – a fantasy Dr Silveira had come up with during my absence – John's photograph.

I must confess I was impressed by the scene, and my eyes stared at the one, who for so long, had been the reason for our concerns and the real reason for our hope and anguish. There was something sacred about the atmosphere, and I would definitely have given into that allegorical form of persuasion, had not a sudden revelation come to me.

Lit up in that manner, John's photograph was very familiar. I had surely seen it somewhere before, flickering in the light of another projector, and suddenly into my mind and to my lips came the name of an American film actor, a second rate actor known only for his looks, I had seen in some film or other. It was as if I had been hit over the head. The last doubt, to which I had clung with a sort of hope, vanished, and I felt come to me with all certainty the irrefutable confirmation of what I had always suspected. In a sudden movement, I got up and put on the light:

'Dr Silveira,' I said with devilish determination, 'I have news of England to tell you...'

I thought he would react in a confused and worried way, but I was mistaken. In him burned a curiosity which could not be faked – the same concern, both enthusiastic and painful which endowed everything which might have any relationship to join.

'Yes, speak to me... Tell be about that admirable, beloved England.'

I felt shaken but made another stab:

'All the more remarkable,' I agreed, 'given the adulation and reverence granted to its heroes...'

I had decided to use the same method he had used with me – unbridled fantasy – to pay him back, using patronising cynicism in return for the contempt he had shown towards our friendship and my very intelligence.

It would be the easiest way to humiliate him, and he would have to understand – if he had not already understood – that I had uncovered his repugnant fantasy. There was something cowardly in my attitude but at least it had the merit of sparing Dona Lucília, whose position as unsuspecting victim I did not wish to aggravate by using a cruel denunciation.

At the same time, it was there in front of her that I wanted to punish him, because he would not be able to ignore the biting and tragic irony, even threatening, of my fantastical description of the trip to John's grave, which I was ready to make in front of his wife. I also burned with curiosity to see what his reaction would be on reaching the apex of my trickery, that is, when he would become fully aware that I, in playing his game, was robbing him of his control. Clinging on to his lie of so many years, he would have to suffer in silence the torture I was going to subject him to, and in this way discover that he could not play with me with impunity. To the end he would be afraid his wife would uncover the truth, or that I might reveal it to her, and that would be the sweetest and cruellest revenge.

But my vengeful project did not come to anything.

After I had described my first visit to the War Ministry in words which gave it a fallacious and bombastic eloquence, and when I was about to embark on my visit to Kitty's house, Dona Lucília got up.

'I am very tired,' she said. Surely she was doing it out of courtesy, so that I would not omit, out of some discreet reluctance, any detail.

I still insisted, rather lamely, that she stay, but she did not agree to do so. My plan was sabotaged and we found ourselves alone, one facing the other, and I began to feel the desire to reveal my game and screaming it out loud. I don't know how I resisted this impulse, but today I still shudder when I think that I could have done it.

A long silence followed Dona Lucília's exit, but it was Dr Silveira who broke it:

'And you saw her?… You spent time with her?…'

I looked at him astounded. His face betrayed no fear or any sort of uneasiness, only a burning and passionate curiosity. This man's capacity for make believe was unheard of, and I was now ready to see how far he would go.

'Yes, I did see her,' I answered, my eyes staring at him.

'And how was she?'

I remained silent for an instant. But almost immediately I started on the most extraordinary and fantastical story anyone could have invented.

Kitty, the blue-eyed romantic with the slender hands, was almost just as he had described her. Only her golden locks had turned white, as a result of the passing of the years and its sorrows. And also deep down in her eyes, could be perceived an endless hollow, a sort of 'absence'.

I could see in Silveira's eyes that my description, first started in a cynical and ruthless way, was beginning to acquire extremes of poetic exaltation which gave it an odd reality. Silveira listened to me, almost in a state of ecstasy, his hands clasped and his eyes shiny, and I myself attempting to hang on to my senses, was beginning to be taken over by my own words, and felt almost moved. In my description, Kitty and I had walked on a golden morning, amongst the flat tombs of the English graveyard, and in order to concentrate better I now closed my eyes. At that moment, I could feel Kitty's body, leaning on my arm, and I could really hear her words, and I only reopened my eyes, when I got to the point where I put down the bunch of red carnations and Kitty, kneeling by John's graveside, read with misty eyes, the solemn inscription given by England in its homage to its bravest soldier: 'To the heroic pilot John Colley, the grateful fatherland'.

I looked at Silveira.

Livid, with trembling lips, silent tears, burning and profound tears, sincere tears, running down his face, and I, no matter how hard I tried, could but believe them.

'My son, my beloved son!...'

Dr Silveira sobbed convulsively and I, having forgotten my plans for revenge, held him in my arms, moved and tried to comfort him.

It was as if lightning had shattered the dark and in one second flat I learned many things I had not known until that moment. I then understood what Dr Rocha had said to me, and I also understood how Humanity always becomes the slave of its myths.

His pain was genuine and John, Dr Silveira's son, was as real as if he had come out of some woman's insides, as real as if he had really existed...

At that moment, a moment I shall never forget, my friend was the living image of Fatherhood – the Fatherhood which is the font of Life's eternal meaning, and governs men and gods...

'Dr Silveira,' I said as a last measure of comfort, 'next year, we shall both go to England together.'

'Yes, my friend, we will both go there together...'

The years went by and we never went to England. In the meantime, every Saturday I have dinner at his house. And the most pleasant moment of the evening for us is when, our eyes gazing at the photograph still lit up by the projector, we speak of John, of his short and glorious life, and above all what he could have become if only Fate and Chance had allowed it.

Branquinho da Fonseca

THE BARON

translated by John Byrne

I don't like travelling; but as an inspector of primary schools I'm always off somewhere, covering the whole country. It's as if I were bravely following a trail of adventures, of new, delightful sensations, like a knight errant. There have been some agreeable moments that I fondly look back on, and I hope there will be still more to leave me other memories, too. Things change constantly as if in an eternal childhood, with its perpetually new outlook and horizons. But, still, I don't like travelling; perhaps it is just because I see it as a duty, and duties are never pleasurable. I get excited at the beauty of a landscape, which I value as much as any human, and I am extremely curious about different races and their customs, and in general about the different mentalities one finds from place to place. In a small country like this such diversity is quite astonishing. However, I am not an ethnographer nor an expert in folklore; I have not studied either of these subjects and soon lose interest in them. So, to wherever it might be, I really don't like travelling.

I have already thought of giving up my job but it would be difficult to get another which pays as well as this. I earn two thousand escudos and I have a free pass on the railway as well as my expenses paid. As I live alone this is enough to get by on. I can save a little so that during my annual month's leave I could go abroad. But I don't; I can't. I want to spend that month quietly, doing nothing; I just want to do as little as possible – to wake up every single one of these thirty days in the same bedroom, to look out on the same street for thirty days on the run, to go to the same café, to meet the same people. If only you knew how good it is, how peaceful it makes you feel inside, how one's thoughts are all of a piece and become altogether clearer. In order to think clearly one has to have peace. Perhaps in the long run one would grow tired of it but, still, Nature demands a certain routine. Trees don't move; and animals only leave their native haunts through the physical need for food or a different climate. My ideas on these matters are as clear as my experience has been conclusive. It is, perhaps, the only thing about which I have firm ideas and sufficient experience.

But I'm not here to philosophise; I'm about to tell you of my journey to the Serra do Baroso. I was going there to inspect the primary school in V... It was in winter, in November; it had been raining heavily, giving the hills a depressing, gloomy air. Stones, washed down by the rain, lay scattered in the roads, the low walls had collapsed and the dry branches were all twisted on the trees. I went by train as far as the nearest town and then took a coach which dropped me by the side of the road in a village whose name I don't remember. It was night. I had been told that there was an inn at the end of the street. It was an old, tumbledown house. I went in and came across a kitchen – a long, dark room – at the end of which was a fire with an old woman sitting by it. I didn't feel at all comfortable; not knowing what I should do, I was embarrassed, but just then a woman came looking for me. She was young but plain; nevertheless she was pleasant and her intelligent gaze made her seem more attractive. Without the slightest hesitation she promptly addressed my problem as if it were something she did every day. She ordered the waiter from the inn to go and tell the Baron that someone had arrived from Lisbon, and to ask him to let the visitor have a horse tomorrow morning so that he could go up into the hills.

'Just wait and see,' she said to me. 'My little message will sort out any problems, transport as well as somewhere to stay.'

She said something by way of vague introduction about the Baron and then we began to talk of other matters. We sat by the fire, warmed and lit by the flames. She talked of the inspection and of the life of the village. At first she seemed sorrowful, but seemed to recover almost immediately. I saw that she was a strong woman, optimistic though unfortunate; I understood the drama of that poor girl. She was quite right, psychologically she was right. I wanted to go straight back to Lisbon and write a report which would vindicate her, take the part of that teacher who, on account of her clear intellectual superiority, was unsuited to that environment. Then we were served some dreadful coffee in large teacups; though I couldn't drink it, she did. And suddenly I saw that this idea I had that she was unsuited to her environment might not be true after all; human beings are the most adaptable of creatures, I must admit.

And so we talked about the inspection and must have spent half an hour – perhaps a little more – thus when we heard a motor car stop at the door of the inn. She got up as if startled, exclaiming at the same moment that it never failed. The small door opened and

through the darkness of the opening appeared a huge man, bending
deeply in order to get through. His shoulders were broad and he had
a large hat on his head; he was wrapped completely in an enormous
black cloak. From afar he said in a drawling, low voice which nevertheless rang through the room: 'Well then, good evening.'

To anyone who didn't know him – or to anyone who knew him
too well – he was an intimidating figure. There was something cruel
about him, in his slow gestures, as if everything around him had
stopped for as long as he needed it to. He had the air of someone who
was the master of everything. He came towards me with long strides
which shook the old house, and held out his hand as if he had known
me for a long time. And suddenly he became a decent chap, like
someone who had let slip a carnival mask. But which, I asked myself,
was the mask and which the true face? He laughed and talked non-
stop. I began to think that my first impression had been unfair and
that the Baron was, after all, a decent sort. The truth of the matter,
though, was that nobody felt comfortable in his company, as I was
beginning to find out. I found him coarse and primitive, but he began
to be more congenial to me precisely because of these aspects of his
character. He was still young, little more than forty. He told me I was
to be his guest and cut short my prevarications with the remark,
delivered in a dry, decisive voice which brooked no contradiction,
that it was he who gave the orders in those parts.

I caught him at that moment with a stern look on his face which
he immediately changed into one of childish delight. I struggled to
understand. He must have felt the need for company, and had come
to *grab* me, pick me up like someone who, at last, comes across
another in the middle of the desert. His greatest joy was to have
guests in his house. He was soon telling me that I should stay a week
and that if I wanted I could send for my friends to come too. I replied
that I could stay for no more than two days whereupon he frowned
and said to me in what I thought was a jocular tone: 'We shall see; I
give the orders around here!' I immediately realised that I had fallen
into the hands of a tyrant, of someone who was used to bending
others to his whims. I replied firmly that I positively could not stay
longer. And then he smiled timidly, artlessly almost, as if he were a
child; I felt sorry for him and explained what I had to do the next
morning before returning to write my report.

He looked at me scornfully: 'What report?'

He got to his feet, making me rise as well, and added: 'To hell with
these things!'

I felt terribly confused: part of me was daring me to do what I wanted to do but could not; it despised in others the things that I am inclined to despise and do despise. But these are the very things that I am a slave to, and this is the worst humiliation I could suffer, the greatest shame. It was the Baron, however, who suddenly poured oil on troubled waters, as if he had read in my face what I was going to say.

'Please forgive my manners, my way of speaking,' he said. 'It was only a joke; I like to bring some humour to these serious matters.'

Wisely we changed tack and decided to go outside. A certain curiosity began to awaken in me about this man's life; he was rich yet he lived there hidden away at the edge of the world, in a village up in the hills. He bade farewell to the teacher and, seizing my arm, pulled me out onto the street. He opened the car door, pushed me in, sat down behind the wheel and said: 'On Monday some friends are coming here from Coimbra and some girls, real girls, like nothing you've ever seen. Do you know Coimbra? Of course you do! Who doesn't know Coimbra? Even my horse knows Coimbra. When I got to the third year of university I began to understand that it could only have been founded by a horse. I came home, put "Melro" on the train – he was a black horse, a real beauty – and took him to Coimbra. I met up with my crowd and...' He stopped to comment on the state of the roads: 'Just look at these roads! I've a mind to drag the civil governor up here and rub his nose in the biggest holes. Anyway, I met up with my crowd and we went together in a procession to the Porta Ferrea and there, from on top of the lion, I bawled out to the crowd: "Is there anyone down there who doubts that this – and I pointed to the University – is the work of a horse?" They bawled back in one voice like thunder: "No!" "So then, I tell you, it must have been his grandfather" – I pointed to Melro. "Therefore today I confirm him in the name of this universal truth: I christen you Dom Diniz!" Then we took him to the courtyard of the University and we awarded D. Diniz his doctorate – in law, of course. And then in his gown with tassels, red tassels – it was a real gown, properly trimmed, which covered him halfway down his legs – he went down into the Baixa, there among the rows of freshers, eating sugarcubes. That night...' Suddenly he stopped talking, drove the car through a huge gate and came to a halt abruptly. 'Here we are. If I were to start off on stories about Coimbra I'd never stop. My friend, I spent nine years of my life in Coimbra, nine of the best years of my life in Coimbra; that would give anybody enough to talk about.'

A door opened. I looked about me but the night was so dark that I could not make anything out. I felt a dog sniffing around my legs and I started because I hadn't realised what it was. And then there came five or six more, of different breeds and sizes, who, whimpering with delight, jumped up at the Baron. He fended them off gently. Behind us came a servant with a lantern which he held in the air and at the top of the stone steps there appeared another holding some kind of oil-lamp which gave a feeble, yellowish light. I was able to see that we were in a rather grand old manor house; its many-windowed façade was lost in the gloom of the night. At the top of the steps loomed a long porch supported by short, thick columns of granite. I have gazed on these semi-abandoned, old palaces from afar, dreaming that they represented comfort, intimacy and well-being, a centre of stability in one's life. Independence and ease, the chance to build one's life as one wants to – those are my impossible ideals. An old manor house whose walls have seen much more than I ever have, walls which have their own spirits; and, surrounding it, a great park of ancient trees, a park full of hidden corners where no one ever goes. To experience the tumult of the great cities and then the silence, the seclusion of one of these long abandoned paradises, where one enters, full of heaven knows what unease, like someone landing on a desert island…

Ah! yes, that would show me a new way to live, to understand, to follow my own path in life. But no; so in the end, then, why do we strive so hard to carve out a way of life which we know is not our own? It is we ourselves who betray our own lives. Life isn't just this, isn't just earning and spending. This is only the beginning; we can take for granted the need for physical necessities. We expend our efforts in trying to get what should be *given* us without even having to think about it; and this is not just because men treat each other as enemies. Life is something else but – and this is where I have misgivings – it is perhaps something which we would not have the courage to go through with. It is better to cover up our weakness in this way. I, too, am a mystic who does not have the strength to give up my life: my soul tells me to break these chains which bind my hands and to head for the mountains, where I can wander amid nature and gaze with the wonderment of one who begins his life anew each day – at the flowers, animals, the sun, the rain, the fresh springs, the trees and birds, the blue sky, the white clouds which the wind brings from afar, the sea, ah! all these things! But I lack I know not what resolve, what power, to master or to renounce things; because, before you can master one thing, you first have to give up so many other things. And yet how many people have I met who are like me, almost like me? Who are torn within themselves, unable to reason or choose or give things up, and who because of this go so far astray and miss so much…

When I got to know him better the Baron seemed to me someone within whom God and the Devil contended. But we did not truly understand each other. His defects, his instability seemed to have won out, absorbing him, taking over the whole man. Sometimes he seemed to have moments, saying something perhaps, when the expression on his face was one of calm superiority and intelligence. He seemed then another person, someone who had drowned within himself, as if in a deep pool of black water. From time to time he would struggle to the surface, in the swirling, filthy slime, but could find nothing to hold on to there. He was a medieval lord, wrenched out of his time, completely unfitted to his environment, like an animal from another climate. And it was this which made him so ferocious, in his expression, his gestures and even the way he spoke; but it all came together in a strange way in which there was also something forthright and good-humoured.

He told me not to take off my coat because it was so cold. The place had no heating and was redolent of the discomfort and damp which pervade unoccupied houses. Nor did he take off that great cape of his which came down to his feet. We proceeded to the dining room, a huge, uninviting space, where we sat down at a table big enough for more than thirty people. I was hungry because it was already well past my usual dinner time. But these matters were not to be discussed; just then a servant arrived with a bottle of red wine which he placed on the table, together with two glasses, one in front of the Baron, the other in front of me. I told him that I only drank with my meals; he replied that this was a wretched notion and, drinking some wine, began suddenly to talk excitedly as if the wine had awakened in him some hidden, sleeping force. And so he carried on drinking, sip by sip, as if his throat were parched and dried out and he had to wet it from time to time. At first I was waiting for other members of the family to appear, but as the time went by I began to understand that the manor house was the lair of the famous Baron himself, who lived there alone with his servants.

All around us, in that house which I supposed must be huge – with its broad, endless corridors, between empty rooms – an unsettling silence which I had never known, weighed more and more heavily; it resonated, too, as though the house had been set down inside a cistern. He carried on with his Coimbra stories, which I listened to, now attentively, now without really hearing him, because I had begun to think about other matters such as the hunger which was now really gnawing at me. I decided to tackle him directly because it was already ten o'clock and I had lunched at midday. But the Baron went on telling his stories, little incidents, reliving them with unholy relish. Perhaps he didn't even care whether I listened or not: he was telling his stories for himself, listening to his own words and remembering those days like a dream brought to life. I was only an excuse, so that he didn't have to talk to himself like an idiot. I realised how much that was a necessary but melancholy pleasure for him. At first he talked and made remarks casually and ironically, but gradually he began to betray feelings so profound that they could not easily be concealed.

It was a kind of yearning for his own self; at certain moments his eyes brimmed with tears. So that I wouldn't see what was happening he got up and began pacing the room, making light-hearted sallies about this common failing we have of reminiscing about our past: 'The past! But what is it, the past? Oh, my friend, the past never was! The present, perhaps, that exists, sometimes…' And, sitting down again, he drank a couple more draughts of wine. I was faint with hunger. The glass remained there before him, full of wine. He was not drunk, but seemed to need to be topped up from time to time, like a boiler beneath which one puts a handful of coal. Another draught. He put down his glass and continued. I glanced at my watch: half past ten. I smiled, out of politeness, but I was no longer listening to him; I could think only of the dinner which never came, which would surely now not come at all. In order to bring the subject up I happened to say, as once more he raised the glass to his lips: 'Don't you find it harmful, drinking without eating?'

'I never eat,' he replied.

I was devastated: so hungry, in the house of someone who never ate!

'But, you know, I was just feeling I could eat something.'

Then he went to the door and bawled: 'Idalina!'

'Excuse my lack of manners,' I said.

'I don't get on with people who stand on ceremony. If you want to be agreeable to me, don't make a fuss. I simply say what I think and do what I like; those are my only principles.'

'Thank you. I shall do likewise.'

The maidservant came in – a tall woman, with a good figure, about forty; she had a vaguely condescending, self-assured air: 'Good evening,' she said.

The Baron continued to talk about this and that as if he had neither seen nor heard her but with some irritation she interrupted him: 'Did you call me?'

I thought he was going to shout at her or even hurl a chair at her head; but no, he smiled gently and suddenly seemed tired.

'My old friend here would like to meet you,' he said, 'and I'd like you to get him something to eat.'

She was by no means ugly; I would rather say she could have been beautiful. And it was easy to see that, there, she was the lady of the house, occupying a position somewhere between Baroness and servant. She left the room smartly. There was a short pause. The Baron, unusually, drank several draughts one after the other without saying anything. I did not understand why that woman, a mere maidservant, had caused this awkward silence. He seemed somewhat distant, thinking about something important no doubt, perhaps something from long ago, something he couldn't get out of his mind. I was thinking these dark thoughts though I myself was in a better frame of mind because I was sure that that well-meaning woman had gone to get me a fine dinner, a dinner from the Middle Ages like the owner of the house himself. He filled his glass again and pushed the bottle away from him, seeming no longer to need it so close to him. He sipped at his glass as if it was a wine he didn't know. I had helped myself to another cigarette and lit it slowly to cover up the fact that I had nothing to say. I wanted to pretend that I was doing something until he should emerge from the reverie into which he had fallen. I didn't want him to feel obliged to explain anything, especially since I would not have been interested and he would have found it painful.

'Why don't you stay here a week?' he asked. 'You wouldn't be bored...'

'There must be something he would like to tell me if only he knew me better,' I thought. 'He needs to unburden himself; it's almost a physical need in his case.'

'I would like to,' I replied, 'but I just can't. I am a slave to my...'

He smiled as if to say: 'These people!' On another occasion he might have insisted, perhaps even forced me to stay. But at that moment he seemed to fall suddenly despondent, to lose the will; he seemed downcast and drained like a mortally wounded lion. And finally, almost as though he was sleep-walking he began to talk in fits and starts; he could have been talking to himself.

'That woman reminds me of certain things – not to do with her – other things; she's just like all the others. Sometimes I got my father to let me have some of his women... or swapped them with him. When I needed some money... or other things. But I'm going to... I'm going to change the way I live...' He smiled with incredulous irony. He paused and, as if he had suddenly awoken, looked at me, sat up straight in his chair, swallowed a draught of wine and dashed the glass so hard down onto the table that it broke into pieces. He then went on in a completely different tone of voice, one now firm and lucid: 'I'm sorry; let's change the subject. I don't want to talk about this any more. Have you ever been in love?'

'No.'

He did not press me to say anything more; but now I was becoming interested in that confession which he no longer wished to pursue. But it was an obsession with him; he had to talk about that subject, about things he could not admit to himself. And now he was putting on his moral front, trampling himself down, loathing himself, as if he would wreak vengeance on himself. As a spectacle it began to be rather unpleasant. I tried to change the subject, begging him to tell me more about his adventures in Coimbra.

'You wouldn't be interested. But I'm not up to talking about Her either, you know.' And, as though he thought better of it, he stopped. 'Ah, my friend, if only I were someone else! To find a new way... but it's not like changing a shirt. I want to, but I can't. It's not just a matter of wanting to. Fools; when I want something, I want it, at once! But this... I only have a picture of Her; I got someone to steal it for me without her knowing. I'll go and get it.' He got up and carried on: 'Pessimism, no; I'm not a pessimist. Women, for me, were just animals, like any other animals. Women? Did I know anything about women? You might think I did; but, really, women, no, I didn't.' He sat down again and slowly poured another glassful. 'When I needed money it was quite simple: I just struck a deal with my father. I would bring a woman back from Lisbon and he would go crazy. He was a like the head of a tribe, a Congolese king. He'd give me the cash and I'd set off out and blow it all in Oporto and then go back to Lisbon. So contemptible, all of it, contemptible.'

The maid came in bearing a huge platter on which there was a large bird, lightly roasted, surrounded by golden potatoes. I thought it was a delusion, a dream; but it was truly a bird, roasted in butter in

the oven. I didn't hear another word he said. The capon gave off a
heady aroma. There was no soup, nor anything else by way of a first
course and so I fell on the bird like a wild man. And some moments
later, already feeling somewhat restored I started to listen again with
relish to what the Baron was saying.

'… Only once was it not like that. She was called Emília. I don't
know where he'd picked up that girl. I'd returned home for the holidays and then at dinner: "Don't touch Emília." "Oh, don't you worry
about that." – But it had to happen – and it did…' For a moment he
fell quiet, lost in thought; I saw him lose himself in the memory,
going back in time to that moment long ago. Then, coming round
again, he looked at me almost in surprise, as if he hadn't seen me;
but soon he was smiling calmly again and, raising the glass to his dry
lips, he proceeded with his story: 'Poor thing; she was just a child.
She was hardly out of her mother's belly. It's hard to believe. In the
end I got down on my knees to beg her forgiveness, weeping. And
in the morning they came across her in the mill pool. But it was only
that one. The others didn't kill themselves; they were only animals…
I'm not eating, but don't stand on ceremony. Eat my share, too. What
the hell! After all life is a matter of eating, and drinking, too, of
course. Oh divine nectar! Let my lips kiss you!' and he drank. 'Let
my heart sing the most holy songs in your praises!' Then he changed
his tone and with a sudden serenity he went on, speaking as much
to himself as to me: 'I never took life that seriously. There's nothing
that can be taken seriously! I am an animal, a pure *beast* you might
say… Whether you say it or not, it doesn't matter, you don't need
to; you need only think it. No, don't choke on your dinner, don't say
anything, just leave me with the feeling that you're not a hypocrite,
sitting at my table. That's just what I am – I am a wild boar. Once I
had some illusions about myself, but not now… If only you knew!
But it's better you don't. We can respect each other; I respect myself
as I am; in the end we are all the same kind of animal. Think of me
the best you can, if that pleases you. Or just the opposite, if you wish.
And if I were to say to you that in the midst of all this gloom there
shines from time to time a ray of light? Would you believe it? At least
you believe in all…'

He said this with a disdain which showed just how much he
despised my lack of sincerity. He was right. But I wasn't thinking
about what he was saying; I was eating. I responded only by nodding
my head, my mouth full. The Baron stood up and walked up and
down the room; he moved away, disappearing into the shadows, his

head bowed, and then returned to the table. I said something just for the sake of saying something, but he didn't hear. He approached me, picked up the silver bell in front of me and rang it. Suddenly he changed the subject.

'You must hear the musicians; you'll enjoy it,' he said as the maid came in again. 'I'll go and get my violin.'

The maid was about to leave the room but, seeming to recall something, she turned back: 'Baron, the violin is broken.'

He turned towards her as if about to curse her or even hit her, his face clouding over suddenly; he managed to control himself and in a cold voice said merely: 'Ah? Broken, eh?'

'Yes, Baron; it happened the day before yesterday.'

'I'll get another one.'

The maid stood her ground, her gaze firm, noble even; the Baron, his first, violent impulse having passed, became calmer and even seemed to hesitate. She took control of the situation and with a certain arrogant assurance asked: 'Where from?'

'Call the musicians,' he bellowed.

And he sat down opposite me with his back to the maid as if that way he could hide from her stern gaze. Grabbing his glass, he drank down another draught of wine. I feared that he would strike that proud woman, or that he would break a chair across her head. But no: he was someone with more self-control than he sometimes seemed. Nevertheless it took some courage or some other force, to stand up to the violence of this nobleman's wrath in that way. There was something mysterious going on between them, that much was clear. She went out after collecting the plate full of bones which the Baron had left. He was speaking to me about hunting when she returned with a platter of pork accompanied by some scrambled eggs. But he did not eat, simply sipping away as he talked. He must have drunk a fair amount of wine but he was not drunk; he remained self-possessed, even under pressure, as one might say of a warship; ready for anything. The table with the glass, that huge, empty, dim house, were the docks, the arsenal of that battleship which would sally forth on the seas at the first order. By now I was observing him with curiosity and not a little fear. Where would that strange man have me go next? In the meantime I had eaten well and drunk with a certain pleasure. I saw that it was already half past eleven. The Baron had gone to a cupboard to get some bottles of various wines and spirits: old Port wines, some liqueurs from France. I didn't want to mix my drinks but he insisted, repeating that phrase, seemingly playful but in fact in earnest: 'I am the one who gives the orders around here.'

And so we tried some of the wines; they were in truth rather special. 'This Port, now, which is 96 years old.' He opened it and thrust the neck of the bottle under my nose; there arose a delicious bouquet which filled the whole house. I suppose I must have thought that something which smelled so heavenly could do me no harm, that, on the contrary, to drink it would be to imbibe all the nectars of paradise. The Baron was talking about Brazil, the jungles of the Amazon and about the women from there – 'the most beautiful women in the world…!'

I disagreed: 'What about the Scandinavians, the English, the Germans…'

He cut in with the real arrogance of the connoisseur: 'That's like eating a lettuce salad – it goes well enough with meat… but I am a meat eater. And in any case women are my worst enemy; it's the only matter on which I and my parish priest agree. And the enemy should always be worthy of us, you know. Fighting with cats? Of course not. I would rather be confronted by a true tiger; it should be a matter of life or death. I leap on the tiger, we wrestle each other, his claws embedded in my flesh, my muscles of steel bending that beautiful, wild, supple body to my will, covered entirely in blood, ah…!'

And he hurled the glass against the wall above my head in a wild, triumphal gesture.

'I have known English women, German women, tigers too…' I said, quite calmly.

'It's merely the skin, merely the eyes and the skin. There's no doubt about it… you have to be there, be there among the teeth and the claws…'

He clasped his hands together. By now we were both drunk. The Baron stood up, glared at me and suddenly, sadly, said: 'Let's drink to a woman.'

I got up, too. He went to the same cupboard and fetched a bottle of champagne. 'Champagne bowls,' he bellowed.

He tried to take the wire from around the neck but without success. The maid entered and placed four glasses on the table; still the wire wouldn't come off. So he broke the neck of the bottle against the edge of the table and the champagne spurted out in a white spume. He seized one of the glasses and filled it; suddenly he noticed there were another three. He looked around for the maid.

'Who are the others for?' he asked.

But she had already left the room. The others were evidently spare glasses; but at that moment he did not see the need for spares and with the back of his hand calmly swept the other two glasses off the table onto the low table below. Champagne was dribbling through his fingers from the bottle. He filled the other bowl and handed it to me.

'Which woman?' I asked vaguely.

'The only one!'

And we drank together, emptying the glasses in one gulp. But to my surprise I saw that the Baron had suddenly become abstracted; with a contemptuous sweep of his hand he threw the glass on one side. Then, silently, he fixed his gaze on me. I did the same, dashing my glass to the ground. By now I knew that in that house everything was broken, from violins to glasses. With his dulled gaze he stared at me without seeing me. Then, as if he had suddenly awoken, he began to laugh; it was a sad laugh, ironic and bitter. He seemed a different person. At once I saw that that man there in front of me was, in truth, another person – one that I hadn't understood, or even seen until now. I looked at him with wonder and pity.

'Come here,' he said in a calm, mournful voice.

And we met at the end of the table. He put his arm through mine and we headed silently towards the dining room door. We went out into a corridor. I don't really know where we went, nor do I know just what we did on that sorrowful wandering. But I recall that we went through several halls, rooms and other parts of the manor house; my memory of it is like a fantastic dream. How long it took I don't know; but what I do remember well – because it has always seemed so odd to me – is that we came across nobody, as if everybody had deliberately vanished from our sight. There must have been servants around somewhere lest the Baron call them. We carried on until we came again to the dining room. He leant against the table and said that he was hungry. He filled a glass with red wine and drank a couple of mouthfuls, grabbed the bell and rang it. The maid – the one with the proud air – came in.

'I want food,' he cried. 'And wine, wine from the other... that... from the other. You know which I mean! What the hell are you waiting for?'

He was shouting, but when she left he began to laugh; he told me that he had known her for more than twenty years, that he had got hold of her in the Quinta das Palmas when she was 'as tender as a little lettuce leaf'.

'I stole her in the Quinta das Palmas. I brought her here like that, over my shoulder, like a sack. I got here and threw her onto the table. My father was having his dinner. I just said: "Nobody touches her!" and nobody did. But these days she's the one who says what goes on… I have never been free of her; she is a tigress.'

She came in again. 'You are a tigress! One of these days I'll shoot you, that's what tigers are for.' But he threw an arm around her slender waist and kissed her neck. 'You were a woman, a woman like no other!' She freed herself from his grasp. 'But today you make me sick!' And he turned towards me. 'I gave her to the servants; but she's ruined them all…'

The maid left the room without paying him the slightest attention. I began to see that what he had said was by no means true and that, rather, the Baron had some sort of respect for her, and that she in turn had some sort of control over him, in spite of everything that seemed to have come between them – whether it was boredom, or he had found another woman. But she had not ceased to be a part of his life. Out in the darkness a church clock struck two as the Baron's dinner arrived, steaming on a plate: it consisted of two large, roasted sausages, well done, with crisp golden skin. Before sitting down he came up to me and put his hand on my shoulder.

'You must never stop being my friend,' he said, mournfully, and addressing me in familiar fashion. 'You see what a poor specimen I am!' His hands shook; his eyes no longer glittered, indeed they seemed empty and lacklustre. 'I am a poet…' he concluded after a moment's pause, with a bitter smile.

And coming towards me, he seized my arm, pulled me up from my chair and led me over to one of the doors. I don't know where he proposed to go or what he proposed to do, because at this very moment, from far away at the end of the corridor we heard a noise like a clap of thunder coming closer. He stopped short, smiling with pleasure; I stood stock still in astonishment. Suddenly he jumped back and, pulling me along, hauled me off to the other side of the dining room. I had no idea what the noise was, nor did I understand anything about these comings and goings of ours. The noise grew louder, like thunder breaking over our heads. I wasn't afraid, but I had no idea what it meant. Understanding that I, though somewhat bewildered and concerned, wasn't afraid, he did not tell me; he preferred to spring it on me, unknown. I began to make out that it was the clatter of clogs. We were leaning up against the wall, not speaking, waiting for whomever might materialise; then, moving slowly, there emerged a thin fellow, with a piece of black cloth over his left shoulder, wearing a large hooded black cape, rather like the Baron's. The latter gave him a sign – a quick nod of the head – and the man put back on the cap which he had previously removed and had been holding in his hand beneath his cloak. Now there came more men, some in long cloaks, others wrapped in coarse blankets of rags or thick wool. I could see that the Baron did not want them to remove their caps or hats; I don't know why – perhaps it was so that strange band would look even odder, even more unreal. They were already familiar with his whims and came in, one by one, in a line, wrapped up, muffled against the cold, as if they had just woken up.

What had they all come there for, at that hour, already past two in the morning? I was a little drunk and I made a vain attempt to understand what I was seeing. And all the while more men came in, as if they were part of an hallucination, one by one, slowly, sleepily, of all shapes and sizes, thin, fat, some with Fu Manchu moustaches, others with little, neat beards, two or three with flowing beards like Old Testament prophets, in a variety of blankets and cloaks. That nightmarish procession of figures formed a strange tableau, and then they bowed down to the ground before me. With their clogs loose on their feet they ambled along like bears, swaying, and, in truth, with their faces covered with shaggy hair, they were bears.

I looked at the Baron as if to implore him to say a soothing word, but he had a faraway look in his eyes; he seemed engrossed. The noise of the clogs deafened me. I no longer knew what to think of it all. The room was full of men who were lining up in front of us. One could hardly see the faces of some of them since they were hidden under large hoods, like monks. I tried to read something in the Baron's face. He looked at me and smiled, a smile of pleasure. There were more than fifty, making a semi-circle in front of us. My head was feeling more and more heavy with alcohol, and I tried, in vain, to understand. It seemed to me that those men were looking at us with fear. Then I saw that it was also with scorn and hate. As if I had stepped out of my body and was observing myself from outside, I saw myself better than I saw the others. And then the noise of the clogs stopped and the maid put three huge glasses on the table, and three or four corn loaves. She also laid two knives and then filled the glasses with red wine from a demi-john under the table, and left. All this took place in complete silence like a well-respected ritual. And then, finally, I heard the voice of the Baron, who had already forgotten me, breaking the silence, and introducing them with an outstretched arm and a sweeping, weighty gesture: 'The band.'

I think now that my face must have registered surprise, prodigious surprise. The band! But an extraordinary band, with no instruments to play! And what strange and wild people they were. I thought that he was teasing me and those poor yokels, but no. I began to be aware of a little man in front of me who was staring at me, smiling scornfully. The Baron introduced me to the man, who had a black cloth over his left eye: 'This is senhor Alçada, the bandmaster.' Senhor Alçada bowed very low; he straightened up once more, and in an absurdly solemn tone, proud of his art, he managed to free his tongue, which till then had been tied by a stammer or by fear: 'Baron, at your service, sir,' he said.

'The Green Jay!' shouted the Baron in a flat voice, as if he had been thinking of something else and had suddenly heard the band-master speak. All these things confused me and I tried in vain to make some sense of what I was witnessing. At a sign from the band-leader, as by magic, all kinds of instruments suddenly appeared from underneath those cloaks: violins, flutes, guitars, citherns, triangles, drums, cellos, mandolins, accordions, harmoniums and jews' harps. I wasn't expecting that. It gave me a sudden urge to laugh, that unlooked-for appearance of a thousand instruments; I felt an irresistible hilarity, and indeed I stared to laugh, but I controlled myself. The Baron looked at me disapprovingly, his piercing smile frosty, and turning back to the Alçada fellow he repeated, deliberately and severely: 'The Green Jay'.

He turned to his throng of musicians arranged in a half-moon and, just when I was expecting a din, one of those infernal rackets, they broke into a vibrant, happy march, full of life and lyrical emotion and in almost perfect harmony. The Baron unexpectedly leapt into the middle of the room and, leaning forward with his legs planted firmly apart, fists clenched and arms flexing quickly and forcefully as if he were beating his chest, sang in a rough croaking voice. It reminded me of African war cries. I was carried away. It was amazing how everything had been transformed suddenly on hearing that great fanfare. Then arose a fine timbred voice from I know not where, singing in a faraway and heartfelt cadence, and the instruments gradually fell silent until only the drums and guitars remained, playing with a strange slow muffled beat. Another voice followed that one, singing in harmony, and a quiet chorus in a deep and distant melody kept up I don't know what refrain, like an echo.

And then the Baron made a gesture and everything stopped as suddenly as it had begun. One of the players came up to the table and grabbed hold of a corn loaf as if this were part of the programme. He cut a slice and passed it to his neighbour. Then he grabbed hold of one of the enormous glasses of wine with both hands, drank only one gulp and passed it on. Everyone did the same. The corn loaves were handed around and each man cut off a slice before passing the loaf on, each man drank a gulp of wine then passed the glass on. The Baron wanted to know what I thought. I don't know what I said but I praised them in all sincerity. Then, seeing that all the men had eaten a slice and drunk a mouthful, he shouted 'The Bang-Bang', and another regional tune broke out. I was dumbstruck. Even today I can clearly recall that feeling of strangeness and lively novelty which that evening with the band inspired in me. Suddenly the Baron, the maid and myself began dancing in the middle of the room. The band continued playing as we went round, heads spinning with wine and music until the Baron fell gasping in a corner like a wounded monster.

Neither the music nor we stopped in this ballet of dancing bears. The maid also fell over in the middle of the room and landed with her skirts up, showing her legs up to the thighs and from that outrageous position began singing along with the music while the band continued unaffected, indifferent through force of habit to these goings-on. I leant on one side to look and laugh, slid slowly down the wall and I too ended up seated on the floor. I saw everything around me move as though I were sleeping on one of those childrens' swings. The Baron, sitting on the floor behind me, was singing in Spanish. But he got up, went back to the middle of the room and called a servant who brought him a large demi-john; raising it high, the Baron began to pour it slowly over his head. The cascade of white wine made me envious. Nothing surprised me any more; they could do as they wished, I found it all quite natural, and I was so hot that I also wanted to pour a twenty litre demi-john of white wine over my head. The Baron, drenched and sliding across the wine-flooded floor, made his way towards me and said: 'I am purified!' 'Indeed you are,' I replied. 'A purifying baptism.' 'It purifies, indeed.' 'Come! I'm going to Sleeping Beauty's Castle.'

He put his arm through mine and we disappeared into the dark corridor. I was being taken I knew not where; he was being carried wherever his obsession took him. I could still hear the noise of the bandsmen's clogs leaving by another door behind us. We were now in the middle of the estate and all the dogs were following us. He stopped short, grabbing my arm:'Ah!… I'll be back in a minute. Wait here.'

And he went quickly back. I saw him heading towards the gate from which we had emerged and disappear into the darkness of the night. In that state of semi-consciousness I seemed to think I had understood what he had said, or rather, what he was going to do. It was truly as if in those few words he had told me more than the words themselves meant. But all of a sudden, as if my eyes had been opened, I saw too that he hadn't really told me what he was going to do; then it seemed to me indefensible, though now I know that it wasn't. However in those circumstances I thought it highly inconsiderate of him to leave me there alone without any explanation. Moreover, where I was I knew not, since I could not see anything around me except for some shapes which could have been small trees, although I don't remember whether I actually ever found out what they were.

Disgusted with such behaviour, I decided not to wait for him; full of energy I began to run in the opposite direction to the one the Baron had taken, hoping in that way to find some way out of the confusion. From somewhere in my subconscious came the voice of freedom and I began to sing the Marseillaise as I crossed the orange groves where my wandering steps had taken me. The dogs were no more, the shadow of the house, too, had gone, and by now my eyes were used to the gloom – either that, or it had grown lighter. To tell the truth I began to recognise things as I passed them and I recall that I tried, in vain, to climb a high iron gate through whose bars could be seen a white ribbon of road. I did not succeed and, indeed, fell twice; I decided therefore to try to find another way out, since I was in the frame of mind to try anything and every obstacle was a terrific challenge.

Then from the heavens into the depths of the night came the sound of a clock striking the hour and the hooting of an owl from some tower that I could not make out, however hard I scanned the sky or tried to pierce the gloom. I lost my way and found myself walking across kitchen gardens where I sank into the soft, damp earth which clung to my feet; at the same time I stumbled over all sorts of things – perhaps cabbages or beetroot – as they suddenly appeared in front of me. It was so tiring that when at last I found one of the paths in the garden I didn't feel so much like singing as insulting everybody. I was thirsty, too. At that moment I heard footsteps close to me and the Baron's maid appeared in front of me; I recognised her voice: 'Sir, do you want me to tell you where your room is?'

'No,' I replied. 'What on earth are you doing here?' I asked, as I moved my face closer to hers. I stepped back a pace, as I smelt the wine on her breath. 'Come with me,' I said, grabbing her by the wrist.

'Where to?' she asked, disdainfully and somewhat condescendingly.

'To my room; you know where it is. But keep quiet,' I replied with a child's excitement.

She took her arm away gently and I let her go; but that brief contact with her flesh had disturbed me, at the same time as it had seemed to disperse the fumes of alcohol which had been befuddling me. I spoke to her as though I had fallen madly in love with her. I was in a fever of excitation, holding her hands again in mine, kneeling on the ground, beseeching her love. She said only a few words; otherwise she remained completely unmoved, not even withdrawing her hands. 'You are crazy. The Baron would kill you. Enough of all this. Come on,' she merely repeated, in an unbelievably calm, flat voice. 'Go; you are mad. The Baron would kill you. Go.'

When I tried to hold her and kiss her she pushed me away with an unexpected force: 'So, then, I belong to the servants, do I?' she said. 'Don't believe everything the Baron tells you.'

And, turning her back on me, I saw her disappear into the shadows. I ran after her, begging her forgiveness. I explained that I had found her attractive and that I didn't think she was a woman of low morals, but only someone with the right to make up her own mind, which was every woman's right, and that this was something noble and worthy. She did not understand me and replied that I was very drunk and that it would be better if I went to bed before I did any more damage. I followed her all the way to the door, which was not far away. After all that walking I had finally arrived back at the house. She said that the Baron was in the garden, looking for me. We had gone in through a room with a low vaulted ceiling and a stone floor. On a large black wooden arch there was a oil lamp, black with smoke; its light wavered, making it difficult to see. I thought it was playing tricks on me. The maid-servant picked it up and began to mount a large stone staircase in front of me. I saw two dogs sleeping at the foot of a chair made of hide; I eyed them somewhat fearfully,

but they did not even bother to look up to see who was passing by.
From the top of the stairs ran a long corridor where the maidservant, holding the lamp in one hand and -- I don't know how – a
lighted candlestick in the other, pointed to an open door:'Here it
is.'

She gave me the candle and, as soon as I had gone in, closed the
door behind me. I didn't care. Perhaps I wasn't even thinking about
her. Desire, whatever it is, is one of those things which sometimes
can just vanish completely. I lit a cigarette and threw myself down
on the bed. After a while I was woken by a fierce hammering on the
door and the voice of the Baron, who was bellowing wildly. I began
to cough; I couldn't stop coughing and my eyes were burning so
much that I couldn't open them. I saw the flame of the candle amidst
a dense cloud of smoke. With great difficulty I got to my feet and
staggered across the room, almost senseless, unable to say anything
to the Baron who continued beating and kicking the door; He was
bawling threats and insults but I only seemed to hear them from afar
as if I was still asleep. The smoke was choking me. I hurled myself
against the door but I couldn't open it. I wanted to cry out but I
couldn't. He was making such a racket on the other side of the door
that he couldn't hear me either. I heard footsteps approaching and
the voice of the maid crying vehemently:'Get away from there! Let
the man sleep!'

Then I shouted for them to open the door and they must have
realised that I was in some trouble. As she had the key, she opened
the door. I threw myself into the corridor and, without a word, she
went in purposefully to find what was causing the smoke which was
filling the room. She had the same lamp in her hand and first of all
opened the window. Then I saw her go immediately to the wash-
basin and pick up the water jug; she headed for the bed and poured
it over the mattress. The wind from the window blew the black
smoke onto us, stinging our eyes and the Baron turned tail, pushing
me before him out into the corridor and asking me what the devil
I had been doing. We entered the dining room. He asked again and
I replied that I had been doing nothing, that I had no idea what had
happened. The maid hurried past, pretending that she hadn't heard
the Baron's questions. So we both went back to see just what had
happened. The room was no longer full of smoke. In the middle of
the floor lay a bedspread and two woollen blankets with an enormous hole in them, made by my cigarette.

'You would have been roasted to death,' commented the Baron, and he began to laugh somewhat excessively. He grabbed hold of my arm – I was laughing, too. He was roaring with laughter, like a madman; he wanted to speak, started to say something, but broke off, laughing uproariously.

'When you came out...' – and he shook with uncontrollable laughter – '... you looked like you were coming out of Hell!' He managed to say this after some moments.

And then we each fell about, laughing, laughing, unable to control ourselves. We went back to the dining room where the Baron wanted to celebrate my escape from Hell with more champagne. The shock had kindled a keen sense of elation in me; in truth I had escaped immolation thanks to the noise of the Baron hammering on the door. Perhaps I owed him my life.

'You owe your life to me!'

And the champagne overflowed the bowls which we raised in the most extravagant toasts. We drank toasts to everything we could think of, to all our wishes, dreams, ambitions, to all our longings and disappointments, to all our friends, to anything which occurred to us at that moment, in complete sincerity. These toasts were really confessions, as though we were opening up our souls. And, in truth, to whom could we speak more frankly than to someone we didn't know and whom we would never see again? Beyond these moments of spontaneous disclosure, when we open up the doors and gates to ourselves, such revelations are so difficult to achieve – perhaps because of cowardice or pride, or because of the general lack of understanding around us – that when something like this happens, we must seize it, although in the end we become tortured, regretful and sad, like someone who has betrayed himself. But, at the same time, it brings an inexplicable relief to whomever opens the safety valve when the pressure within him has become too unbearable. Among other things I told him was the story of an unhappy affair of mine.

He was the first person I had ever told, ten years after she had gone and screwed up my life. Nor will I ever tell anyone again. I believe that at that moment I was, above all, telling the story to myself. I relived that sad story as if it had been the happiest period of my life, something I never wanted to forget, and which gave me the greatest satisfaction to recall again, in living speech, listening to myself as if someone else was telling me the story. The Baron, motionless, looked at me steadily; when I finished I saw that his eyes were full of tears. Neither could I see for tears. After all, it is something so simple, so common. I stopped and there was a profound silence in the room. Then he made to rise, but fell back in his chair. He raised a glass to his lips once more and drained the glass in one gulp. It seemed to give him new strength. He got up slowly. I watched him rise and he seemed to grow; it seemed to me that he had grown in size and stature, that he was huge, like a giant. His chair fell behind him. His gaze was fixed and distant. He walked towards me and slipped his arm through mine, as though he was now following an impulse he had always managed to suppress, but which now he had to obey. 'Let's go,' he said.

We were quite calm. We trod on a dog which fled with a piercing whine, breaking the silence of the night; it echoed through the stillness of the house, making our flesh creep. We left the dining room but returned there subsequently by another door; we did not know where we were going, as we walked together, our arms linked, silent and inseparable. At last we descended a staircase and pulled back the great iron bolt of the door, through which flowed the cold night air. The dogs ran around in front of us; we walked among low trees – perhaps apple trees – in the middle of which were some creepers. We went around the house, still silent, as if there was some sort of understanding between us. I didn't feel I had to ask him anything; he was bent over, looking for something. I noticed that we were walking across the flowerbeds in the garden where there were lots of flowers – roses, huge white lilies and beds full of blooms. At last the Baron knelt down and began to pick some violets. The dogs were licking his face and he spat, but not angrily, and pushed them away gently. They were, indeed, violets; I asked him if they were to eat.

'Have you read "The Madonna of the Holy Field"?' I asked.

He did not reply and continued, in the dark, to grub for the tiny flowers, lost among the leaves of the creepers.

'You're right,' he said suddenly, getting up. 'Violets are so sentimental. A rose! that's the thing.'

'For whom?'

'For Her.'

'Ah, well, I too would…'

'Only me,' he shouted, angrily.

In a low voice, as if I was talking to myself, in a tone of bittersweet melancholy, I replied: 'I'm sorry; it was for the other one.'

'Who is the other one?' he demanded, stopping and looking at me in the dark; he spoke sadly, intimately, like someone who remembered some lost hope or old longing.

'And this? Your…'

"'My…'" And then he fell silent. He disappeared into the shadows. I couldn't see him although I could hear his voice there not far from me; it was as if he had suddenly ceased to exist and only his voice was left floating on the night air.

'You don't know her…' he said. 'Why should I feel I have to tell you her name?'

I detected great emotion in his voice; we were still both quite drunk, our feelings easily aroused, as happens in that state. We said nothing, preferring the long silence of our intense communion, until what was particular to each of us began to stir. The Baron began again to look for a rose. I too was cutting roses, tearing my bloody hands on the thorns, aimlessly, since I had nobody to whom I could give those flowers which I was gathering at such cost. I began to ramble on about women and love, essentially a tragic, demented monologue. He went on with his search, restless, silent and indifferent to my ravings. Suddenly he interrupted me: 'It's like Her!' he exclaimed almost triumphantly.

He had plucked a small button of a rose and held it up in his hand. I followed him.

'I wanted to run away with Her,' he said, stopping abruptly. 'But I no longer want…' He paused and then carried on, his voice full of sadness. 'She was afraid, she was afraid of me.'

'But then women must always be afraid of us,' he continued, in a voice full of tears. 'You are an innocent. If we are not afraid of a woman, she's not worth anything.' And he added, sadly: 'Let us pretend that we are in agreement.'

We continued to wander among the nocturnal shadows, silently, walking alongside each other. I wasn't at all surprised when we quickened our pace, as if we knew what we were about. The deep silence lay heavy around us, and over the whole world, too. There was only the slightest breath of air among the leaves, and the sound of our footsteps and those of the dogs. But then the Baron stopped short and, turning round, roared out: 'Who goes there?'

Even the dogs scampered off in fright. I could see nobody and so I ventured to say that he must have been mistaken. But he would not have it.

'Who's there? Who's there?' he bellowed in a high, apoplectic voice.

And he ran off into a thicket of trees. I followed him, and we made sure that there was nobody there. The Baron, though, was so convinced that there was still someone there that I began to waver.

'I'll beat them like dogs!' he cried. 'Idiots! I'll soon put a stop to their tricks, following me around like this. I'm not wet behind the ears. Rabble!'

Then, abruptly, he signalled me to be silent. I heard nothing. But he drew his pistol from it holster and fired six times in the direction from where he thought the noise had come. Then all was silent; even the dogs had vanished. I alone remained. He got hold of my arm and explained that it was the servants. He hurled the pistol away as if it was now useless, and we retraced our steps. We trudged in silence for some time. By now my eyes had grown accustomed to the darkness so that they began to penetrate the gloom. He was carrying the snowy white rosebud in his hand; I trotted along at his side as if I knew where I was going, but in the end what attracted me was this mystery I could not even begin to imagine. I was heading for the unknown and it was this which drew me on without my even knowing. The fresh night air was light and pleasant on my face. The dogs had returned to our side, where they stayed, like shadows creeping beside us.

I heard a branch crack and at that moment I realised that there were, indeed, some people following us. In the state of mind I was in I thought it meant something else, so I fell silent, thinking that was the safest thing to do. I checked that I was carrying my revolver in its holster and I carried on alongside the Baron who quickened his pace with each step, like someone running away. I pricked up my ears and, gazing intently, tried to pierce the darkness. The dogs ran off at times and then came running back suddenly, scaring me. Eventually we came to a road, where it seemed that the night was not so dark; either that or dawn was already breaking, I don't know which. Whatever the reason, it was not totally dark. It seemed, too, that nobody was following behind us along the road. The Baron broke the silence; He leaned over, close to my ear, as though even there we needed to talk in whispers.

'It's there.'

'What?' I asked, in a low voice, taken unawares.

'Shush, don't be concerned.'

'About what?' I asked.

'Let's go… No, you'd better stay here. Only if I call…'

'Take it easy.'

There didn't seem to be any sense in what he was doing. Nor, perhaps, in what I was doing either. But we all see the mote in our neighbour's eye and not the beam in our own. And in fact we carried on together as if we knew where we were making for. We followed the high wall of some farm or other, inside which we glimpsed the shadow of a house. Finally the Baron told me to go on in front on my own and stop by a gate up ahead. Some dogs on the farm began to bark furiously; alongside us the Baron's dogs barked back. He shouted at them to stop and aimed a kick at the nearest one. The dog ran off howling, a metallic howl which pierced the night and made me shudder. We had hardly gone any further when I realised that, for some reason, he was uncertain what to do next. He paused, looked behind him, all around, without apparent reason. He began to whistle, calling the dogs. The other dogs on the farm barked even louder; there must have been three or four of them. The Baron continued to the end of the wall, and stopped, as if he did not mean to go further. We had already come far enough. Then he told me to hold the dogs. But how? At the same time I was somewhat afraid for they did not know me and so I excused myself, saying – and it was true – that I could hardly manage to hold four dogs at the same time. 'True enough,' acknowledged the Baron, and, leaving me behind, disappeared. I tried to follow him but I couldn't even see him. I called out; he shouted back, far away, lost in the night. It was a voice which didn't seem to belong to him, which seemed to come from the other side of the world: 'Waaaiit there…'

I walked in that direction, but didn't find him, so I sat down at the side of the road and lit a cigarette. I stayed there calmly smoking, aloof and forgetful of everything in a sudden happy indifference. I don't know how long I had been there when I heard steps. The farm dogs began barking again. It was the Baron. He explained that he had gone to a vine to pull out a wire, an explanation which made me burst into gales of laughter. He looked at me in surprise, not understanding the reason for my laughter. I didn't know how to explain it myself. I was in such a good mood that I surprised even myself. He stepped back and commented in the slow, deliberate voice of the inebriated: 'You're drunk, you're very drunk indeed.' I took offence at this, which proved that I really was drunk, and answered him in the same disdainful manner: 'But my drunkenness is just today, while yours is for God knows how many years.'

As if he hadn't heard, he stopped at the foot of an olive tree and began to wrap the wire around its small trunk, affectionately calling to the dogs who were with us. 'Mondego… Here… Mondego…' He took hold of the dog's collar and threaded the wire through it, and then the next one; 'Tejo... Here boy.' I watched the operation, standing there motionless, until he had them all tied to the wire. Then he told me: 'Stay here, don't leave this spot.' 'Why?' I asked. 'What do you mean why?... Well then!' and he showed me the rose which he still clutched safely in his left hand.

I was already lucid enough for that to begin to seem ridiculous, and I laughed in his face. He gave me a great shove and I fell on my back in the middle of the dogs. While I was trying to get up they licked my face devotedly and I hurled violent insults at the now absent Baron. I got up and ran after him. The dogs started to bark and howl. On the other side of the wall I thought I could hear voices intermingled with the barking of other dogs. I began searching for the Baron away from the roadside, as if I were hunting a wild animal, running, tripping on clods of ploughed earth, in the ditches, falling; I staggered to my feet, crazed by a furious thirst for revenge. But it was in vain: everything was fleeting shadows, tree branches whipped my face, down which the sweat ran in great drops, and leaves caressed my cheek mockingly. I was snorting like a bull. Suddenly I remembered my revolver and took it out of my pocket. Out of breath and unable to continue, I stopped to think and work out a plan.

I realised that I was beside the road again. I took a few more steps, sat down in the gutter and resolved to wait for him there. I put the gun on the grass beside me and with a handkerchief began to mop my sweat-drenched forehead. I was tired. I took a cigarette from my pocket and began to smoke; it didn't taste right. I threw it away and sat staring at the red glow until it disappeared. I began to sink into a great drowsiness. I looked without seeing; I heard without hearing. A tumult of ideas which I could neither control nor understand filled my head. It was a mad stampede of light and shadow, of visions, now indistinct, now so clear that they hurt, all experienced by an 'I' freed from that other one lying there, stupefied and comatose. But from afar came the confused sound of many dogs barking together, and little by little it brought me back to reality. I felt that I was beginning to be able to think more clearly, to come back to my senses. Mechanically I grabbed the revolver. I was about to lay it on the grass again but decided to keep it in my pocket. I thought over everything which had happened up to then and I understood that I had read too much into things, distorting the facts. It was all a game.

Where could the Baron be? Perhaps still looking for me, in some distress. I remembered that white rose held high in his hand, a symbol of purity and refinement, and I saw the beauty of his gesture;

I did not know for whom it was destined though he had asked my help in the matter. And I had betrayed him, pursuing him with a gun in my hand. I had to go and help him; I got up and started to run down the road, the fever of remorse growing ever stronger in me. I ran faster and faster. At that moment I did not have more than a confused idea of what my companion was about, with the rose in his hand; but now that gesture was working away within me, like the thirst for a higher ideal, like a dream which won't let you go. He hadn't told me who it was for. Ah, he called her Sleeping Beauty! I thought she must be very beautiful. I confess that it was only later that I understood that all this was part of his preparation for entering that place.

Finally, though, I tired of running. I don't know why but I began to recall how much I had wanted to travel to Brazil. It was an obsession which I had had for a long time and from which I derived much pleasure and a great inner strength. I stopped thinking about the Baron and began to stride out in high spirits along the road, singing in the night. The sky was full of stars and my voice rose towards them. Some force was carrying me along, I knew not where. At the same time as the Baron was jumping over the high wall, drawing close to the castle and scaling the ramparts to Sleeping Beauty's window, I was striding out along those unknown, endless paths, scattering my hymns to night's immensity.

It was only the breaking of day which drew me back to my senses. I began to shiver; my feet were hurting. I looked around, in the half light of dawn, trying to make out the Baron's manor house but all I could see were the great valleys wrapped in shadow and mist. At that moment I felt both a sense of wonder and the bewilderment of waking up somewhere completely unknown. Where was I? How far had I come? I worked out that I could not have covered a huge distance. I hurried back the way I had come. I walked and walked, already tired out and dispirited but I did not find the palace, nor any house or hamlet, not even a single person. It was as though I had landed on the moon. Only bare hills in the grey light, and the white, never-ending road, curving away before me. I must have walked for hours, until I could go no further. My feet hurt, my whole body, too. My head swam; it felt as if it had been crammed, suffocating, into a helmet which was too small for it. My throat burned too, with a thirst that grew with every step. I sat down, or rather fell, beside the road which led down a mountain. Wearily I scanned those hills which were now emerging from the morning mist; impassive and majestic, they bore witness to my agony. In the distance the sky took on tones of pink, streaked with violet. It was a splendid, fresh sight. A tiny, dark bird appeared next to me, on a dry branch of gorse, chirped dolefully and flew off, disappearing I know not where.

I got up to carry on though it was painful even to straighten up my legs and back. I felt as though my bones were broken. But then Providence lent a hand: on the curve of the road there appeared a miller, his donkey loaded down with sacks of flour. It was, without doubt, one of the best moments of my life. I felt reborn. I went to meet him and asked him to lend me his donkey. He didn't want to; and he took some persuading. He insisted that the animal would not bear my weight, that he could not leave the bags of flour there, that I should stop pestering him 'for the sake of the most Holy Sacrament'. I asked him how much the flour and the sacks were worth; more than twenty escudos was the reply. I took a fifty escudo note from my wallet and put it in his hand. Not wanting to show his satisfaction he unloaded the sacks with much lamentation – 'let this be for my sins' – then disappeared off somewhere briefly, bringing back a cart from wherever it was, saying he did not want to tire out the donkey. He went to hide the bags behind a thicket of brambles and then returned. Since the donkey didn't have any stirrups and the pack-saddle was very broad the miller gave me a hand up. Once seated I gave a click with my tongue and the co-operative beast set off up the road at a jog-trot. I straddled the enormous straw pack saddle and looked back at the poor man like someone gazing at his guardian angel.

The sun was already quite high by the time we reached the manor house. The servant came to open the gate. 'Ah, Sir! Well then…' he exclaimed in some surprise.

'Well then, what?'

'I mean… Do excuse me. We were afraid that… as my master, the Baron…'

'He's here?' I demanded.

'He's out of danger.'

'Out of danger? What danger?'

'You mean you didn't know, sir,' he replied. 'He met with an accident…'

'An accident?

'Yes, indeed, sir. So, you weren't with him then, sir?'

'I was, but… Well…' I hesitated. 'And how did it happen?'

'I know nothing more,' he said. 'I'm sure Senora Idalina will be able to tell you…'

I went to the Baron's room. He was laid out on the bed; he had been shot in the shoulder and he had cracked his skull. I saw that he wanted to tell me something so I approached his bed. With great difficulty he managed to whisper through his lips: 'But she was there… in the window…'

And he closed his eyes, as if exhausted from the great effort. The doctor pulled me by the arm and requested me to leave the room so that the Baron might enjoy complete rest.

Some time later I had some news from him. He sent me a message that he was waiting there for me.

The Baron! Yes, one day I shall have to go back there and visit him and hear that formidable band of musicians once again. And – who knows – we might even sing to the stars again and I might help him to put another rosebud in the high windows of his Sleeping Beauty!

Miguel Torga

ALMA-GRANDE

translated by Ivana Rangel-Carlsen

Riba Dal is where the Jews live. Throughout the year Father João vainly blesses, absolves, baptizes and teaches the catechism.
'Who is God?'
'The All Powerful, Creator of heaven and earth.'
From the swiftness and skill with which they answer these questions, no one would guess that behind the catechism pulses the blood of the Old Testament. But it does. And at the moment of death, when a man does not care whether it is the Torah or the Gospels, before the priest comes to give the finishing touches to the cleansing on his departing soul and learns the dread secret from the fearful man's cowardly tongue, the smotherer is summoned.

Of these servants of the Old Law, entrusted with the duty of abbreviating this world's sufferings and safeguarding the honour of the covenant, none is greater in memory than Alma-Grande.

Tall, gaunt, hook-nosed, he lived in Destelhado on the heights, where the wind from Galicia still whistles restlessly all year long. Whoever called on this father of death knew that he first had to climb the hill and struggle against the wind like a ship on stormy seas.

'This damned wind!'
So it was. As surely as Alma-Grande would be sitting in front of the fire at the house in the corner, one could bet that the harsh breath of Sanábria would be sweeping the hill. All one needed to do was call out his name in front of the house.

'Uncle Alma-Grande! Uncle Alma-Grande!'
'Coming…'
In no time, the pincers of his hands and weight of his knee released the dying.

Dauntless, he would enter the house and silently cross in front of the gathered, who for three days had waited impatiently in that room for the last breath of the sufferer. He would go straight to the bedroom and close the door. A short while later he would leave, his expression at least as peaceful as the one he had left behind. Those waiting outside the door would look at him with terror and gratitude. Once in a while, after the nightmare, a voice would rise timidly from the depths of a conscience and protest. But the next day that same voice was as likely to rise above the wind on the heights of Destelhado and call for him.

'Uncle Alma-Grande! Uncle Alma-Grande!'

'Coming…'

And in no time he would come out the door.

When Isaac's hour arrived, it was Abel, one of his sons, who climbed the slope. The boy was flustered by the unusual turmoil at home, by the strange way his mother had sent him to call Uncle Alma-Grande, and because of the wind.

'What's the matter with your father, boy?'

The child looked hard in the dry face of the smotherer.

'Fever…'

'Well, let's go then…'

'What are you going to do to him, Uncle Alma-Grande?'

'I'll just have a look at him.'

All the way down the street, only the wind spoke. Hoarse from so much bellowing, monotonous and tireless, the wind expressed the intimacy between the two: the boy, excited, battling with confused, persistent forebodings; the old man, accepting, as a river accepts its flow, a fate which entrusted him with the burden of hastening death.

At the house, tears began at the threshold, but Alma-Grande's entrance seemed to dry everything. In the wake of his slow, ponderous tread down the corridor, mute despair and arrested breathing followed.

'What's he going to do to him?' Abel asked once again, as the bedroom door closed behind Alma-Grande.

In answer to her son, two silent tears slid down Leah's face.

Inside, stuck to the sweat-soaked bed, Isaac seemed to have reached his end. He was white, his eyes lost in the hollows of his face; he looked like a drowning man and seemed to be merely awaiting orders to depart. He had fallen ill fifteen days earlier with such a high fever that Dr Samuel had given him up. He had come to see him, came back once again, and advised the family to order the coffin. Isaac, however, was like a cedar of Lebanon: tough to the core.

After the doctor had given up, Isaac was sick for six more days, but did not die. His eyes remained bright and lucid. He kept moaning that he was dying, but his piercing, jet-back eyes continued to shine brightly. Finally, however, a strange shadow settled upon his face and his wife, Leah, lost hope.

Two more days passed and when, in the living room, Dona Rosa reminded Leah that it was time for him to make his last confession, Daniel, one of Isaac's brothers, approached his sister-in-law and between a couple of words of comfort, dropped the name of Alma-Grande. At first Leah resisted the idea of calling upon his services, but the prospect of Father João coming into her house to administer the last rites settled the argument. As soon as day dawned, in a tone that frightened her son, she sent Abel to fetch the smotherer.

When Alma-Grande entered, Isaac was in the throes of that final battle one always fights lying down. The enemy within seeking defeat, while his opponent, a noble being loyal to his heritage, bravely defends the besieged bastion. Beads of sweat rolling down Isaac's temples and the quickened rhythm of his breath were evidence of the conflict. Whoever witnessed this battle with clear eyes needed nothing else to feel the grandeur and solemnity of the struggle.

But Alma-Grande had no eyes to see this. He was insensitive to the nuances of life's mysteries. Without a shudder, he moved toward the bed like an automaton performing a routine task. His role was not to look, but to place his hands around his victim's neck, his knee upon the chest, to dismount in a few minutes – an instrument that had correctly fulfilled its function.

In his castle, Isaac resisted. The swift bellows of his chest diligently pumped air into the furnace. Hot, thick, energetic sweat continued pouring from that human volcano.

The house was like a tomb inhabited by mute petrified living beings. Only in the bedroom was there any motion and excitement.

Silently, Alma-Grande advanced. But when, with outstretched hands and bent knee, he was about to fall on Isaac, a voice different from all the other voices he had heard in similar moments, a voice that seemed to come from another world, said: 'No! Not yet… Not yet!'

How often had the smotherer heard these words, these cries of despair, these desperate anxious appeals, without checking his sacred mission! How often! But this time, the appeal and the moans sounded somehow different. 'No! No! Not yet!'

The blindfold, which until then had curtained Alma Grande's eyes, began to tear. Hesitating between the darkness of custom and a dawning light of conscience, the smotherer felt like a charging torrent that had lost its way.

'No! Not yet… Not yet!'

Something terrible was happening. To the struggle that Isaac had until then carried on against unknown forces, there was now added the duel between the two men, one knowing he was going to kill and the other knowing he was about to be killed.

For a moment they were eye to eye, intently measuring each other. Sweat ran down Isaac's face; hot blood pounded in Alma-Grande's temples.

It was the sudden creak of a door that shattered their intense concentration. At the sound, Alma-Grande fell upon the dying man like a suspended weight suddenly released. With a dull thud, without a word, his grasping hands searched for Isaac's neck.

But the door had creaked in, letting someone in: a presence that Alma-Grande sensed – a wrathful presence standing beside him, straining to grasp the scene.

Isaac's final effort to remove the groping claws coupled with Abel's astonished presence took away the customary strength from Alma-Grande's hands and knees. The murderer inside him, the animal that drank life in deep draughts, vainly struggled to the surface. Vainly, his conscience assured him that his purpose in life was to kill. He was not bold enough to command those hands and those knees to kill in front of a witness.

He straightened, his face displaying a pallor like the dying man's and, lacking the courage to face the boy's alarmed, piercing eyes, he turned and silently left. He crossed the living room with lowered head, a far cry from the tragic majesty of other times. He was leaving life behind him, and life gave him no stature, for his mission was to kill.

Seconds later, when Leah entered the bedroom like a guilty animal, she found her son sitting on the bed, stroking his father's forehead. The child struggled in an ocean of uncertainties, but the same heart that had dictated his furtive and worried entrance into the bedroom now impelled him to place his hand on the scalding forehead of the one who had given him life.

Perhaps it was also this innocent, filial gesture that caused Isaac's blood to flow in his veins with confidence. Twenty days later, without having confessed, Isaac was having his broth by the fire as if nothing had happened.

Nothing, in fact, *had* happened, as far as anyone else in the village was concerned – except, that is, for Isaac, and the boy, and Alma-Grande. Others had passed from agony to death and from death to resurrection as unconsciously as someone passing from summer to winter and winter again to summer. Only the three knew, in their different ways, that the drama had been darker and deeper. Isaac had seen death's claws for himself first hand; Alma-Grande had for the first time stared into the darkness of his pit; and as for the child, he had glimpsed things he could not yet understand.

Time went slowly by, and with it all memory of Isaac's illness was erased from village memory. The family went to Mass – and celebrated the Sabbath in private – as usual.

The three, however, kept peering into the mirror in which the sinister image of the recent past was reflected. Ever more painfully, Isaac looked into his soul and recognized revenge. With increasing guilt, Alma-Grande looked within and saw fear. The innocent boy saw only anxiety and confusion. The three formed an island of despair in the calm seas of the village. No words passed between them, although the child asked for and received his father's blessings every morning and every night, as was the custom, and Alma-Grande issued a monosyllabic greeting when he happened to pass by Isaac in the street. Otherwise, they were guarded with one another, as if preparing for the hour in which, for all eternity, they could dispel the heavy cloud that darkened their consciences.

That moment finally arrived.

Alma-Grande was returning from Bobadela after visiting his daughter and grandchildren when Isaac, who had followed him like a bloodhound, ambushed him on the road. The only witnesses were God and Abel who, without being suspected, had followed and now watched the scene from behind a boulder.

'Thou shalt not kill…' So says the Gospel, but in real life, under another covenant, morality has different guidelines, as Alma-Grande well knew.

'Thou shalt not kill…' And yet, Isaac stared at Alma-Grande with the same implacable gaze that had met his own eyes in his own time of agony.

'No… No…'

But Isaac was younger and stronger. Soon Alma-Grande lay on his back on the ground, his neck clamped by the other's hands and his ribs under the infinite weight of Isaac's knee.

'No… No…'

From behind the boulder, the boy could see Alma-Grande's congested face and hear him gasping for breath against the choking grip.

Powerful, inexorable, the vice tightened. After only one more gasp the three were at peace. Isaac had had his vengeance; Alma-Grande had lost his fear; the child finally understood.

Joaquim Paço d'Arcos

THE STORY OF VENÂNCIO,
SECOND OFFICIAL

translated by John Byrne

The noise was discreet but perfectly audible, persistent, continuing wearisomely on through the whole night, keeping him company, as it had on previous nights, and as it would on all the nights on which he proposed to stay working late.

Under the woodwork and the floorboards, within the walls, between the shelves crammed with books and papers, the mice were eating up the fabric of the old building and all its venerable furnishings. By day no one heard them. The weighty voice of the Ministry which occupied the large old house drowned out all the voices, all other sounds. The public themselves who headed for the little windows in search of information, or who tried to insinuate themselves into the offices to sort out matters which were the province of the Department, did so with the utmost respect, diffidently, speaking low, submissively, lest they arouse the simmering displeasure of the civil servants, with invariably disastrous consequences for the poor petitioner. During the few hours designated as 'hours of opening' there reigned this sovereign body, whose decisions were law, whose judgement superseded justice, whose inertia was the most effective shield against the dangerous changes in the social fabric, or in society itself or even in government – a body which constituted the great, sprawling family of the civil service.

The mice, subdued by the presence of the gentlemen who worked in the building, by their chatter, by the squeaking of their footsteps on the decrepit floor, did not dare, above their secret and corrosive toil, to attract the attention of those whom they did not wish to antagonise. And so they took advantage of these few hours of human activity to enjoy a well-deserved rest. In this way the sovereignty of the old house was shared, in perfect peace, between the civil servants and the mice. Until very recently, each one of them had different spheres of influence. But now, braving the light of day, emerging from the holes in the floor and skirting board which they had patiently made, the rodents began to stick their noses into the deep slumbers of the archives and to mock the service with the voracity with which they ate up the sheets of paper, the notebooks, the heaps of official papers which had been accumulated by the service during the execution of its secular mysteries.

This contempt for the limits – tacitly accepted for years and years – of their respective spheres of activity had led the Minister, yes, the very same, following a proposal by the Director General, to set up a Commission to look at measures which, of necessity – so long and profitable had been the truce between the two parties – they would have to take to get rid of the rodents. The method of setting up the Commission called for lengthy and conscientious deliberations on the part of the statesman charged with organising and empowering it. It was necessary to add to the prestige of certain names the regal qualities of others and the dynamism of yet others. It was helpful to use the opportunity to draw into a cordial collaboration certain figures who had strayed from the fold either through political disenchantment or personal disaffection; it was advantageous to remember the experts who would suggest – based on their undisputed expertise – the best means to combat the dreadful species of muridae; such means had already been tried and tested by those various international bodies which, working together, had changed the world in the last decade, making it peaceful, prosperous and happy. It was moreover worth bearing in mind the sensibilities of those concerned – experts, politicians, members of staff, the indispensable figures who gave the thing tone and those who, accustomed to wield authority, would carry the burden of the struggle against the implacable rodents.

In this manner, after about three weeks of consultation and procrastination, during which the list of Commission members was definitively established seven times and had to be changed from top to bottom seven times – after these twenty-one days during which the Minister suspended almost all other work in order to dedicate himself to the sensitive task which demanded so much tact and knowledge, the eminent gentleman of the State was finally able to send to the *Official Gazette* the decree naming the Commission charged with the supreme power to recommend the means of destruction of the mammals, of the rat tribe, to use the wise words of the government citation.

The Commission was composed of twenty-nine individuals, all of them equally illustrious. The President was one of the most eminent luminaries of the Academy; only after much supplication did he agree to lend the lustre of his celebrated name to this mission of undeniable national interest.

With the publication of the decree Venâncio was deeply and understandably annoyed. He had been the first to draw attention – he had informed his superior immediately – to the danger that the mice were beginning to represent to the old house, to the archives, to the Ministry, to the institutions, to the country which harboured them. Three or four files of the greatest importance – one relating to the property of the mother-in-law of the Director General – had been practically destroyed by the alarming voracity of the disrespectful rodents. The Head of Section had informed the relevant authority, and step by step the matter had gone as far as the Minister's office. The reaction of His Excellency has already been related; how he was not lacking in the judgement necessary to put the problem in its proper perspective – the national perspective, in fact. And how his cogitations brought forth the notion of this vast body which would not disgrace us tomorrow in front of FAO, or UNESCO or BIT (IBW) or OIS, in those vast amphitheatres where voices echo throughout the world and where every problem can be tackled with the same unity of purpose which would be employed in the slaughter of the teeming, insatiable rodents.

Upon learning that a Commission was to be set up to deal with the problem which he had uncovered, Venâncio began to nurse the entirely legitimate ambition that he might be part of such a distinguished working party. Apprehensively, he placed his humble petition before the Chief of Section.

'I see no reason why not,' his superior replied benevolently. But it was only after a great deal more pleading that he condescended to speak about the matter to the Head of Department.

This worthy had no longer any reason to favour Venâncio, especially since it was the Chief of Section who had gained the glory from the second official's silent endeavours: 'What the Devil do you mean with this idea? But, very well then, if you are so keen on the matter then I can commend it to our Director General.'

These words did not even amount to a promise. When they were recounted to Venâncio by a third party he weighed them in all their slippery worth; he realised that he would need to back up his assiduousness with a letter so that the matter might not be still-born.

Into the composition of this epistle he poured all his devotion, all his deference, all his powers of persuasion and blandishment, in short all the dreams of any down-trodden bureaucrat. He referred to his long years in the service of the Department, the numberless duties, burdensome and oppressive, which had rained down on him from all sides; the incontrovertible confidence which he had always merited; the loyalty which he had never ceased to demonstrate; the leave which he voluntarily sacrificed every year in the public interest; the overtime for which he was never paid; his wife's illness which left her a suffering invalid; the rewards which he had never received because they were systematically creamed off by others; the promotions never achieved; his personal devotion to the recipient, to his revered Chief, to the great servant who had conferred both glory and efficiency on the Department; and at last, humbly, diffidently, he came to the point: might he be included in the number, which he had heard would be great, of the members of the Commission? It was he after all who had pointed the finger at the mice! It was he who, during those silent evenings which he had devoted to the work of the Department, had, alone, observed their midnight labours and who had, furthermore, endeavoured to put a stop to their vandalism, their depredations, by means of the stoppers which he had made to plug up the holes in the skirting boards.

The Head of Department, tickled pink by the honour accorded him by his subordinate and by the respectful tone of his letter, happened to mention the matter to the Director General during the hour set aside for State business: 'I have just had a letter from Venâncio, you know the poor devil who works in the second section. What do you think about this then: he wants perforce to be appointed to the Commission.'

'What a ridiculous idea!' he replied. 'What on earth for, to what end? To a Commission of those we have specially chosen... what on earth would the Minister say. Did you ever hear of such a thing!'

And so the exalted bureaucrat had the basic good sense not even to bother his Excellency the Minister with such a preposterous idea.

Venâncio's wife was a lady whose acute modesty had, over the years, deprived her of any lingering charms; chronic illness, too, had aged her (prematurely). However she held an almost religious respect for her husband's vast toil; to her eyes, peering from behind a veil of long, self-effacing adoration, Venâncio was a pillar of the State. And so she shared his well-founded pain at his undeserved exclusion, which followed all the other rejections which had been the reward for his long and dutiful career. But this time, from the depths of her own distress, she found the courage to try to console Venâncio for this most recent, though surely not final, disappointment.

'What good would it do you anyway to be a member of this Commission?' she asked. 'If only they would give you some money... but this is only for the glory...'

'What are you women doing, talking about matters you don't understand!' replied the second official, hugely irritated. 'Women don't understand these things; it would be a poor soul who only thought of what he might or might not get out of it. As if there were not other satisfactions in life!' And the wound which not being part of the Commission – the Commission which had been set up by his own Minister – had opened up, began to spread through the bureaucratic soul of Venâncio.

But the gall, all the accumulated bile of that gratuitous affront, only finally overwhelmed him on the afternoon when the Chief of Section, without removing the yellow cigarette end from his bottom lip, said: 'I've just been to the Terreiro do Paço for the opening of the Commission. What a splendid ceremony; and the Minister spoke so well. As for the President's reply, what a delight that was!'

Venâncio bought all the daily papers just to see if there was the slightest mention of the matter in the press. The Week had, on its third page, the official photograph, with the flower of the bureaucracy, of thinkers, of experts and of politicians gathered around the member of the Government. And it did not stint in its references to the fact that for the twenty-nine members of the Commission this was a matter for much congratulation.

Venâncio was eaten up by the purest and most justifiable envy.

The Commission met the following day, but some of its members were already missing on account of the fact that their many other duties made it impossible for them to devote themselves completely to its work; and the President, too, was due to take the waters. It therefore postponed until after the summer, on the unanimous vote of the members present, the study of this problem, the urgency of which the Minister had emphasised during his vigorous, statesman-like speech.

Venâncio continued to work through the evenings in the large old house where the Ministry, with its branches spreading out all over the city, had set up the Department and the Archive. But bitterness had entered implacably into his soul. Nevertheless he still felt bound by the weighty responsibilities of State. Without his dedicated toil of an evening everything would grind to a halt; and the machinery of State would topple. He weighed the catastrophic consequences of what would surely happen in that case. And, out of civic duty, the pure duty of a conscientious servant, he, alone of everyone in the building, carried on his silent, methodical labour throughout the evenings and the night.

The Chief of Section could thus claim in front of his superiors that there was not a single matter which was not being dealt with in good time. And he took care, secretly, to praise Venâncio: 'My good fellow, you are a regular glutton for work! One of these days you'll get your just reward.'

Venâncio, however, did not believe a word of it. Only habit, disguised as duty, continued to bind him to his servitude. But if in the sight of other men he seemed to be the same, he had utterly changed his attitude towards the rodents. He no longer targetted them. He ceased to make the pieces of cork with which he stopped the holes and which, due to him alone, had been the last feeble obstacle to the catastrophic invasion of the mice.

With the heat of the summer the members of the mouse family, of the rat tribe – in the memorable words of that which never errs and which is called the *Official Gazette* – the engaging, companionable rodents, feeling in greater need of fresh air, gained a new audacity and began to flaunt themselves, unconcerned, at quiet times, on top of the furniture, along the shelves, on the Archive shelves.

Venâncio left them in peace, since they did not bother him. And they, cunning and shrewd as they were, understood the advantage of a peaceful co-existence. And thus a modus vivendi was tacitly established.

Venâncio, to whom his superiors had not accorded the rewards he deserved, could not but be sensible of the fine qualities of the unassuming rodents. He began to feel a special affection for two large rats, more furry, older, slower in their movements and more easy-going; they were also less greedy because they had already done, already accomplished, everything in this world. They seemed to be, like him, two pillars of the State and perhaps it was this shared conviction which brought them together.

And so it was that Venâncio found himself bringing to these two affable companions, on those nights when he was working late, an old sweet tin full of delicate little tidbits: crusts of bread, thin slivers of cheese, tender bits of smoked sausage.

This was his most closely guarded secret and, unknown to his wife, he would prepare the morsels; distributing them now became part of his routine, in the same way as his work, as methodical and as scrupulously executed as his official duties.

The drama came to a head when the Director General wished to do a favour for his mother-in-law, a favour which family obligations required of him, and from which his wife, as the mandatory heir, would come to benefit. He asked that the files pertaining to the esteemed lady's properties be brought before him.

A flurry of activity swept the Ministry. Rooms, offices, repositories and filing cabinets were searched from top to bottom.

'Perhaps they have been sent to the Procurator,' suggested the Chief of Section, with the natural and creditable awe of one conscious of his responsibilities.

No; there was no record in the check-out book of the files having left the building.

And so the search, the exhausting search, proceeded.

To Venâncio fell the disagreeable task of conveying before his superiors the half-digested remains of the files which the Director General wished to consult. They consisted of a heap of papers, chewed through, indecipherable and useless.

When the Head of Department brought him the disagreeable-looking heap of paper the Director General exploded in shrill, almost blind, fury. 'But is this the work of the mice? What is the Commission doing, what steps are they proposing, what measures have they taken?'

The Commission, which had been set up almost a year ago, had never re-convened. The President's illness, the countless duties of its members had not allowed it to carry out the tasks it had set itself. The President, on the telephone, had once again proffered his explanations to the Minister.

The Director General did not dare take up the cudgels against that Commission on which the flower of the country was so liberally represented. He quite rightly ordered, however, the most thorough inquiry; this took a most unfavourable direction as far as Venâncio was concerned. The cleaning lady testified that various scraps of food had begun to appear in those places where they could only have been put with the express intention of attracting the rodents and providing them with nourishment. And since Venâncio was the only official who worked overtime, only he could have carried out such a feat without embroiling others.

In front of the official entrusted with the inquiry Venâncio did not have the resolution or the spirit to resist the evidence which had been built up against him. He floundered through a calamitous confession to his implacable interrogator, the latter representing the State against whose sacred heritage the former had conspired.

The Director General – whose mother-in-law had made his home life hell, blaming him for the destruction of the archives – took the conclusions of the inquiry to the Minister. And this great public figure, who never wavered in the performance of his duty, in the execution of justice, was implacable as, indeed, conscience required him to be.

Venâncio, who had conspired against the security of the State, causing it irreparable damage, was dismissed from his post as a civil servant. There were still those who thought that forced retirement constituted sufficient punishment; but His Excellency did not yield and insisted, purely and simply, that the second official be dismissed, on the grounds that the country had had enough of rodents.

Two years later the Commission, which should by then have come up with measures to combat the dreadful rodents, was dissolved; the President was duly lauded since, in spite of the fact that circumstances had not allowed him to bring to bear on the matter all his great powers, nevertheless outstanding figures must be honoured and accorded the recognition of the country and of posterity. It is in the exaltation of such examples that eternity is stamped on the annals of History.

Manuel da Fonseca

MARIA ALTINHA

translated by Patricia Odber

Every year, women who live down south, beside the sea, cross the hills and spread out across the plain, heading towards the harvesting and work of the rice fields. They come bringing cheerful songs and noisy chatter, and the people of the small towns gather in the squares to watch them pass on their way to the big farms. And, in the first days of toil, at the time when the harvest overseer has the most longed-for words for those who go bowed between the ears of corn or buried in the mud of the rice field, when the sun disappears and the cicadas and crickets begin a chirping that is lost in the distance, the women from beside the sea sing new and colourful songs.

Around the fire, itinerant farm-workers and day-labourers hush their rough voices and stay listening to them, their gaze lost in the night, thinking of the lands beside the sea, from which the women have come. Because the songs of the young girls from the south have the brightness of the waters and the quickness of the waves. And their bursts of laughter are as natural as a spring of water shot through with sunlight, jumping on a rock. They bring the freshness of the sea to this desolate and barren land.

For this reason the townspeople gather to watch them pass, and the farm-workers and day-labourers fall silent and listen to them, after work, when the night spills stars on the earth.

Maria Altinha left her village for the first time, and the long journey was a new experience for her.

She had left them all behind. The hills and almond trees and walled paths, and orchards of loose soil with trees laden with fruit. And the orange trees and the little white houses and the water wheels squeaking on the hillsides. And the blue lulling whispering of the sea and the scent of the sea borne on the wind to the window of her room. And her mother making little baskets of palm leaves at the door of the house, and her younger brothers selling them in the villages – everything, everything was left behind, far, far away. Now, it was that flat and dusty open countryside interrupted by great oak pastures from time to time. Always flat, wild and barren.

But what did it matter? Afterwards she would return to the village with the money earned from her new job, and neither her mother nor her little brothers would go hungry when the winter cold came.

As soon as she reached home, her mother would fold her in her arms, weeping, and she, with a crooked smile, would show her little calico bag full of money. And when night fell, with the rain drumming on the roof and the wind raging outside, around the hearth they would listen to her recount the things of those lands; her brothers asking questions and watching her with shining eyes, amazed by her answers.

Afterwards, the youngest, overcome by sleep, would let his little head droop in her lap and the other would follow suit. Only the eldest would persist in listening until that weight greater than his strength came and pulled down his eyelids and closed his eyes. She and her mother would put them to bed and go to bed themselves. And the wind and rain would cause no fear because, along with some job or other that would turn up, the savings brought back from the plain would be enough for the whole winter, without hunger entering the house.

Because of this, her clear voice overflowed with joy when she sang and the labourers stayed behind to hear listen to her until sleep came.

Valdanim had no sooner swallowed the hard lump of bread, than he dragged himself to beside the house joined on to the barn where the women slept. There he stayed, his cigarette unlit, watching Maria Altinha and smiling at her with enormous teeth below his moustache, his arms resting on his knees.

There were songs and laughter – in those first few days the women from the south won over the men of the plain.

But, now, little by little, everything changed. The group now dragged a heavy choir up the slopes and the womens' voices faded. They began to feel the painful work in their very flesh; from morning to night, under a scorching sun. The scalding air of the plains had dried up the freshness of the sea. Only the plaintive songs sounded out at dead of night.

Valdanim took his ease, tilting his head back, eyes fixed on Maria Altinha as if she were singing for him alone, although her voice was lost in the melody of the other voices of the gang. Now, Valdanim would sing to her and, now when he saw her, it wasn't just that fixed smile with enormous teeth below his moustache; now it was an impudent phrase as well:

'Maria Altinha, one of these nights I'm going to tell you what's what.'

But the girl didn't reply and Valdanim rolled himself up in his blanket, thinking that a situation like that didn't require fine words, but it did call for a strong pair of arms wrapped around Maria Altinha's waist. And a torpor took over the man's body, he seemed to be drowning. He pulled his blanket over his head, his eyes turned heavenwards and closed gradually. In a moment, Maria Altinha was in all his senses. And he fell asleep. A night-long sleep, with neither nightmares nor dreams. Around dawn, that painful awakening, his body twisting in a fever of anxiety. And, still half asleep, it was time to set off with the gang heading towards the water meadow.

What really woke them all up was the cold pond water climbing up their legs.

They looked like condemned men and women.

The low sky limited the darkened horizon all round. Hills and bare summits, occasionally a shrivelled cork-oak with twisted boughs, standing alone. In the middle of the rice field, legs buried up to the thighs, bent over, in a row, the women stretched their arms down into the water, stirring around the bottom. Here and there, a man.

Since the sun had come, tearing the damp veils of dawn and afterwards burning like a fire until dusk, the women with their skirts hitched up between their legs, sleeves rolled up, waded through the swamp weeding the rice.

Mosquitoes buzzing made ripples on the muddy water, a bitter stench clogged their nostrils and seemed to penetrate all the pores of their skin. As they plunged their hands down to the depths, little concentric waves were sent out around their arms, and air bubbles came gurgling up to break the surface, stirring up the stench right under their nostrils. Because the women's faces almost brushed against the mud, whenever they took a step forward, hanks of hair kept falling forward on to their brows; so the women tied back their hair and scratched the mosquito bites with their wrinkled fingers.

The foreman, in the ditch, looked hard, giving orders. Here and there, a man. The blazing sun full on their backs, the horizon dark.

They seemed like condemned men and women.

One dusk, heavy with sadness, all that could be heard out in the fields was the scolding of cicadas and crickets. Maria Altinha felt the onset of the first fever. For ten days she couldn't go to the field. Ten days on her own, trembling with cold and sweating on top of the sack, covered with the blanket, in a corner of the storehouse. The carter came from the township with the little round box full of wafers and Maria Altinha was unable to go to the rice field…

One day she did the same as the others. She went into the rice field yellow with malaria. When her teeth began to chatter, she left the water and lay down on the ground, trembling from head to foot. It was a lost bushel; the foreman stood there and drew a line on the paper.

When Saturday came, that week had only three days' wages for her.

One afternoon Valdanim left the field long before sunset. He couldn't do any more, he had a pain. The foreman allowed it, reluctantly, drawing a line through the paper.

Limping, Valdanim took the path towards the hill. But once past the hill, he stopped limping and hastened his pace.

Black thunder clouds darkened the sky. A tepid breath of air touched the skin of the harvesters, making them shiver in a cold sweat.

Valdanim ran for the hill. Behind, further and further behind, remained men and women buried in the rice paddy, stooped over, with their hands stirring in the depths.

They looked like condemned men and women.

Lying on the sack, Maria Altinha seemed to be asleep.

That day she hadn't even got up to go to work. That brusque trembling had come and, alone on the hill, she'd struggled trying to close her teeth, clenching her fingers in her overalls. A deathly cold stole over her limbs and her teeth chattered in unison with the strangulated moan that came from her chest. In a fruitless, painful struggle, her stiff body struggled to control its unruly, continuous movements. All alone, far from home, far from her mother!…

Afterwards the cold slowly disappeared, and with it the trembling. She was exhausted, her body broken, her head throbbing as if the flames of a furnace were burning inside. And that heat went down her body. She was burning up; the sweat soaked through, covering her in a sticky broth. Nightmares, a thunderous noise came and went, now intense, intolerable, now soft and caressing, soporific. She spoke with gestures, wept, laughed. Her eyes, opened wide, tried to see but in the dark only fast, shapeless things went past, hallucinations. There came the noise, growing until it burst like a thunder-bolt in her brain. And it faded into a distant whisper. The heat had gone too, and the nightmares ended. Those drops of sweat remained, her body left with no strength for anything. Now Maria Altinha seemed to be asleep.

She could scarcely hear the cautious footsteps that drew near and a voice that whispered close to her ear. Hands stroked her hair, her face, her breasts. Enormous hands. Everything was indistinct, lulling as in a dream. Then came that sharp pain in her lower belly: a stabbing, tearing her in half!

Maria Altinha shouted, but thick lips bruised her mouth with brutal desperation.

Now the townspeople don't recognise the women who return from the harvests and rice fields when they watch them pass by, in the square, on the long journey back to the south. They go away all dried out and yellow, as if they were old women, without any chatter, without a smile, their faces frozen beneath their handkerchiefs.

There she goes, that girl who sang and laughed so much, withered, silent as a shadow. Only inside her thoughts twist round inside, in endless bitterness. Winter is coming, with the rain and wind, and hunger will come to that humble little village house. And her youngest brother will cough all night long and mother will weep in the corner and there is nothing she can do, nothing!...

The other women seem to be thinking the same; so silent and hidden in their handkerchiefs that their faces can scarcely be seen.

That is why the townspeople go disappointed from the square, and they are wont to say of those folk who come from the south, from beside the sea:

'Every year it's the same. They come here singing and go back weeping.'

José Marmelo e Silva

TESTIMONY

translated by John Byrne

The Bible says that Cain killed Abel for a trivial motive. Homer sings that the beauty of Helen destroyed Troy.

A neighbour of mine suddenly committed suicide.

Opening the papers, we read that a man was killed in such and such a place, struck down with a hoe – or stabbed, or shot – for no real motive: for a glass of wine, for the sake of a couple of coins. Sometimes when we think about it, it seems as if sanity is something which just bobs along on the surface like a bit of cork on water.

Gentlemen: the doctor doesn't waste time studying the effects of an illness except better to discover the root cause. Why not adopt the same method with our own misfortune? I compare it to the mouth of a river whose real source is often our mother's breast.

During my military training in Mafra very strange things began to happen to me: turning a corner, passing by the shops, the butchers, the cafés, the chemists, it was not uncommon to find myself the object of pointing fingers, of brazen murmurs, even from the young bucks.

'That's him, that cadet!'

'For something so trivial!'

'For nothing at all!'

'The poor dead thing, six feet under!'

It's true that there was no doubt that I had behaved irresponsibly, but why did it have to be my arm that did the deed, and not another's? The local gossip, which at that time centred on the Cova Funda, called me a cynic, a 'revolting cynic'. For these poor people, here is the confirmation; because, looking deep into myself I found the seeds of our own evil. And let me tell you, Lia's grief transcends any trivial concerns: we just pin this label onto the most poignant dramas or attribute them to a kind of fate – glorious for some, deadly for others – but irrevocable for everybody.

Lia knew so little about it because it was she herself who sent that soldier to the coach, when I and my colleagues arrived in Mafra; we gazed at the Convent almost disdainfully, almost indifferently – as though we took it for a very different kind of monument – while a hubbub of children buzzed around us: 'Hey there, cadet, have you already got a room?'

'Cadet, do you need a room?'

'Cadet, there's a room…'

(Damn it, everything was redolent of the barracks, even the people, even the colour of the houses!)

Why was it she who sent that soldier, who came up to me, took my suitcase with no hesitation and said: 'Our major Escoto's widow is waiting for you, cadet.'

Why did she send you, indeed, I ask.

Fate is what marks out all human dramas; it is Fate that brings disgrace, but disgrace is no more than the mouth of a river which often has sprung from our mother's breast.

Lia's mother had attached herself to an elderly man when she was very young. This man, the deceased A. N. Scoto, was a distant relative of ours; but ever since he had been a student he had lived such a rash life (or, as I heard tell when I was little, such a scandalous life) that we at home lost the thread of things at the precise point where his second wife fled to Paris, and he got divorced a little bit later. It was only eight years ago that we heard, vaguely, that he had died in Mafra; I had never met him. After all, the soldier told me, he had married for a third time, in Porto, and had had two daughters, notwithstanding his advanced age, and…

Indeed, I am hardly up the stairs, the door opens by itself and Lia appears, one of them, radiant with my arrival. Here she is close to me, between the old furniture in the little sitting room, opening to me the door to her soul as if I was the one whom she has been awaiting for so long with a sharp, unfailing anxiety. There she was: serene, very white, small, with the high forehead of 'papa's' portrait and with such a serious, pure demeanour that I was stunned. And of course, that certain type of 'mama' was a complete contrast; excessively fat, sleek – though some might use a stronger term – quite coarse, it's true, but her uninterrupted, unrestrained flow of speech was at least excusable, for at some point I sensed in her one of those not uncommon types who have acquired some sensitivity at the cost of much poverty and suffering. In addition, she had read a few novels and suffered from asthma.

She was often terribly short of breath – it was wretched – and her husband had spoken a great deal about us, had retained an interest right up until his death. She was from Trás-os-Montes, she was called

Conceiça (Dona Conceiça). After great tribulations which God had so unjustly inflicted on them, Lia had secured the position of schoolmistress at Cheleiros. And, in short, because they had to take in a paying guest for the spare room, they didn't doubt that I would give them the pleasure of accepting. They thought of me as family, obviously. They were already counting on me last year. They knew all about me, through my colleagues.

That was fine by me. But I confess that I found her speech a bit of an ordeal, like a new chapter in the romance of the major. We had always lived well. My father is a notary in Portalegre and my mother inherited property in Castelo de Vide, which we have been selling off little by little. I would prefer not to reveal any of this now, but it does explain how that belated kinship awoke in me a reaction strong enough to reject it. Finally, when I was able, I addressed myself directly to Lia; I wanted to shake her out of that seraphic gaze.

'Your sister isn't here; of course, she must be already married…'

Lia's face clouded over; she faltered: 'No sir, my sister… but why did you say that, cousin?' She asked the question so clumsily, with such a lack of art, that I averted my avid eyes.

Dona Conceiça heard and she stopped telling the story of her life – 'from the time when I was a queen', detailing all the cities she had visited, 'even Milan!' – and sighed: 'Juja…'

I understood immediately that I had touched on one of those sensitive, secret areas with my dreadful, indiscreet curiosity. Embarrassed, I waited in some apprehension, and perhaps the fact that I seemed to be expecting something impelled Dona Conceiça to sigh deeply, forced her to fight for air once more: 'Juja…. she died,' she said sadly, opening her heart.

'What! She died?' I blurted out, like an idiot.

'For us…'

'"For us", no, mama,' Lia retorted generously, recovered now. 'I love her just the same, perhaps even more, poor thing!'

Lia fixed her brimming eyes on some distant point, and Dona Conceiça confided in me the cruel secret which made her lips tremble: 'She left me for Lisbon…'

Lisbon, pronounced in that way, meant a forbidden world – something like sensuality, wonder, mystery. In that choked moment I had a glimpse of Juja, tempting – the Rossio, a car, sparkling lights, luxury, pomp, a room – and I ardently desired that she, the adventuress, might not be a cold, saintly beauty like her sister, not so refined and autumnal.

Lia was twenty five years old; in truth she had been waiting for me. Since her papa died, the only door in the house left open was the one to the kitchen garden, and from the garden one could see pines, a vine, windmills, waving lilacs and the endless sea, nothing more. Looking down from the top of the house she could see the shining black road flow away, the road of pleasure, love and display because it led to mass, balls, walks, teas, the carnival. It went in the direction of the towers and cupolas of the Convent and on to the railway station, to Lisbon, to the whole world – that black road. Lia had also been along it, but now that her life had quite simply lost its lustre it was the road which held her back. They moved on, abandoning her, those who marched abreast and brought up the rear. It was then that she, dressed in mourning, locked her house and shut herself away. But her heart kept vigil, night and day, afraid lest a man with golden hair and celestial blue eyes knock at her door and retreat in despair when she didn't come to open it.

And so I brightened Lia's black fate, imagining all this with a cruel smile as soon as I found myself alone in my room, breathing heavily with satisfaction. In fact, there were hundreds of eligible men for every eligible woman in Mafra; and within my first hour there I was, luxuriating in the knowledge that Lia's eyes were tenderly watching me at my toilet – as, humming, I washed, polished, combed – unchangingly passive, promising, eyes longing for other longing eyes. Lia wasn't a passionate woman; nor was she blonde. She was different and I was weary of Lisbon, and of its clinging 'floosies', tanned and sensual. Mourning had locked the window of that house and the door, and so Lia grew like a luxurious little stem in the dampness of a gloomy, basement room.

The Captain welcomed us with some hackneyed speech but his intention – coercion – was still clear enough through the mask of the old soldier. There was no mistaking the harshness of the words – 'You are soldiers' – and a little later he repeated: 'You are soldiers like anyone else.'

In order that we understood this simple fact, he made us stand in line at the office door for the whole afternoon – in the hot sun of a Sunday afternoon. We couldn't say a word. The Convent had been equally repellent: the sheer weight of the place leaves everyone feeling crushed; but, at night, the Esplanade Bar resounded with great guffaws. Nor did the captain want any music in the streets, so we went out with the other so-called gentlemen, making up the most disrespectful verses. At that point I turned for home. It was Autumn and the night was growing cold – I made my excuses. My aim, I realise now, was while appearing light-hearted and hesitant, to worm my way into the life of two innocent creatures.

I found them playing cards in a small room, overlooking the yard, which they used as a kitchen, sewing room, and as I could see, a small dining room. They invited me to take a seat, and I put down my copy of the *Século* which I usually read in bed. Ah, begged Dona Conceiça, with a not unsweet tenderness, could I not lend them the story column for a few moments?

I held it out to her but Lia grabbed it hastily and set about searching through it impatiently, ruffling the paper with her bare, ladylike hands, like the wings of a white dove; I couldn't help smiling as I observed her in surprise. I couldn't clearly define how I felt but it was pleasant, nonetheless. I only managed to place it when the mother, also agitated, justified her daughter's behaviour in all earnestness: 'This for her is like a little bit of heaven. It's the greatest pleasure in the world.' And all the while Lia was devouring some horrific chapter of the *Phantom Submarine* – I think that's what it was – with a look of delight that was almost sensual. The horizons of that ingenuous girl seemed so narrow, so limited to me that just by crooking one finger I could call her mine.

Let's not mince words: our pleasures are utterly relative and reveal a great deal about our souls. Dona Conceiça, 'en famille' like this and beneath the table lamp, had rather lost something of her over-bearing, monstrous ways and anxious and imploring, demanded: 'Just tell me Lia, were they saved?' The cards trembled in her fat fingers, she repeated the question, each time in m ore honeyed tones. Lia waited just enough to heighten the effect and at last, sighing deeply she nodded that yes, they had been saved – all of them!

What a relief, thank goodness! Dona Conceiça couldn't read at night, it upset her. I offered my services, but Lia, radiant with the defeat of the pirates didn't want to play anymore; she hardly realised, woe betide us, that she was about to set in motion the disgrace that would end in such a violent downfall. She started up the ancient machine with its battered horn; it stood, badly lit, hidden away in a corner of the room.

How could they still have kept it? The music, equally old-fashioned, burst out of there, just as indistinct and tired. However, Lia was enjoying herself, she sang, twirled around once in the small free space, watched me furtively. Without her lips moving, I heard her heart calling: 'You seem so kind, ask mama, and come and embrace me!' And when I hesitated: 'Come on, don't waste any time.'

Her anguish dragged on until her lingering gaze said to me again: 'Please, I haven't danced for eight years. Why don't you come? I know full well why not, you don't think me worthy.' I went. I kissed her eyes – at least in the mystery of her life which, to our misfortune, some higher purpose had marked out for sacrifice.

Lia was not a good dancer but she abandoned herself body and soul – docile, content like a lost lamb in the arms of its shepherd. I noticed Dona Conceiça later; she was pretending not to spy. What for? There seemed to me to be no point in this cruelty to Lia, in not letting her live.

'Give me my coat, daughter, I'm feeling cold.' Lia let go of me and ran towards the coat. I saw clearly that as she handed it over – it was a black fur coat, quite shabby – the poor girl received a terrible look of reproach; in her dismay she barely managed to return the glance to me, dismayed. Thus provoked, I put on a new record, a new needle, overcoming Lia's hesitation by means of one simple gesture as we slipped into each other's arms. Dona Conceiça took out her rosary, her lips trembling with fury and, in that way of hers, again brought up the matter of the lack of air. Perhaps she needed to go to the window... like hell she did. She squinted out of the corner of her eye, she prayed. Did she want to convince me? I kissed Lia on the mouth while her mother was fussing about. And Lia didn't hear her, but pressed herself closer, wanting to be next to me and to forget herself. What desire! And then she raised her white neck to me, her gaze too; I thought to find in her the same sense, the same gratitude, as in an animal that we had led to the water and which greedily drank; but Lia's gaze showed me that she was disturbed, deeply so, naively, impossibly, desperately so. Her state reflected a drama which she managed to express in half a dozen simple, choked words: 'You wouldn't harm your Liita, would you?'

She had delivered herself to me. Like a bubble of soap that had come, so vulnerable, iridescent, to rest intact in the flat of my outstretched fingers. Liita! Indeed, the whole moment seemed unreal to me; that pathetic phrase, so improbable. Lia, worthy of sorrow. I had committed a brutal sacrilege.

'Cousin José,' Dona Conceiça butted in, crossing herself and gathering up her beads, 'you don't mind if I ask you something, do you?'

'Oh, my dear lady, by all means... Please...'

'It's just that... could you come and play a hand, if that isn't too much; and talk with me a little bit, too.'

(How kind! She was trying to beguile me.)

'But don't you want to go to bed?' I said.

'I don't sleep. I wish I could, but I can't, my heart won't let me.' And then, looking at my left hand, she added: 'What a handsome ring our cousin has! What a beautiful sapphire! My husband had a ruby, but the ring was the same..'

'You have noticed, too,' said Lia, in surprise. 'It's the symbol of everlasting love, isn't it, Mummy?'

The truth of the matter is that I don't think of Lia at all during the night. Lately at the Apollo I have been mixed up with a chorus-girl. She was a bit common; at that time she was called Georgette and had run away from her father in Oporto. She was related to 'a former Governor of Angola'. You can't imagine what a bloodsucker she was. It was no use my changing my digs or my café; when it came to tracking me down she was like a policeman. She followed me tenaciously to the Baixa, to Estoril, to the Arcádia. How many times had she made me miserable, sticking to me like glue. I can see her now: her fine lips, swollen, proud. She lived in the Rua do Arco, with some fat, rich fellow, in a place with a tiny verandah. Fair enough. It was she who attached herself to me once more, laughing, making a fuss, tapping her tiny foot instinctively, in delicious desperation, until she fell on the bed crying about something or other.

At that time that I felt I loved her, because I felt she was a woman. But the nasty piece of work cottoned on to this very quickly and from that moment started to feign her weeping! I didn't kick her or hit her: one night I just left her, naked, her lips swollen with poison or blood, in cavalier fashion, for good. The relief was as if I had pulled out, painlessly, and not without some pleasure, a corn or callous rooted in my soul. Horrible creature! I had hardly awoken when I cast her aside. I shook her off like some confused nightmare, at the crack of dawn, before daybreak. Jumping out of bed, I remembered Lia; perhaps she was still sleeping. How good it would be to go on tiptoe and surprise her in her soft white sheets. To go into her room and enfold her sweetly, as imperceptibly as the dawn light enters and enfolds her. At first diffused, fearful, less bashful little by little, now bolder, more insistent even to the absolute dominion which arrives with the crowning glory of the sun.

But this is mere imagining; apart from anything else Lia sleeps with her mother. What other fancies will my imagination bring me? I am holding at bay other, sadder matters, either from shame or remorse. On this morning they had, as they had told me the previous evening, to set off for Cheleiros, it being Monday, a schoolday. And so we were able to go together to the barracks. I remember that Dona Conceiça was complaining about the drizzly wind, about the distance and that I resented the fact that Lia put up with all this; she seemed short, walking by my side, nestling close to me when she could, carrying now in one hand, now the other, a small bag of clothes. She lifted her melting eyes to me repeatedly as if to plead: 'Who will help me one day to escape this torture?' She would have liked to stay with me once and for all, slave that she was, and creep away before sunrise. The promise of her lips was mute, the desired embrace of her arms invisible; she had to be content with just holding out to me the tips of her delicate fingers as she left. There we went, the countryside still asleep. The convent was like a great stain against the eastern sunrise. I slaked Lia's thirst there at the side of the road with the living water of which the Evangelist speaks.

'Can you be there, cousin?' babbled her mother. 'It's an hour or more on foot.'

'Perhaps,' I said.

I have to say it again, quite sincerely, frankly (We said goodbye, see you soon, simply enough). It made me believe that she would enjoy more than anything seeing Lia really loved -with marriage at the end of it, why not? I was from a family to which she had always aspired: I had a degree – in arts; I was the heir to some great pile – probably mortgaged, although nobody knew for sure. Lia with her gifts, rare enough these days, of education and honesty – a heart of gold, unsullied, beyond price. Certainly she wouldn't have all that much experience of looking after a home; she would have enough problems there. But for that there was cousin Conceiça, the 'mummy'. With nothing else to interest her, she could be the lady of the house.

In short: the neighbour from the ground floor would do my room; I could have the use of the yard; I could make myself at home. At home? How? There was no electricity in the house and it was a kilometre from the barracks. What nonsense. Only now, saying these words to myself again, do I realise how ridiculous the situation was. 'So it was because Lia was there, then!' gloated one voice. 'She'll come to spend Saturdays and Sundays there.' Even so. I would go out I decided. And I went off to that pile and thence to the parade ground.

'Half turn!… out turn!'

'Shoulder arms!'

All morning on parade; all afternoon in class. By evening I was tired out. The peace of that sheltered house suited me well; perhaps that was where the spirit of one of my father's relatives roamed around. Little by little, from the old bed, from the desk, the walls, from the worm-eaten, unwaxed floor, or perhaps even from the echoes that lingered, Lia's downfall had begun to creep into my soul.

Major A. N. Scoto's orphan carried out her duties with the air of someone who, although innocent herself, had to atone for some wrong – there was nothing else she could do – in order to save her own life and that of her 'mummy'. Why did she persist in calling her 'mummy'? She earned 250 escudos a month and they had this place in Mafra with its rent fixed long ago and, thank God, covered by subletting the ground floor. (Lord forgive me: I'm telling all these things, unvarnished, just as I saw them; what would be the point, truly, of trying to cover them up?) Furniture, gold – bracelets, earrings, maybe keepsakes – even clothes, everything was little by little swapped, quite deliberately, for their daily bread. The piano, too. A major's uniform. With some of this money Juja ran away to Lisbon where in some street she would buy some fruit and a ticket for the lottery, which she would perhaps just give to some lover.

During lunchtime on the second or third day – I'm not sure which – I turned up at the house while the neighbour was making the beds. She was a simple, gaunt countrywoman, with troubles of her own. She asked my pardon, and hastened to add: 'The orderly brought a box for you, sir. From the young lady.'

I opened it; there was the explanation on a little piece of white paper: 'I'm sending you these grapes for your tea. I'm sorry it's nothing much. Lia.' And I thought to myself, tenderly even: 'It's in the bag!' I felt like laughing. I know: it's not pretty, but it's the truth.

'Tell me something,' I asked the woman all of a sudden. 'What happened to Juja? Did you know her? Can you tell…'

'One night a suitor came and took her off in his car. Have you heard about it, sir? I beg you not to say anything about it, I don't like intrigues, nor am I trying to stir things up; but it was the way her mother treated her, she's a hard one, that one. She didn't let the girl go out with him, her blood boiled just to see him come to the window, she'd belt her for the least thing, just like she hits Lia, who is an angel, poor thing. and so she that's what she did, may God forgive her… And now she's working in the theatre, I think she's a dancer. Everybody blamed the mother because she never lifted a finger, everything had to be done by the daughters, like slaves they were. When she's drinking, no one can put up with her. She even locked them up in a dark room. Worse than a devil….'

'What?'

'Oh sir, on my soul, it's the truth. She goes around all evening making a great fuss, saying she can't get enough air, that she has a pain in her heart, but it's the cheap brandy that does it. She always gets one of those bottles of the stuff from Cheleiros, the strong stuff. You'll see some things, sir, it's pitiful. And you've hardly got here and I'm telling you this. And isn't she renting us the ground floor and now she wants to take the kitchen away from us?'

It was the sad situation of Major Scoto's orphans that gave me pause. I had never thought of marrying. I have always been, once I was aware of these things, a free spirit, practical, it might conventionally be said, perhaps somewhat selfish. The more I live and find things out, the more the vision of the wedding night recedes in space and time. And my future, moreover, is not so grand as I have made it out to be. Now in the second grade of the military I have to work to eat. Once this is over I shall return to Portalegre and ask my mother for a few coins every day for coffee. As usual.

Lia is a good girl. I couldn't help but pity her, so desolate in love, with her anxiety to do the right thing. So often I am torn between the most tumultuous, contradictory feelings. 'Perhaps it would be a blessing,' whisper my desires. 'Perhaps an outrage,' says my heart. 'Now wouldn't it be an act of charity?' says my reason, discreetly. 'On the contrary, a crime,' cries the law. 'And it was only a flirtation, in the Portuguese fashion!' says irony, butting in, ruthlessly.

I ended up thinking all this senseless, disturbing, cynical, shameful. In my distraction, though, I saw the orphan's eyes again; and, thinking about them, I started to feel that there was something anguished and tragic in their mysteriousness, something which went beyond a mere promise, so easy, so unsettling. And so I wanted to find some honest solution for her pain. I didn't know what to do. Above all, as the sad afternoon faded way over the distant sea, with its glimmers of red, it was then that I, on my way to the poor, lone house, fed up of marching and kitbags, of the captain's sadism and tired, even, of my companions, felt the clamour of a thousand interior contradictions. But by the next day it was raining and I felt alone, flat. On Sunday I would go to Lisbon; I might even meet Juja, have a good time, you never know. Mafra meant the Convent and the Convent was a fortress. Soldiers, soldiers, soldiers. And suitors. What pedantic creatures, without a lover, without anything. The good old days in the king's service. Delicious kisses in the half light of corridors, in the velvety darkness of the underground, in the exciting profanity of the cells. That fortress so heavy, so powerful, now seemed to me to have been raised by a genuinely regal, sexual force. In order to crush it, in order to tame that unmistakable force, whether motivated by an acute fear of scandal, or by a rigid adherence to the Faith. In the very same corridors, centuries later (1938) some filthy washerwoman would direct her obscene overtures to the most needy, the boldest tommies. And then she would go and complain to the Company.

That was when Guerreiro, Pinto Basto, Casquilho and Maia, my old comrades, hit upon the idea, on Thursday night in the café, of a raid on Lisbon, on the Alto district; in mufti, as if we were making a case for armed pacifism. It was a very curious thing but the further away I tried to get from the idea – it was just so absurd – of going from theatre to theatre looking for Juja, forgetting about my friends and everything else, the less I could bring myself to do it. We had hardly arrived, however, when in the Café Portugal I told them what I wanted to do; they laughed in my face, coughing and ahemming behind their hands; on the way out Guerreiro, trying to dissuade me, was reduced to insulting me. And he had good enough reasons; it really was very silly. I went with them, through that part of town, from place to place, to the sound of fado. We drank; I found the whole evening pointless. I was thinking about Lia, and Juja, too, overwhelmingly, and about my father, growing old in Portalegre. I felt sad, Lisbon far from my thoughts. Pinto Basto's girth, fat and comic, with his face like an outmoded baby Jesus, just seemed ridiculous. But at bottom I was looking forward, too, to getting my own back on Guerreiro for his triumphal, gloating smile. And Maia? An idiot – because of those things he'd written. Casquilho was priceless: he had got it into his head that the social revolution would be started by little allegorical verses. Crazy! In the end I left them in a bar, quite drunk. The fado meanwhile continued to haunt me out in the street, now to the right, now the left, in the babble of the radios, in the cough of a woman, in the way a drunk was walking, in many other things. I went down in the lift at the Glória, there in the Baixa. I wanted something to amuse me a little; nobody at all among that crowd was looking at me. I felt somebody push me. Someone else... But what sort of sense was there in coming to Lisbon in my khaki drill? I was thinking I would glimpse something in all those women going by, whether honest or not, something of Lia, of the major, of Dona Conceiça. One of them might perhaps be Juja. That was a mistake: there at the door of Maxim's I bumped into Georgette. What a damn nuisance. I wanted to hide, but that was out of the question.

'Aren't you at the Apollo any more?' I manage to ask her, leading her away from all the confusion.

'I needed a change,' she said frankly, shrugging. 'But haven't you fallen out with me?'

There she was, pouting; the kid collar of her coat gave her a delicately ingenuous air. 'Listen: maybe you can tell me something. Do you know some girl from Mafra, called Juja, or Maria de Jesus? She might be a chorus girl...'

She looked me up and down: 'Is she a petty bourgeoise? Or some girl from the provinces?' she snorted, with ironic interest.

She managed to make me feel small. 'Come on, don't be jealous,' I persisted. 'I'm asking you if you know her.'

'Jealous, indeed,' she retorted. 'I might even be able to help you find her. Is that what you want?'

'Good night!' I flung back at her, stalking off trying to look imposing.

She didn't run after me, or stop me. She didn't care. She had other fish to fry or she had moved. She wasn't hurt; she just laughed at me. Putting my hand on my heart, meanwhile, out on the streets, wandering around hopefully, I touched the narrow seam from which God had made Adam. The idea which obsessed me amounted to no more than wanting to meet Juja and have my way with her, thereby possessing at the same time something of Lia – without the responsibility – and the unknown soul of a lost woman. I was a coward.

All that morning it rained and thundered. I missed the roll-call and had no dispensation for my absence. In the meantime as the shooting practice in the country had made us filthy and I hadn't been to change my uniform before dinner, I didn't go to the café but headed for the house instead, intending to return later. I was surprised then on climbing the steps to find a ray of light in the corridor. I went in; they were already there and had just finished eating. I say 'eating' rather than dining better to convey the impression I received on seeing the table, without a cloth, plates half licked and a cheap bottle of some dark-looking wine. Her face flushed, Dona Conceiça got to her feet.

'Guess what Liita fancied today?' she explained in a loud voice. 'Potatoes, with salt cod and cabbage.'

And she, what would she have fancied? A sickening smell of cabbage and potatoes came to me. Lia, her lips greasy, wearing a gown, a yellowed gown made of ticking, added unnecessarily: 'Mummy's such a glutton: she never leaves a thing…'

'For me,' she was going to say. Perhaps she was still hungry.

'The doctors, you know,' Dona Conceiça cut in, just in time. 'I'm not supposed to eat; but I get so hungry… And my heart isn't getting any better. Everything's ready, Lia, put the plates away. But your cousin must be soaked – quickly, get him a glass of aquardente; now you must go and change…'

'Very well, excuse me.'

'And I put up with a kilometre of rain; for what?' I say in my room. 'It's today.' I am elated. 'It's today.' Lia was crying out for me; the loudspeaker began to play. I made haste, so that I could feel her lips touching mine, they were burning, her eyes were more anguished. I had to do something decisive, right now.

'Tonight, come and talk with me in the corridor,' I pressed her, secretly.

'Ah, but I can't,' she replied sadly, glancing suddenly at her mother.

What more could I want? She hadn't asked why, nor seemed offended, like some silly girl. And for the rest I wanted to get her to agree – although, I must admit, something deep down in me would have preferred a refusal.

'Don't be afraid. You can come at any time; I'll be waiting for you.'

'She never sleeps,' she murmured despondently.

Perhaps it was the great lump of a mother, then, whom I should get out of the way. The chronic difficulty she had in breathing meant that she was always close to us, sometimes seated, sometimes standing, like some stupid bell tinkling out the feeblest claptrap. She asked us to stop the music, so that I had to listen to her, so that I would come to the conclusion that in Lia I had the wife who would be perfectly suited to all my plans: 'If only you knew how much this poor soul suffered because she wanted to help a girl from Cheleiros to get married...'

'Excuse me, Dona Conceiça, but what has this to do with me? It only gets on my nerves, you know. Listen, go to the garden, go and get some air. Leave us alone for two minutes, that's all we need...'

The most extraordinary thing was that Lia was also listening to all this nonsense with transparent enjoyment, her hands on her knees, looking down, in an attitude of modesty and self-denial, saying something here and there, deliberately, as if spelling things out, a habit she had picked up from teaching children.

'No,' added Lia, carefully, 'this young girl – as it happens an extremely interesting, a very good little thing – went to meet me one evening at the school, where I happened to be making some maps, and she told me, in tears as though someone was about to kill her, that a certain Senhor Rogério already owed her his sacred word of honour.'

So she paused for a moment to see whether I was surprised by this. I smiled. My weariness cried out enough, enough. But it wasn't enough. 'What did I do, what did you do?' I asked, making me think: 'Do you know what I'm saying, Lia? You are a fool, an idiot. You're not of this world. Good night.' I wanted to tell her this quite openly and send the mother packing. Just like that, that they didn't belong in this world. But my knee was stuck fast to that of the orphan, there on our side of the table.

'In short, Lia, you are a saint,' was what I actually said. And I tried to give the impression that that was it, an edifying conclusion. In vain: it only encouraged them. This Rogério and the peasant girl ended up getting married and I yawned, unable to contain myself. Lia was the godmother.

'And have the godsons turned out well?' I asked, by way of revenge.

Lia was shocked: 'So, so...'

'He's already tried to kill her twice,' said Dona Conceiça.

'Oh, Mummy, don't say that; nobody ever saw him!'

'But what if it had been true?' I asked, deliberately. 'Wouldn't you have regretted what you did?'

And I waited, as if I were offering counsel. Lia took her leg away and shifted on the chair.

'Regret, no,' she said. 'I would feel pity for her, the poor thing. But she had got her honour back without delay, that's the main thing.'

Was the poor maiden keeping it for later to remind me of the same obligation? I still wanted her, I had no scruples, enraged as I was by the high price being put on her boring, useless virtue. I got up. 'Please excuse me, ladies,' I said, turning the screw. 'I have to go to roll-call, and tomorrow I'm off to Lisbon. Should you want anything…'

Lia turned pale. I bade them goodnight and turned to go. As she ran to close the stair door she slipped me a note. It read: 'I need to talk to you. When Mummy is asleep…'

When Mummy is asleep…

The note, which I carried in my breast from Cheleiros, was a declaration. Before lights out in the barracks Maia snatched it from my hands, ran among the beds reading it out loud while the others held me. The place was in turmoil.

'It's the old, lost romantic spirit which is reborn!' cried Casquilho the poet, getting up and throwing his arms in the air.

They started throwing bolsters around, hitting each other over the head and shouting obscenities. How crass they were! As soon as I had got back the crumpled note I fled. 'I loved you before I knew you. And now that I have your word…' Yes, my darling. And I ran out into the wind and rain, towards Lia's arms, for better or for worse.

It was for worse, it hardly needs to be said. Because I had being holding back, only a decisive action – even if that meant abduction – could have saved Lia. Now, this did not appeal to me; nor did I sense the road to the precipice beneath our feet. Then again some things were so unexpectedly revealed that night that I didn't even have the time to realise their real import. There was no forewarning, no missed heartbeat, not the slightest thing to tell me that I had Lia's fate in my hands that night. Only the lamp at the front of the house seemed to flicker oddly. But how can the play of light and shadow in the night mean anything in human terms?

When I got there the silence was absolute. So different from that of other nights I think to myself. On tiptoe I go to my room, my heart pounding. Today there would be no sound of rats gnawing or squeaking, of any spirit moving along the dark corridor, of thieves about to attack during sleep. The virgin is about to be sacrificed; around her moves no mysterious darkness. I get into bed, my pyjamas on. I glance at the paper, nervous, expectant. How I want to be able to hear Lia's heart beating, her heart which will soon bring me the sign. In the engraving two girls in London are fighting a duel – it's something from a play. Lia is struggling desperately against her fear of her mother. She's heard my muffled steps. 'There goes the love of my life,' she will say, starting to tremble. No. No. She's incapable of that. Why am I deluding myself? There's nothing dividing us except the little reception room with its old furnishings. So easy to come to me! So far beyond words! 'Mother, why aren't you sleeping? There's no need to lie awake, it's late. Close your eyes. Close them for now your child is grown up and wants to leave the cradle, as birds want to leave the nest once their wings have grown.'

An hour went by. Perhaps Lia has fallen asleep, too. What a letdown! I get up and a sudden, strong gust of wind bangs a door, whistles through the house; nervous, I turn to go back to bed. No. I get up again. It's now! The whistling wind will cover the sound of our steps, the sound of our mouths. I shiver and fall again on the bed. If only I knew what to do!

Dona Conceiça's eyes are closed but her breasts heave, they do not sleep, they are full of menace, the chain which holds Lia. Her virgin's body moves gently with sweet impatience. Her thighs unfold, her form turns around softly. Her right arm falls carelessly. The street-light dances on her bed, throws lines on the wall, reveals Lia's hair hanging loose, her face, her burning mouth. And I, like a wraith, have crossed the room separating us, and like a thief now through the transom I see her sorrowful longing to be set free. Lia hardly dares even half-open her eyes to peep cautiously at her mother. She fears her as if she were some despotic lord. But she has made up her mind: neither fear, nor virtue, not even the memory of her father can stop her. The secret of her self-possession is mine. Lia will come. There she is beside the bed. Her trepidation equals my desire. But if it so why hasn't she come straight away? 'What stupidity!' I say, in a rage. Wasn't it utterly thoughtless of Lia to let Dona Conceiça rest her cheek on her soft left arm. 'That will awaken the tigress...' And my blind passion was such that I wanted that virgin with or without her damned arm. The widow had been sleeping on top of her now for ten years, not from any tender sentiments, it seemed to me, but because she was a tyrant. Meanwhile the struggle began again. Lia had closed her eyes; her resignation seemed infinite, pulling her arm away slowly, gently. She looked so angelic, one might have said! Just then, fatally, Dona Conceiça's left hand rose involuntarily, moved and then fell on Lia's neck. It was terrifying. Even in sleep the octopus did not release its prey.

Lia's stillness once again dispirited me. It was useless; everything was working against us.

And then… the unexpected: the fearful hand slipped away. Outside the storm had died down. The lamp had ceased to flicker. Without a sound I opened the door, Lia shuddered and, recognising me, got up like a zombie, and came towards me, deathly pale, not uttering a sound. I took hold of her belt and we took two, three cautious steps into the room. Her mouth immediately sought out mine and she kissed me eagerly, still standing. I leant her against the wall and it occurred to me that I could overpower her momentarily and carry her in a moment to my room. My fingers ran up and down her back, I opened her dressing gown and touched her. I felt her respond instantly. Lia seized me, desperately, violently, her eyes now open, now closed, hastening the consummation.

Despite her convulsions she dragged a promise from me: 'You won't ever forget me, will you?'

'No.'

Her directness shocked me. Perhaps Lia's excessive vulnerability might awaken my own conscience. I was afraid, too, that her panting, her short, passionate gasps for breath, would wake the monster, Dona Conceiça; suddenly there was a sound in the corridor. We froze, rigid. We could hear the sound of footsteps quite clearly. Lia was about to cry out but I shook her and nodding at her bedroom door, pushed her towards it. 'Go on!' Her eyes shone with the light of tragedy, she came towards me, her face disfigured. I heard the sound of the bed – I daren't breath – and Dona Conceiça's voice: 'What's the matter with you, child?'

'Nothing, Mummy.'

And everything relapsed into its former silence.

My terror was overwhelming. I leaned against the first thing that came to hand, stunned. I don't know how long it took for me to be able to think: 'It wasn't Dona Conceiça who got out of bed – it was him! He had awoken on contact with Lia. It was her father's spirit. It was him; he has come to save her.' And I felt something like a kind of relief within me that I hadn't fallen into the abyss. It was truly a crime. I felt the sweat cooling on my face and if, by happy chance I hadn't left the candle burning in my room I could not have set foot in there. I staggered in that direction. But, heavens above, when I got to the door the improbabilities reached their height: there was Georgette, calmly taking off her gloves, putting them on the marble dressing table, just like a lady. My astonishment and then sudden anger are evident, visible. It was she whose footsteps has stopped us. I fell silent. I saw in her something mysterious, ghostly, something which stopped me throttling her. She stopped for a moment in front of the mirror. Could this really be me, not dreaming, and Georgette in the flesh? Full of doubts, I approached her and she held out her hand: 'Good evening,' she stammered.

I don't return her greeting, but I take hold of her fingers as if to determine whether they are really hers.

'But what nonsense is this?' I throw the question at her. 'Have you gone crazy, or what? Do you think that this room is just another, like those in Lisbon? Be off or I'll break your head open.'

She wasn't at all cowed. On the contrary: she smiled bitterly, her gaze resting on my state of dress – I was wearing an overcoat on top of my pyjamas, looking somewhat ridiculous. Then, clearly in great sadness, she began to explain.

'You know how it is. I began to ask around about the girl you were interested in. I came to tell what I had discovered; I had no intention of staying.' She sat down on the bed. 'I asked the carriage to wait outside for fifteen minutes.' The usual prattle. 'Very well,' I replied, my cynicism coming in handy. 'Quite simply I would rather you didn't bother yourself to that extent.' I wanted to see what her real motives were. 'But when all's said and done you've come just at the right time. If you wish you may stay here with me tonight.'

She tucked one leg under the other. 'It wasn't me you were expecting. Where have you come from in this state?'

'It was Juja, actually,' I said. 'Did you speak to her?'

'No, I didn't. But tell me: where have you come from?'

I said nothing. Everything about her was intriguing, even the fact that she wasn't wearing make-up. Her lip, with the fever of another time, curled in unaccustomed bitterness. And each time her sadness seemed even deeper, in her narrow eyes, the carelessness of her gestures, her pallor.

'Juja… died,' she blurted out at last, tenderly.

And she buried her head in the bolster. 'So it was her,' it occurred to me in a flash. Is it possible? Was Juja a false name? Was this adventuress the orphan child of some relative of mine? The one I loved and then discarded like a slave.

If it had been something I had read I wouldn't have believed it. It was all some bad joke, a dream even. Nevertheless, Juja was there before me, unmasked, sobbing over her ruin, her naked soul, torn to shreds. I began to stroke her as though she were my unhappy sister; I kissed her hands, the hands of Juja before she turned to prostitution. And then her brow, her sad, damp eyes. ('A petite bourgeoise?

Some girl from the provinces?') That Juja was dead. Why look for her in streets or in the theatres? I felt like weeping to myself. We were on the same bed, alongside each other, devoid of all desire.

After a few moments she began to stroke my hair and wanted to know things about Lia, about 'Mummy', about how I had come to that place, whether they had enough to eat. And, on the same subject, whether there were still figs in the garden. Ah, how she missed those figs sometimes!

'I guessed at once that you must be here in this house and that Lia, with her weakness, would be very fond of you. I came more to warn her. Why don't you marry her? She's a saint.'

'She is indeed,' I replied.

(That room was formerly her father's. She thought I was in the other one, hers. The light had attracted her.)

Then the damned horn blared out in the silence of the night and she got up and went to put on her gloves. At that moment I seized her by the shoulders.

'Listen, Juja, listen, darling,' I begged her. 'Don't go away. Don't go. Now you know I love you. The one who died, that was Georgette. Don't leave. Can't we forgive each other, my love.'

From the depths of her soul there came but one word: 'Impossible. Impossible.'

'I beg you, darling, not to go…'

She turned round to face me; I wanted to hold her with all my strength. 'We must not… It would be the death of Lia. No. No.' And she fled to the corridor.

My arms fell limply by my side. From the window I could see her going slowly towards the car, and then turn, once, twice, to Dona Conceiça's room – the one which had been hers, as an adolescent. And there I stayed, empty, wretched, crushed, listening to the noise of the sea.

'Off you go,' I'm saying the following morning after exercises to some soldier. 'Ask the widow Scoto to give you my trunk and take it to the Pensão Moderna. Hurry now!'

After much persuading off he went. I was extremely nervous, waiting near the Convent, going from the road to the gardens, from the gardens to the road. Wagons came by, loaded down. I had never before this time wanted so ardently to set off for the unknown, money in my hand, to be spent in whichever port I fetched up. My desolation was like that tennis court, above the gardens, which during the night had filled up with dead leaves and puddles of water. Never-failing autumn! Juja had left an envelope addressed to Lia on the dressing table; there was some money in it. I left another envelope, with a brief note of explanation and a month's rent. I was broke. I ruled out going to Lisbon; among other things, I didn't want to risk meeting Juja again so soon. Above all I needed to rest and think. I was far from thinking that other, even worse, surprises lay in wait for us. When my trunk arrived I settled into my new room, but for a while I had the feeling that something was missing, whatever it was, I didn't really know. My mind wasn't working properly; I was vexed, eaten away inside. This obsession that people have, to rifle through their pockets, once, many times, looking at things, summoning up memories, and... nothing. Propped up on the bed, daydreaming, all sorts of things, I suddenly remember: 'The ring! The sapphire! I had it in my dressing room.'

I spring up and run out into the street and dispatch another soldier. Instead of the ring, however, he brings me an off-hand note from Dona Conceiça. It is clear enough. If I were to give all the details they would fill a couple of police notebooks but I can sum it up in two lines: from the inquiries conducted by Captain Silveira – he questioned the soldier who had brought my case and the lady who lived on the ground floor, while the owners of the house, Dona Conceiça and Lia, made a statement – we gained the exact impression that the theft, if it had taken place, could only have been carried out by a third party. The lady had spent the morning washing clothes by the well; the soldier, who had undoubtedly gone into my room, refused to admit what he had done, however, when the sergeant with typical subtlety had gone to the mess and asked who had been to do a favour for a certain cadet, so and so, who wore glasses etc. The ring was worth more than 800 escudos; I had used it in certain emergencies. More than this, it had been in our family since the marriage of my great grandfather. But my unease did not spring from either of these reasons; rather, it sprang from the mysteriousness, in itself, of the disappearance. It was even possible that it had been Juja! In truth, she had admired it many a time in Lisbon. Who knows? I must admit that I don't even remember whether I still had it when I got washed that morning. I would have to be patient.

The days passed, and although I had my room in the Pensão I continued to eat in the mess, to save money, and mixed rather more with my colleagues – in the café, in the street, in the corridors of the Convent.

'What is the hardest thing to bear?' asked a certain Paulinho one day. 'Do you know what it is? It's not the captain, nor the knapsack, not even the lectures; it's the lack of women. There are more than a thousand fellows in the barracks... And each one left to fend for himself!'

It even got so that one of our great pleasures was when some sergeant's daughter, full of herself, not a child but not quite a woman, took a perverse delight in smiling back at our stares whenever our paths crossed. More: the captain would arrive unobtrusively, solemnly, on his bicycle every weekday morning at half past six. Come rain or shine we would assemble on the parade ground to salute him as soon as he got up in front of us. And there we would go, behind him, to the beat of the drum, in squad formation, kitted out, sweating, making for the 'theatre of operations', knee deep in the Mata Grande. It was the time of day when two or three elegant ladies would be on their way to tennis, with their bare brown legs and white pumps. The damned attack! 'Throw yourselves to the ground in short, rapid intervals... Make the best use of the lie of the land...' The ground was soaking and full of gorse. At the end of the afternoon's instruction what we really wanted was to sleep; the naps we took during lectures were not enough. But it was just at this moment that the 'élite' would come sauntering along the road while we remained there with our tongues hanging out. One or other group of three or four little sweeties would stroll up and down, with the ingenuous air of someone who had come to gawp at our discomfort. They had their fathers – officers, our superiors. (At another time Lia would have been one of them – and Juja.) They came along that road... They knew well enough that the cadets of this year would leave sorrowfully, like those of previous years, who had promised to return and had not. But was it even worth thinking about? They were there during our brief stay in Mafra with a little bit more hope than the daughters of station masters as the trains passed by.

And anyway, I thought to myself one afternoon, what if any of these doll-like creatures – for whom life has not been so hard, who know how to play tennis, flirt light-heartedly, smile and perhaps embroider, maybe even give caresses, who are learning how to paint their eyes and dye their hair, and have these childish names – Mimi, Mideu, Midá, Bina, Lili, Fifi, Jujú, Lulú – and who are above looking for a 'good hard-working boy', what if any of them should pay attention to the misfortunes of two of their old friends, the orphans of

Major A. N. Scoto, an old friend of their parents…

'Have you got your invitation to the ball?' one of the groups asked me, interrupting my thoughts just then.

'What ball?'

'A ball in your honour, given by us. By the way, where are you going?' asked the blonde one, Binita, whom I already knew. She was a darling.

'Don't bring anything else up,' said another one, laughing.

'It's true, isn't it? It was you who had the ring stolen? So, has it turned up?' asked the other two.

'I'm still waiting,' I joked.

'Do you know what they're saying around here?' asked Binita.

'For heavens' sakes, girl, don't say it; it might not even be true,' warned her friends.

'Tell me. I don't mind,' I said.

They hesitated for a couple of minutes, pretending to have misgivings. 'Ah, no, it might be no more than gossip.'

But finally they came out with it: 'Perhaps the widow Scoto, you know, out of necessity…' And they all four smiled in superior fashion.

I didn't hate them for it. In any case they all had that golden skin I love so much! A little later as we were waiting in line for dinner a first sergeant cadet, a native of Mafra and therefore in touch with things locally, managed to be much more to the point: 'It was the widow Scoto who pawned it. That's what they're saying…'

Gradually my disquiet became unbearable. What was more I had an odd kind of fillip across from my room: a girl in pyjamas – nothing more. At any moment when she sensed that I was around she would open the door onto the verandah, showing off her charms to me, walking around, inspecting herself in the mirror, shaking the duster, stretching out languidly on the sofa, assuming the most provocative postures as she lowered herself onto it. She used to hum. She would appear on the top floor, drawing my attention with her dry little cough, and then to amuse herself, sit by the window, reading.

This girl in the pyjamas was married; she carried on this game deliberately, perversely. She swung like a pendulum between moods, sometimes sentimental, at other times crazy. Sometimes she would laugh out loud at something in the paper; yet another time I saw her crying.

As for what the Pensão had to offer, our chambermaid was fat and ruddy. Even so whenever I put my hand out to touch her she would stand up on tiptoe, flustered, and call out: 'I'll call the boss right now. I'll kick up a fuss.' And out it came, her little speech, calling out down the stairs: 'Worthless sort!' She would leave the bowl of hot water at the door of my room while I bellowed out from inside for her to come in. 'You are not worthy, sir!' she cried, waddling off in haste down the stairs. The landlord, who was still a strong young fellow, began to look at me suspiciously. How could I not, in this situation, think of Lia, Juja and other unattainable women?

It is true that Lia wrote to me, a week after my flight, a sad letter to which I did not reply. 'Although my first note did not mean anything to you, since you left it behind when you went,' she wrote, 'I am not offended, as you might suppose. I am indeed madly yours and I remain – and will always remain – so.' The truth was she meant trouble. 'I hope,' she continued, 'that one day God will notice me, as much as He has so far forgotten and put me to the test, and allow us to be united eternally in the same supreme happiness.' There was more: 'Our house is always there entirely at your disposal; I hope to have the good fortune to see you again.'

With this appeal ringing in my ears I chose instead to go to Lisbon in search of some little adventure – it was a matter of being honest with myself. Just as Juja had done previously, I frequented the cafés and looked around me; in vain. Before dinner I went up the Rua do Salitre, my mouth burning, where I later found myself at the door of the rich old chap; when the old boy came out he saw me there. 'Excuse me, sir,' he explained, quite spontaneously, and not unkindly, 'but she doesn't live here now. She's going around with some young officer.'

Perversely, the old man's words cheered me up: I dined well, had something to drink and enjoyed a happy little adventure.

When I got back to Mafra that night I was appalled by the pitiful provincialism of the spectacle: a blind girl was singing sad songs and playing a guitar. The tables were full of uniforms, decked out with silver and gold, a few business men, and a great many of my colleagues. The lubricious gaze of all these people was fixed on the poor girl who, with her white, nebulous eyes, had aroused their pity. There was much clapping, muttered phrases: 'Good show, encore, encore!'

The eyes that should have been blind – the eyes of all that lot; and the eyes that should have seen – the eyes of that poor singer.

As for Lia, I don't know whether somebody put a curse on her life when she was in the cradle. But the world fell in on me that tragic night, crying out, 'Someone help, she was killed and for no reason at all!' – when the only reason was the inevitable notice of execution. Everything had been so well prepared beforehand; it was like a sort of momentum which, as the gradient grew steeper, pitched us irremediably overboard the moment it met the slightest obstacle. I would not be able to explain even to myself what it was that happened between Lia and me that fateful night of the ball. Did I at some point swear I loved her, or make promises in vain? I didn't seduce her. I merely praised her fine hands. How could the poor girl have gone so far as to take acceptance or rejection as a matter of life and death?

I was dancing with Binita, with that pagan beauty of hers. 'Will you not choose a bridegroom for yourself from among these three hundred students?' I asked her somewhat indiscreetly just as Lia appeared with her "Mummy". She was wearing a white dress, her face white too, heightening the blackness of her imploring eyes. The music died away and with it the rhythm of the steps. I could only see that anguished look of hers, already so familiar to me, only more charged, more intense. And I was afraid of her and of me. Perhaps I could ask her to go with me to some dark, hidden place… and put an end to it all.

'You're quite wrong,' said Binita, getting into step. 'Marriage doesn't concern me for the moment. More than anything I want to live a bit. I'm just an ordinary girl, with no special plans. But should a boy turn up one day who has a future and who likes me…'

'What if you don't meet him?'

(But wasn't Lia's appearance rather odd? She's beginning to haunt me. Dona Conceiça, too, though how could that be?)

'What are you saying?' asked Binita again.

'That I agree absolutely,' I replied without the first idea of what I was saying. But then seizing on one I said suddenly: 'It's obvious, Binita, that this isn't a declaration, but you know that I have some sort of future and that I could like you, like…' – I glance at Lia again; Binita catches me – 'just like… something precious.'

'Just like a sapphire ring, isn't that it?'

I choked. We danced another few steps. In my mind the inaudible dialogue merged: 'Why didn't you reply to my letter? Mummy knows everything, that's why she agreed to come here. If you knew how much I have suffered!' 'But that's crazy, Lia, I don't even love you; I feel only pity, forgive me!' That's just stupid; what would I gain by being so brutal. I could say: 'Please forgive for not coming round; exercises, you know, lectures.'

The foxtrot finished and I went with Binita for a moment; I sought refuge in the smoking room. What if I left? To go to Lia would mean losing Binita, from whom I had drunk of the sun: ripe, golden. Notwithstanding, I go towards the door. Halfway along the corridor there is a verandah, its door open. This bit belongs to the firemen. The cold discourages me. 'Idiot! Lia's passion is making me do things…' I turn round and go back to the buffet where the men were jostling.

'A glass of port? No, sorry, it's anis.'

'Good evening. How are you both?' Cool, diplomatic. 'Oh, do sit down,' her mother would say, 'over here.' There were thirty girls; I had to leave them, all of them, that young one, that dark one, even Binita. The music had begun again – a tango, if I was not mistaken. 'Let's see if Lia's would like to dance.' I peer at her. 'No,' she says to the crowd. Her anxious eyes scan the whole room. Perhaps she had said: 'I have a partner,' meaning me. Must I go? It's horrible: the music shakes my whole body. Nearby two older women bend close. 'A beautiful dress,' they murmur. 'Who knows… the ring…' I return to the smoking room and bury myself in a chair where Guerreiro is surprised to see me.

'Leave me, I'm tired, on edge,' I say as he approaches.

'Have you danced with anyone?'

A lot of the young men were complaining about this ball, "in their honour" and with only half a dozen girls worth a second glance. The air was thick with smoke. Gradually I was able to make out among the other voices that of our teacher of tactics, second lieutenant Alferes: 'It will prevent a scandal, Vieira. We're talking about a close friend. It would be a disgrace…'

'There was nothing in it, I promise you,' replied the other. 'But how can I resist, damn it? I can't. she's stronger than me. Can't you see the way she looks? Yesterday she sent for me, talked about a camping site, a long way from here. What can I do?'

On every side I sense conflict, a great struggle. Lia's despair reaches me from the ballroom; it seizes me, makes me feel small.

'There was no other way she could see me again so she went to extremes – it was blind passion. In the end, it's another load on my shoulders – that was all I needed. But Dona Conceiça, how had she got her to change her mind? It seemed incredible. It wasn't just in a moment of vexation: Lia made the dress, she had plenty of time –

and with Juja's money, there's an irony! Even they have let themselves be corrupted. And wouldn't the rumours about the ring and the pawnbrokers have reached them by now? There are plenty would confirm the story…'

At this moment, though, the speed of our downfall had already brought the three of us to the edge of the precipice. In truth everything happened so quickly and so directly like a car which crashes and plunges headlong over the edge. It was much later when Pinto Basto was standing next to me. 'Some stuck-up bitch,' he said, barely able to speak, 'that one there who won't dance with anyone. What the hell is she doing here, can you tell me? We'd be better off, dancing together, just us men, with each other. We're a bunch of sex-starved…'

'What's this got to do with me? Go and bay the moon…'

'Bay the moon yourself. Have another drink, it might put you in a better mood. You think you're irresistible, don't you? Well, I'd like to see you go up to her now.'

His outburst made me smile. Guerreiro and many others were there so I make up my mind to teach Pinto Basto a lesson in front of them. To begin with I just gave a little push in the belly. All the shadowy thoughts suddenly disappear.

'A bottle of port?' I say, proffering my hand.

'You're on,' he accepted curtly, 'if you can get the one in white to dance with you.'

He enlisted a couple of fellows as witnesses. Guerreiro burst out laughing. I make my way through the room. The room seemed full of all sorts of things happening but I did not know what exactly. Instead of one I would have happily lost a thousand bottles of port to have been at that moment no more than that chap who had bet he could persuade the girl in white to dance. A man without a past, a novice, without remorse. Born on a sofa, not long before, just to dance with a ravishing woman, whose name I did not even know – the lady in white. Well then; I was merely part of the bustle of the room. With a couple of sharp taps the orchestra demanded attention. Anxious glances. We're in the sticks. The leader was showing off his stiffly starched shirt front: 'We have a request for an English waltz – *The Blue Danube!*'

Some of the girls came forward. For a few moments I saw the white dress, whirling round at my command, reflected in the still waters glimpsed between the branches of exotic trees. Then the face of Pinto Basto, half-drunk, half-reluctant, swaying with the bottle of port: 'You were up to it, you bastard. Congratulations.' And I felt Lia's body, her soul, in my arms; mute, dying to speak but not daring to, heart-broken, pitiful – her mouth.

'Have you been enjoying yourself?' I ask, blithely. No reply. Whatever it was, it seemed to choke her. I hastened to her aid. 'You must have been very hurt, only to have shown up now…'

'I don't think about it any more. From the start you didn't attach any importance to what I wrote.' She stumbled again; her voice was too loud. Everybody seemed to be watching our embarrassment. I felt ashamed: I had callously encouraged Lia open her heart to me.

'And now, another disaster. I've been relieved of my job at Cheleiros. Mummy smacked some children who were being cheeky to me and just because of that those people were up in arms. They swore statements against me, saying I didn't teach them anything, that the children hadn't taken any exams, all sorts of things, all made up. And what's more, the inspector took against me; he couldn't speak to me without reducing me to tears. I wouldn't be friends with just anyone, you know. It was all because of this. I haven't the energy. They called me stupid, proud… I don't know what's going to become of us.'

The steps of our dance became mechanical; the people around us seemed to melt away. I was responding to the music without thinking. And, callously, without a word of comfort I asked myself why Lia had got dressed up in silk and had launched herself back into society, chasing a man of my disposition.

'But good can come from misfortune,' she managed to say, starting again. 'Mummy has agreed to our engagement and has no objection to my being with you.'

'What on earth for?' I say, quite brutally.

Once again her anguish overwhelmed me. (The orchestra still played.) I waited for Lia to compose herself sufficiently to ask, as though from afar: 'Is there any chance that…?'

Clapping. (At last!) The violinist bowed, well pleased. My gaze meets Binita's bluish green eyes. They have struck up the *Danube* again. This is unbearable. 'No, I shall disabuse her for good. They were clinging to me like castaways in the hope that I could save their lives. The "Mummy" would cease her vigil, squinting out of the corner of her eye, moaning about how she couldn't breathe and her broken heart, she would deliver her up to me provided that she could live and have her daily bread. What an enormity! Perhaps she was even counting on the protection of the law. How could I not believe now that it was Dona Conceiça herself who had stolen the ring? Had she really been asleep that final night?'

Lia was that same girl who had been breathing so heavily, lost, panting. I remember now and look at her to see if I can rediscover my desire. But her black curls were scorched, the shrunken yellow of her neck contrasted with her powdered, milky features. Binita, her body full of the sun, radiant and fresh, gave me a quick glance, smiling. Never had poor Lia seemed so abject, so destitute, and Binita so elegant and beautiful.

And then, this terrible thing happened: Lia put her left hand on her breast. And there shone the sapphire.

'What, Lia,' I exclaimed without thinking, 'Was it you who stole the ring?' And I set about trying to wrest it from her, like some common thief.

The fates had ordained it: the music had stopped a moment earlier and the words burst like a bomb through the whole room. People came running from all sides, in haste. I realise now that I had blundered, I recognise what, in her heart, Lia's intentions were – 'It's a symbol of everlasting love, isn't it, Mummy?' – but it was too late. Green with rage, that monster, Dona Conceiça, ran towards her and struck a heavy blow on the nape of her neck. 'You shameless hussy! You have disgraced the ashes of your father!'

There was a sudden swirl of movement as Lia dashed off down the corridor like a madwoman. The black, overwhelming shadow of her mother was running after her; so many men, so many people, but nobody thought to stop her. They stood, dumb-founded. At last somebody managed to grab Dona Conceiça.

(Meanwhile, all around: 'Imagine, just for the sake of a ring, for something so worthless!' 'It's a terrible disgrace, poor thing!' 'It was inevitable.')

The verandah was open and so did not stop her abrupt, tragic fall; and there was Lia spread out flat on the ground like a bird with its wings broken. A cry of alarm – so deep, a cry we would never forget – lingered in the night.

That was in the autumn and now the birds are twittering in the eaves. To tell the truth I must add that the nurses managed to save Lia. Having just received her very touching pardon a few days ago and the news that she is restored to health, I am moved to relate to you all these sad, weighty things. The mother, that poor thing, fainted and never recovered consciousness that fateful morning. And there is yet another, graver, question: What will become of Lia when she leaves the hospital, her heart grieving, with nobody to look after her and the only member of her family left, her sister, the chorus girl? Will she head for Lisbon, too? Or for whatever God ordains?

Perhaps the best thing – don't you think? – would be if I were to persuade my parents to offer her some sort of light job in our house.

Maria Judite de Carvalho

SO MANY PEOPLE, MARIANA

translated by John Byrne

I've only just got here but I hardly remember coming. I can only recall in any detail the man who was run over and the large, white hands of the driver who brought me here; his short fingers had hardly any nails, and his hands seemed to dissolve on the steering wheel like starfish left stranded on the sand by the sea. Two bloodless hands. And all the while the owner of them, of these hands, was perfectly alive. He even insulted the old man when he paused in front of the wheels. Like me. So long ago… 'Get yourself some glasses, you old rogue!' The old man seemed lost, and his faded eyes appeared not to see. It was as if he was far from that street where his body just happened to be walking and where he had stopped, the object of insults and laughter he couldn't hear, from the driver and from those people who had paused on purpose, just to mock him. 'Look at him, he's well gone! Hey, old fellow, have you had a drop too much or what?' He was so alone, that poor old man, so alone!

Was it true that I had gone to the doctors? Had I really left the house? But that's how it happened. Here by my side I have my bag and on my knees the hat I bought six years ago, the one with – I only noticed today – two moth holes and a silly feather on the right side. A hat that didn't suit me and that I didn't feel right in either. How could it have been any other way?

The world is suddenly an assortment of strange things that I notice for the first time and that exist with an utterly unexpected intensity: the peach tree in the garden about to blossom, the old chair with the upholstery sticking out, where I like to sit, the bed with the flowerlike ornaments, that belonged to Dona Glória's mother. Wavering images that in the end lose themselves in the flood of my tears.

There are so many things that we never think about just because we haven't the time: hope, for example. Who's going to waste five or ten minutes thinking about hope when he could be using the time so much better, reading a novel or talking to a friend on the phone, or going to the cinema or writing minutes while he's at work? Think

about hope, what a waste of time! Don't make me laugh. Hope…
well, there's always someone, I suppose… and like sand it gets into
the pleats and hems of the soul. Years go by, lives too, until the last
day and the last hour and the last minute and then it turns up to
make what we have been expecting so sudden and startling, to make
what was already bitter even more so. Just to make things more difficult.

The specialist asked if I had any family; I told him I hadn't. He
seemed slightly disappointed, as if my personal situation was in the
end only the most painful detail of all that was about to happen and
about to be said, the first stone in the smooth progress of my case.
He regarded me, the analyses in his hand. 'Absolutely nobody?' he
asked again, as if he only had to shake my goodwill about a bit for
me to admit to someone. 'I shook my head and smiled, my eyes
serious in the beige framed mirror behind his reddening nape. The
feather in my head waved from right to left. Then, I don't know why,
I felt somehow ashamed of that feather. 'Very well then,' he said,
reading the analyses again. Why all this sham? Perhaps he just didn't
know how to begin… As if now he knew any more! What point did
it serve? Why all this delay? Perhaps just to use up some more time
with me… it could just be. I had paid 500 escudos as soon as I got
here – what it had cost me to scrape together those 500 escudos! –
to the fine-looking woman with the florid face; her uniform was
pristine, her smile conventional, to be switched on and then off again
like a flame that had been blown out because it was no longer
needed. 'The professor has not yet arrived; pray be seated…' Maybe
things weren't so bad as the other doctor had hinted by his silences,
by his half uttered words of encouragement, by his laugh which was
just a little too open and smug, which sounded as false as Judas. Who
knows? Perhaps…

There was still hope.

Once again the red and white smile, the wide, mascara-lined eyes
of the woman.

'Mrs Mariana Toledo, my good lady.' There, before me now, stood
the great Dr Cardénio Santos, studying yet again those complicated
hieroglyphs, those mysterious signs known only to the initiated and
which were a kind of cipher of death. I found myself looking closely
at his face, as if this were more important than anything else, even
more important than the words which he was getting ready to throw
like a veil over the truth. It was a ruddy, moon-shaped face with two
small piercing eyes set into the soft flesh. It was no more than that,

except for the fact that it was the face of a good doctor, one of those rare geniuses who never in all their born days make a wrong diagnosis. Never; a fact of which he was quite aware, of course.

'Well then,' he said, 'your case is not hopeless, far from it... What is needed...'

But all I needed was to know. I managed to force another smile; I tried the stratagem I had worked out at home. 'That's fortunate,' I said. 'I've been planning a little trip, but I haven't bought the ticket; I didn't want to buy one before coming here.'

I felt that he was puzzled. I guessed, even without looking, that he was looking at my threadbare coat, the feather in my hat, my darned underwear, the general impression that I had let things go. 'I don't think that's quite wise,' he finally said, in spite of everything.

'I don't lack courage, doctor,' I said. 'How much time do you give me? Without coming into hospital, of course. If it's nothing infectious I'd rather die in my own bed, in the house where I live at least.'

It was a palpable hit; he wasn't on his guard. He was still struggling to find the right thing to say, of course. He laughed and I felt a surge of admiration for him, for at least his smile seemed genuine. 'You are not one for half measures, are you?' he said. 'You think you are going to die soon...'

'I'm asking you, doctor,' I replied. 'It's so very, very important. You can't imagine just how important. I'm not off on any trips. You only need to look at me... Do I look like someone who goes off on trips? It's as simple that... when you are alone like me, without anybody, you can't afford the luxury of being deceived. I need to know exactly what to expect.'

He began to mumble something: 'Well, then...' And then he delivered the truth, wrapped up in pompous, difficult words, all very technical. When I had stripped them away I found myself face to face with death.

Hope persists in spite of everything, protesting that it can't possibly be this way. Perhaps he's got it wrong, who knows? They all make mistakes, even the professors of the Faculty of Medicine. The very idea, how could he have got it wrong, what with the figures all there, quite clearly, on the analyses. But perhaps the laboratory; it wouldn't be the first time... I can remember a while back reading in the paper... What nonsense! It's all quite correct, what the doctor said, all that's written down. But hope, not wanting to let you down, clutches at straws, no matter how insubstantial, no matter how inconsistent.

But it's 20 January today and starting three or four months from now I shall be awaiting my death.

I feel so lonely, more than ever, even though that's how I've always been.

Always.

One night when I was fifteen I noticed that I was crying. I still don't what it was that had caused these tears, it was all so long ago, wrapped in the white folds of the past. I remember only that my father heard me and got up. He perched lightly on the side of my bed and began to stroke my hair, wanting to know what the matter was.

'I am lonely, father,' I said. 'That's all it is. I was crying because I'm lonely and because it just occurred to me... Silly, isn't it? I'm just lonely. And what about you?'

Regretting that I had been so open, I tried to laugh in order to stop my tears but he didn't join in; at least this spared him from the anger that I would feel for him the following day. He didn't laugh and his voice when he finally spoke was very gentle, and almost sad.

'You have realised this too,' he said softly, 'you, too. There are people who live for seventy or eighty years, even more, who never realise. Yet you, at fifteen... We are all lonely, Mariana. Lonely and with so many people around us. So many people, Mariana! And nobody is going to do anything for us. Nobody can. Nobody would want to even if they could. There's not a chance.'

'But you, papa...

'I...' he replied. 'The people in your world are different from the ones in mine... At bottom perhaps some of them are the same, but there it is again, even if you did come across them you wouldn't recognise them, not even physically... So is there anything can we do to help ourselves? Nobody else can, my child, nobody else can...'

Nobody else can.

Certainly not my father who, poor thing, died a few months afterwards, nor, later, António and after him Luís Gonzaga. My life is like a tree on which all the leaves are withering, followed one by one by the branches until not one remains. And now, deprived of all its sap, it will fall.

The maid, Augusta, spends days uttering great overblown sighs and then exclaims: 'I just want to die!' But she is healthy woman, very good-humoured, with a decided taste – which she doesn't bother to hide – for policemen. The words which accompany her sighs don't make sense; she doesn't have nightmares of the dark or of the heavy earth like I have. She doesn't know – and even if she did know she would think it childish to ponder such things – that she will bring forth the very worms which will devour her. She did not see, as I saw, that mound of earth over my father's tomb, the earth of the graves which were being dug alongside. The grave of my father who only months before stroked my hair with his warm hand. Nobody else can, my child, nobody else.

I didn't believe him because I was just a little girl full of expectations of life, so many that now I can't remember them. I felt alone but I knew that it wouldn't always be like that. I was absolutely certain of it. And then when a few years later I left school behind for freedom and met António I thought that my father really knew nothing. To tell the truth I didn't even think about my father. There was little enough time to think about António and me; it just slipped away through my fingers, time that I wanted to seize.

We went through a few difficult years: my in-laws hadn't wanted us to get married so they ignored us which was easy enough for them because they lived out in the sticks. Now that all my selfishness, all my resentments, all my lesser or greater hatreds are going to die with me, I want to know whether they were right or at least understand why they acted like that. Perhaps – who knows – I wouldn't have been that pleased if my little Fernando had married a simple typist, penniless and with no family, who was neither pretty nor accomplished, and who did not shine in any way. How do we know what we might have done or thought if things had turned out differently? If my son had lived to be a man for example; if I had been rich like António's parents. Money changes people in the most extraordinary ways: those women who were spiteful in secret or their own quiet way start to show it openly the moment they get hold of money. They become aggressive, indifferent to others, all of which they are now forgiven.

For six years we lived in some attic rooms in the Rua das Pretas; António taught maths in a girls' school in the Largo do Andaluz and gave private lessons at night. I copied things on my typewriter and did the odd translation when one turned up. What we both earned, together with the few shares that my father, very prudently, had left me, was just about enough so that we did not die of hunger and could pay the instalments on our furniture.

Sometimes at the end of the afternoon we would stroll down the Avenida da Liberdade and through the Baixa as far as the river. On sunny days there were always children by the wall, watching the boats in wonderment or running happily after the pigeons.

'Perhaps everything will be better in a year's time,' I said, suddenly uneasy, to António. 'We could even have a baby, don't you think? I would so much like to...'

He replied that, yes, things might perhaps get better. And then held me close. We would have a baby and then go to Paris. Did I agree? Sometimes he felt angry, remembering the estates in Gouveia, the buildings in Viseu, the gold bars which his parents had locked away in the safe in the bank.

'When the baby is born we'll have to call it Fernando, won't we?' I said to him once. 'That was my father's name...'

He laughed automatically, without really laughing: 'OK, that's fine by me, girl, it's up to you.'

His eyes were shining very brightly.

Life is a funny business. One day António's mother died and we went to Gouveia for the funeral. His father was very low, brought down by the death which he thought would never happen. Crying, he embraced his son and apologised to both of us. He too felt suddenly alone and this was so frightful that soon he began to beg us to stay, us whom he had so despised. (He was a boor who only needed animals for company.) And not just to beg but also to suggest some kind of pledge, to be sure that he wasn't being cheated. Crafty old peasant! A few escudos which we had been going to spend in Paris, António's dream. And then he wanted a well-furnished house, with his own room. He said all this and then looked at me in triumph, because he thought that would be my dream, too. I smiled and said nothing. I smiled and thought of little Fernando.

Limp. And disgusted with myself as if I had tasted my own flesh. Like a bit of bread which you chew for a long time, which in the end starts to taste foul. Tasting myself, my own juices. I spat myself out disgustedly onto the bed and there I lay, wrung out and drained. My state of mind is somewhere between calm and despairing with a vague anxiety mixed in somewhere. At times I am afraid of this loneliness which is far greater, vaster than any I have felt before. No matter where I turn I always come back to myself. But I have already seen enough of myself and I realise that really I have nothing more to tell myself. Nothing more.

From time to time I am afraid but the room protects me. When I shut the door a moment ago I felt that it made a different sound, that it didn't swing there as it usually did but stopped short there in the silence like a full stop. Time, too has stopped. The hands of the clock still go round but all the hours are the same. There are no longer hours for eating, nor for sleeping, neither for work – has it got this far! – nor those which were once mine alone. Now that they are all mine I don't even notice them. There is only night and day, but the morning has ceased to be the beginning of things and to give a sheen to them. Everything has stopped: even the cars in the street and the voices coming from down there, because I don't let them get through to me; even the rain which beats on the windowpane because its patter will soon be silent too.

I am in my room. It is no longer dark and has lost for ever that smell of an unwashed body which can't sweat, having no more fluid to shed, as well as the smell of old paper and ants, that smell of so many old women, which pervaded the house from the beginning. It was a smell which followed me around, even enfolded me in the street, penetrated my nose and my mouth, and which I surely never lost in these last few years simply because I never even noticed it. Little by little the room stopped being so frightful. Now I needed to look around carefully so that I could see the low ceiling with the peeling stucco eyes, which watched me ceaselessly, which examined me over the shoulders of the ugly old furniture; and the fussy wall-paper of which Dona Glória was extremely proud, perhaps excessively so.

From time to time she turns up, her speech full of the diminutives that she happens to favour at that time. Why don't you take a little turn around the block? Do I want her to bring a little something from the street? Is there nothing I fancy? It's such a beautiful day, the sun is so warm.

Me, go out? And what if I should meet someone I know? I can just hear them speaking to each other as if they were there before me. 'Poor child,' they sigh, 'how thin and pale you are. You really ought to see a doctor. Why don't you go to old Whatsisname? He's pretty good, don't you think?' Then follows the litany of those saved by old Whatsisname. Or perhaps: 'You know, I barely recognised you. You'd better do something about it while there's still time. Do you remember Cicraninha? Well, she suddenly turned very yellow, had hardly any strength… but when she went to the doctor it was already too late. Nothing could be done. Poor thing, she's now buried up at Limiar.' Or in the cemetery at Alto do São João or in Prazeres.

Even if they didn't know, even if I hadn't told them I was going to die they would certainly still have a good cry over me. People love to have a good cry, especially over someone else and with good reason. 'You're ill, child, I'm telling you. I mean, your face... How many pounds have you lost? How dreadful for you...' And they would have that vindictive expression, devoid of all surprise, which those who are unhappy, whether truly or imagined, (which is to say almost all human beings) even the best, the so-called good ones, cannot disguise. 'Things happens, you know, you must be patient. Take me, for example...'

I don't give a damn for examples; I don't give a damn for other people.

The nights are the worst. So long, so endless, full of phantoms, some of them old but recently returned, almost faceless and speechless, others new and old at the same time, ethereal bodies which haven't begun to decay, which don't want to because time is still hastening by. António, Luís Gonzaga, Estrela, too, of course. Estrela more than anyone. I think about them involuntarily, even when I try so hard that it hurts to stop them entering my head. They come, nevertheless, and lodge and linger there. They are all happy, hugely happy, after having shooed me out like an insignificant animal that's been annoying them. What, them? No, of course not, I know. If my live was like that what could they do about it? It only hurts because they've managed to find happiness at my expense. It's I and my silence which has given them all this good fortune. One word, one cry, one tear would have been enough, but I could not force any of these out of me. Now it's too late because I'm dying. It would have been too late anyway, even if death had not come along.

Fortunately in Portugal you can buy sleep without needing a doctor's prescription. One, two, three tubes of sleep. But in Paris... The prescription, please... You can't Madame... because of the suicides, Madame... because of the suicides, Madame... BECAUSE OF THE SUICIDES...

From how far away that voice comes to me! Just as it was, the very same, from six, eight years ago. I think the chemists was called Heudebert, or was it Saint-Michel? It was on the left side of the boulevard as you went down to Sena. I've already told you Madame, It's impossible. I'm very sorry.

I started to roam the streets. A fine chilly rain began to fall and I went into a Biard because I suddenly remembered that I hadn't eaten since the previous evening and this now seemed a matter of extreme importance. Then I went down some steps into a Metro station though I can't recall what it was called. Nor do I know from which station I emerged. In any case I stayed down there a long time, an hour or two. It was late at night and there were a lot of people. They carried me along, in comfort, where they chose. I enjoyed that teeming night so much, going nowhere. Dubo... Dubon... Dubonnet...   Then the night ended. Barbes ou Place Clichy? Eat Lustucru pâtés... Children adore Banania... Marignan – The Lovers of Venice... I was pushed along two corridors and then it was night again. Don't you want to go out? Well then, allow me... allow... allow. A girl at my side was reading 'Confidences'. It's funny to recall her face so precisely, as if she was someone close to me. Omo washes whiter... Jean Marais about to kiss this motionless profile, with long blonde hair... Gentlemen, shave with...

A few days after I went to fix up our visas so that we could go back to Lisbon. António had of necessity to accompany me.

Some hours earlier it had been night, a cold February night, with the lights pouring out onto the boulevard's thick asphalt and neon letters making luminous pools in front of the cinema and the cafés. There was a light mist like the breath of the city. We went into the Royal; already there was a friend from Lisbon, Costa, who had a grant to study at Recherches Scientifiques, and a group of Brazilians, his friends, as well as a Portuguese woman, whom I didn't know. She was called Estrela Vale and was a sculptor. At first I didn't pay much attention to her. Then I began to watch her, guided – this was something new to me – by António's gaze. She was short and slim, her small, round head was covered by heavily lacquered black hair, and the lips of her delicate mouth were sucked in and outlined in cyclamen red. Her dress was cut very low and she had a beauty spot at the base of her long – extremely long – white neck. She spoke a great deal, but slowly as if the words too were shaped by her and she made them meticulously and with great care.

The beginning of everything was not a matter of somebody's appearance, nor was it a certain look or a particular conversation, but rather a few words arising from nothing much, and perhaps for this very reason fated, something that, curiously, I immediately knew for certain. Ordinary words, meaningless like so many that we say and which will fade away in time and be forgotten. But these remain, however, engraved on my memory. Everybody was talking. Apollinaire, what a great poet, have you read *Les Alcoöls*? Julinha Reis, have you heard of her? Julinha Reis, yes... And then suddenly everybody was absorbed in a conversation about whether a given person was really married or not. Estrela raised her glass of white port to her lips and António, forgetting about his beer, gazed at her. After a while he said in a voice I didn't recognise: 'How pretty it is, your beauty spot. It looks like a flower in the wind.'

I was utterly astonished: it was so unlike him, that phrase. He always called things by their real name. Could it really have been António who had spoken, who has said this?

The woman put her hand on her neck to run her fingers over the recently born flower and started to laugh a lot for no reason at all; it was as if she was full of that kind of complete happiness which some-times people sometimes feel and which when it wears off – it comes so unexpectedly – leaves behind the memory of a sullen mouth and an angry look where no light falls. But what do I know what Estrela thought, what Estrela felt… António carried on looking at her unmindful of anything or anyone else. She was laughing, she was laughing so much. I still can hear her laugh, a secret kind of laugh, which came from deep within, which bubbled lightly without over-flowing.

Why do I remember that night so well? Everyone's voice jostled for attention, now one, now another rising above the rest, not minding how they clambered over the others in their desire to be louder and therefore justified. And all along I heard the low laughter of Estrela.

After an hour or so the fat Brazilian with the face – what was he called? – already maudlin with whisky and overflowing with a cloying tenderness that he could not contain for the family he had left behind in Curitiba, began to talk about his wife (he called her 'my lady') and his beautiful children. All the while he stared insis-tently, as if one thing followed from the other, at Simone's huge décolletage, which hardly covered her nipples. António was talking to Estrela but his voice was so low I could not hear what he was saying. The others, inattentive and indifferent to things which did not concern them, carried on talking desultorily, their voices slurred with drink, and repeating laboriously the few words they could manage at that time of night.

We crammed into the swarthy Brazilian's Renault and Simone's Vedette to go home; her car jolted across the dead, old city, all over the place, getting lost in the narrow little streets or the wide boule-vards which she confused even in the daytime, because to her they all looked just as grey and ugly. Simone didn't like Paris. She agreed when someone said that there were fine things there; far be it from her to disagree. And the night life was wonderful. Yes, of course…

But they really shouldn't come to her talking about elegance – people from Rio dressed far better – or about French cooking or the beauty of Paris. What beauty? She was fed up, to the back teeth, my friends, of steak, chips and dirt. Her eyes, so dark that they had no iris, danced in the little rectangular mirror. Her slender hands with scarlet nails were tapping the steering wheel impatiently because once again she was lost.

'Rio is something else,' she said suddenly, dreamily. 'Just that huge sea, eh Etelvino? You remember? That huge endless sea?'

In the back seat, on my left, Etelvino Cruz's teeth were like a gaping hole in the night. 'So why did you come here?' he asked in a thick voice. 'Why don't you get the first plane back? Have you come here just to find fault? That's crazy, kid.'

They talked and suddenly I was alone, so alone that I began to feel like crying, just as I had years ago. But now there was no one to run his hand through my hair. Sure, António was next to me but I knew that he was really with Estrela in the fat Brazilian's – whose name I now remember was Garibaldi – car.

Simone now began to sing; her voice was deep and husky and her songs were invariably sad. They told of mistrustful eyes, hungover, eyes like berths at night where boats are beached, like deep pools in which men disappeared for ever. Her voice swelled, poured out as if she would never stop.

Costa who was sitting beside her begged her to sing something lighter. He thought the one she was singing too depressing. Simone shook her head violently, her hair Indian, jet black, so smooth; she said it was impossible. The drink had made her melancholy and there was nothing she could do about it, even though she regretted it herself. She was so sad one night that she thought about killing herself and took six Gardenal tablets. She didn't know anyone else who had done that. Jandira, the blonde girl next to the door, snuggled up to Costa, said that it was only with the fourth whisky that life began to have any zest, and she suggested that we end the night in a bar in Montparnasse that stayed open all night. Simone stopped the car to tell the others and within a few moments we were all settled around another table. António sat down beside Estrela and in a low voice resumed his conversation. Simone, her eyelids lowered, seemed to be pondering death as the only remedy for life.

It's funny how I remember all the little details of that night. At one point Jandira began to sing a samba while António danced with Estrela. Their faces were close together and their bodies seemed as one. They didn't speak. 'I'd give anything for a bean stew,' exclaimed Simone in a sudden flash of inspiration.

'Right. There's a restaurant near here where they do a bean stew,' said Etelvino.

'You don't say! You're not kidding?'

'It's true; Salustiano told me where it was but I wasn't paying attention. Now that he's gone away it's hard to find out just where it is.'

António and Estrela sat down again. Etelvino shook a matchbox to the rhythm of the music. 'Waiter, a half, please.' It was I who spoke.

'You've already had too much; you'll soon be drunk,' said António. 'You know well enough that it goes to your head.'

I downed the beer in one, then another and yet another. Everything started to seem different. People seemed more attractive suddenly; I even wanted to embrace them. The tender feelings that welled up in me for Estrela were so strong that I almost wanted to cry. It was more or less at that moment that I noticed that one, thick, white hair; I couldn't take my eyes off it. Estrela, too, began to look at me insistently, no doubt because my drunkenness had made her feel more at ease. Then she looked with great interest at António. How could this man have married that woman? It was easy enough to read her thoughts in her sharp gaze and in that puzzled, vertical line between her plucked eyebrows. I bent over the table and I pointed to the hair.

'Wait a moment while I pull it out for you,' I said. 'You might make a mistake and pull out one you didn't want to. You haven't many like this.'

My words came out with difficulty, slurred. But they came out. There was a silence broken by Jandira's nervous laugh. Then António helped me to my feet, put my coat around me, wrapped my scarf around my neck and told the others not to put themselves out for us. There were plenty of taxis nearby, added the waiter.

At the door we passed the man with the bibles who was just coming in. Remember eternal life… I laughed at him, as if he were just a comic actor, and then turned back to say goodbye to Estrela with whom I felt, I remember perfectly, on exceptionally friendly terms.

I believe that as soon as the effect of the drink wore off, in other words the next morning, I thought about killing myself. That doesn't mean that I had decided to do it, far from it. There are very few people who kill themselves and they are those who don't talk about it but sooner or later they kill themselves. The others, those who spend their lives talking about it, are nothing more than moral black-mailers, blackmailers who use death as a threat. I'm going to kill myself because I know you are this man's or this woman's lover. If you leave me I'll kill myself. In general they get away with it because human gullibility – especially that of men, when their vanity is at stake – is limitless.

I only thought about killing myself so that I might suffer more. It was a kind of game of chess which I played with an opponent – António – who wasn't there and who didn't know what was going on. And even when I went into the chemists on the Boulevard Saint Michel it wasn't because I wanted to kill myself, but because I wanted to sleep and I thought I wouldn't be able to without a seda-tive.

Much later, though, I wanted to. There was a day when I really wanted to die: the day when Estrela came back to take from me the only thing I still had -- the memory of the son I never had.

Even today I'm still amazed at how soon I was sure of what would happen with António and Estrela. Something – I could tell, I knew at once – would have to give and nobody lifted a finger or did the least thing to stop it happening. Neither Estrela, nor he, nor me. I was certain, indeed, but full of doubts. I told myself, and with more conviction with every day that passed, that perhaps I was mistaken and that it had been nothing more than a passing fancy already forgotten. Within me, though, the conviction had already taken root, without my noticing. My doubts were forced and even as I formu-lated them I didn't believe them. And so I felt a modified amazement, mixed in with a kind of bitter satisfaction, which made me think of another side of myself – see, didn't I tell you? see, wasn't I right? – when one afternoon António informed me without looking at me and while rummaging around in a drawer for some-thing which, whatever it was, he never found: 'Estrela Vale came back yesterday. I met her just now in the Baixa. She's come back to stay.'

'The only thing I don't understand is why he talked to you about her,' Lucia had to say to me much later, Lucia who had always been my friend (and would always be, I supposed). Lucia has a nodding acquaintance with António: to her he was just a man; to me he was António, that was the difference. He was head over heels in love with Estrela, I had realised immediately during that night in Paris. He wanted her only for himself and he wanted to give himself only to her, as I understood him later. That was António all over. Even when he was a bachelor he had never had a woman whom he still didn't like or didn't like him. He couldn't have been any other way.

We lived then in a first floor flat on the Avenida de Berne, which his father had furnished with particular bad taste, full of decorative art, while we were away. He still hadn't arrived from Gouveia but his room was there at the end of an enormous corridor, still empty but already with a huge picture of a woman, entirely naked, hanging on the wall.

I asked Estrela to dinner and that night all the doubts that I had been building up soon dissolved in the face of the evidence. António could not hide his feelings; who knows, perhaps he didn't even want to. She sank her slender, lithe body into an armchair, her head always very straight, her lips half open even when she listening. She was full of stories, the kind of gossip that used to annoy António, but which on the contrary he now seemed to find delightful. Did we know that Costa was Jandira's fiancé? She was going back to Brazil, of course. Her father was extremely wealthy, he had factories of some sort... She would never have thought that Costa would have gone after money like that...

'But Jandira...'

'What about Jandira. She's crazy, thick as three short planks. As for Costa, well between you and me, he's not exactly bright...'

He was Costa's friend but he laughed at Estrela's words. Now, what about Costa... let's have some more, yes, let's have some more... And Simone, what became of Simone?

Well, she'd started taking Gardenal again one night when she'd been drinking heavily and now she was going around with the doctor who'd treated her, Jean-Claude. Garibaldi, meanwhile...

António was drinking in her words.

She came more often. I needed to see them; I felt the need of both of them. It was quite strange; while I was watching them I felt extremely calm.

Lucia, who turned up most days, didn't beat about the bush: 'Mariana, your husband is deceiving you,' she said.

'Deceiving me? What an unpleasant expression. António has never tried to deceive me. Of course he doesn't tell me everything, because there are some disagreeable things I don't want to know, that's why.'

'And you have decided to carry on like this, not wanting to know?' she asked.

'I suppose so I'm waiting for him to say something,' I replied.

'You'll wait a long time.'

'That's fine by me. But I'm almost sure he's going to say something.'

Lucia shook her head in incomprehension: 'And you still invite this great big…' (She stopped short of the word just as in her life she had stopped of anything that offered the slightest difficulty.) 'And you still invite her even though she's after YOUR HUSBAND? In YOUR HOUSE?'

In her indignation she spoke in capital letters. Lucia had an overdeveloped, even medieval, sense of propriety. Perhaps it was because her great uncle had been a count, even though ruined. Several times I had tried to show her just how far fetched was her way of looking at things, but Lucia either could not or would not understand me. I really believe she couldn't. In her early childhood her mother had instilled into her certain infallible opinions which had to be passed on to her children in their entirety, together with whatever her husband managed to add in this respect.

How is Lucia nowadays? In those days she promised a great deal. For her *my* husband was a man who belonged to me body and soul; and *my* house was like an impregnable fortress to be defended if need be by firing great boulders or pouring boiling oil on any future assailants. Poor Lucia, she never noticed that in the majority of cases the possessive form is purely decorative.

We went to Gouveia for a weekend because António's father was feeling ill. It turned out to be nothing serious, he was already up and about, working as usual and worried because his olive trees had hardly blossomed. It was a lovely day and we went for a walk. António, why I don't know, perhaps as an excuse not to talk, to fill the time doing something or other, decided he would take some photographs. I remember that I was leaning up against a tree and that I had slipped my arms around the trunk. There was a sudden crack and I trembled.

'It's over,' I said pulling my hands back.

'What's over?' he asked in a feeble voice, unsure of himself.

'I don't know, something. I was looking at you and I felt pretty good just the way I was. Good, in spite of everything. Then you took the photo and we both changed our positions. It would seem that there was nothing making us do this…'

'What a silly idea! It had to be; we couldn't spend the rest of lives like this.'

'No, no we couldn't,' I said.

'Listen, Mariana,' said António, coming closer. 'For a long time I've been wanting to tell you, to explain to you... but it's so difficult, Mariana. I never thought it would be so difficult. I look at you and I can't... maybe it's better this way... yes, it's definitely better...'

'I know what you're talking about.' It was me speaking, but my voice didn't waver. It was perhaps a bit dry, a bit high, but I couldn't have done it any other way.

António was silent for a moment and then he spoke: 'I thought you must know, that it was quite out of the question that you didn't know.'

'It was only natural, wasn't it?'

'Of course.'

It was difficult, so difficult, he had never realised it would be so difficult. I had to help him or there would have been a kind of breakdown in my own relationship, already so strained at times, with myself.

'António, you know I'll go along with whatever you want.'

Today I feel so much at peace with myself and so can once more write about myself; for after all who but me would waste time listening to me? Who, now that my life is completely empty? Empty of António, Luis, Lucia, my friend I always had, my friend forever... forever... the illusions I had. Empty even of those bit players who come and go after saying their little piece and who, after all, we need so much.

Around me there is only death, closer each day, as well as the silence of the house, the silence of the noises of the house, of the harsh, monotonous voice of the owner talking with the neighbours who gather in the evenings to talk about the other neighbours, about their embroidery, their maids (the enemy within our doors, Dona Glória!), of the cars passing in the street, the woman crying their wares, vegetables or fish. At some times there is silence, at others there are noises I don't want to hear, because they are not mine, they haven't been mine for a long time now. They are the noises of the others, of the living. I close the window and bury my head beneath the pillow just so as not to hear them, so as to be alone. And so, too, that I can let myself weep and feel really unhappy. It's as if I had finally reached the top of the mountain and therefore felt completely calm, ready for the descent. But there are also days when, on the other hand, I go out onto the veranda just to watch people. I already know the barber who spends his days at the door of his shop, the 'Smart Barbers', to get some fresh air or some sun, depending on whether it's hot or cold: I know the pretty girl who lives in the next building and who goes out sometimes in a car with a bald gentleman of a respectable age and appearance; and the children who spend their time playing on the pavement when they come home from school. It's when I see them, when I hear their eager young voices that I shut my window and retreat into my own life, which is mine alone and which goes on within my room.

I spent I don't know how many years wishing I could run away from a loneliness that terrified me merely to think about it; I passed my time believing in people whom before long I let fall through my empty hands. Luís Gonzaga used to say that I expected too much of God's creatures. Perhaps he was right. Then there were days, months between, black and empty, with no beginning and no end, days to be got through, leafing through strange lives in detective novels with their happy endings, the villain always punished and evident virtue amply rewarded, watching stupid films, smoking cigarettes which I lit one after the other but which I didn't enjoy, wandering the streets. Alone. So it's come to this...

Now here I am, not even able to read. I know I'm going to die and this certainty is enough, like a sedative. In the face of that certainty everything else vanishes. But sometimes everything else crowds in on me too, depending on the colour of the days. Grey days pass limply, disconsolately, tempered by tears. I spend the black days in minute analysis of myself and of all this inglorious existence of mine. I fall to thinking whether this life might have been different, better, and, if not longer, whether I might at least have seized my chances, had I done things differently, had I gone down other paths. But no; it was not I who decided. It wasn't I who opened the hands which were, I can see now, already empty. I was forced to act and to keep quiet about it, too. Sometimes I would be going along a wide street and see a way open and then suddenly there would be a wall. I would already be too late to go back and so I had to find some way out of there, or stop altogether and just stay there. It wasn't I who put the wall there, nor was it I who did things before the time was ripe for them. Everything was there, ready for my arrival, just waiting for me.

I have already spent five years of my life in this room; I couldn't have done anything else. Now that I know what awaits me I find in it something death-like, at least something half-finished, undefined. It's not yet death, but neither is it truly life. I suppose it never was. I would no longer be capable of living a real life because I've lost the habit. What's more this experience, this life, was always just a bit too difficult for me. I never got used to it, which is odd, because everyone else thinks of it as the most simple, natural thing, the most natural and simple thing that ever was. I always stood on ceremony and so didn't do things the way I should have, as other people did, even the slowest and most ignorant, at their leisure. I spoke loudly when the most elementary rules demanded I speak softly, I kept quiet when I really should have said something, I just didn't know how to *be*. In fact I never knew how to *be*. I always chose the wrong time to speak or to be silent. I got it all wrong, I mixed everything up to the extent that I couldn't find my true self. People like Estrela, even Lucia, know how to choose their moment, know the value of coming to the point – in other words they know how to live. Me, I always got it wrong. Even the moment of Fernandinho's entry into the world, had he been born, was wrong. Estrela herself told someone that in her view the time could not have been worse. The very same Estrela.

My son died within me. One afternoon I was crossing the Restauradores when I caught a glimpse of Estrela. She was wearing a yellow suit, which fitted her exactly, and from a distance her head seemed even smaller and even darker. Without paying attention to what I was doing I stopped to look at her. At this moment the car came and hit my legs. I fell to the ground and lost consciousness, but before I fell I think I screamed.

It was this that caused me to lose my son and meant that I couldn't have children in future – my looking at Estrela like that. Naturally she never saw me, or even stopped, because she wasn't that sort of person to stop in the street if someone screamed, she probably didn't even notice. Her fault was to have passed by close to me for the second time in our two lives. At times it is enough, though, just to look at someone, to utter a mere word, to laugh, to pass by, for the other person to die.

Later, many months afterwards, I learnt that at the time of my accident Estrela was abroad with António. However, this is of secondary importance. I could never get rid of the notion that that woman was Estrela. Her, or a deceptive shadow, what difference does it make? It was her I saw although her real body was at that moment in Paris or London. It was because of her that Fernandinho was never born.

I don't want to leave anything behind me. I've spent this afternoon tearing up various papers, among which I found a picture of me with my arms hanging down, leaning against a tree… Why had I kept it? I don't know, I don't remember any longer. I put it on top of a chest of drawers because I enjoyed looking at it.

So many papers, so many sheets of paper that I've written all over. Diaries, letters which never reached their destination because after all, thinking about it clearly, they weren't worth sending… Papers covered in fine, fancy writing that I don't recognise. Firmer, balanced, well-rounded. My writing now has become puckered and shapeless along with my face and hands, along with my own body with its flabby breasts and neglected, faded flesh.

This basket is full of my life. Torn bits of paper, fragments, bits of things someone has written to me and that I can't remember having heard, words I said to someone now forgotten. Everything mixed up like my memories. Postcards from Luís Gonzaga with Italian stamps and views of cathedrals. Words from someone unknown sent to someone who is no longer me. The weather has been very pleasant… Rome is a wonderful city… and all my best wishes to finish with. I can't even laugh about it any more.

Perhaps it was because of the postcards I had been reading that I dreamt of Luís that night. His presence, whether real or imagined, always made – and still makes – for pleasant company. For a long time he was always in my mind when I woke up, looking like he did when we first met or when we said goodbye to each other for ever. And it was forever notwithstanding the postcards which he continued to send me for months and months. It was a time when I used to wake every night and enter the feeble light of my room, still unfamiliar to me, fragrant, and tasted my dreams in my mouth. I didn't want to wake up because I then began to think about myself. I closed my eyes, wanting to return to the nothingness from where I had just come. There were images in my head that I couldn't make out. I wanted to know who I had been dreaming of but I couldn't. Sometimes, though, I managed to drag from the deepest recesses of the night one or other obscure, shadowy, almost buried figure. Are other people's dreams wan and drained of all colour too? I asked Luís about this one day and he said that his dreams were like mine. But then Luís accepted everything, didn't laugh at anything at all, and found nothing strange or unreasonable. He always turned over every idea in his mind at length, trying to understand everything, even those which were so silly as to be beyond him. And when this and other things happened, in his voice and his way of smiling he seemed so much like my father.

I first met him in Lucia's house; he was vaguely related to her. He belonged to a rich family from the Minho, very religious people. Being the youngest and weakest child he was destined from child-hood to be a priest. So he went to study at the seminary, but when he finished there and before taking holy orders he felt a great uncer-tainty. Did he really have a religious vocation? He then came to Lisbon to study classical philology. But quite early on, on the first day that I met him at Lucia's house, Luís Gonzaga told me quite naturally that it was perfectly possible that he had always been destined for the priesthood.

Now when I write his name or his face comes to me, I feel less alone. It's the same when I get one of his postcards. They don't say anything but it's in his handwriting and it is sweet to think that somebody has bothered to remember me for a couple of minutes.

For how long did Luís Gonzaga continue to write me postcards? In the last one I got, six months ago, he said that after five years spent in universities and retreats he was coming back to Portugal and hoped to be fortunate enough to have a small parish in his own part of the country. Then there came a hackneyed phrase, hoping that I too had found my direction in life.

My direction... Perhaps I really had. Could there have been another one, one better than those I had sought?

Perhaps he will carry on writing to me from beyond my life, who knows? No, there are so many things which will stop him doing so. His good name, for example. What would they think and say if they knew – and they would know, of course – that he was writing to a woman? And one needs to take care of one's good name, as Lucia already well knows. What use is friendship when your good name is at stake? Friendship... Perhaps for Luís it is only a case of his finding within himself a memory which is merely pity. Perhaps it's out of pity that he continues to write to me... No, what an idea. So what about one's good name? And self-interest? It's just as well not to forget self-interest. We only give others the bounty of our remem-brance provided they are grateful for it. And I think that I only wrote to him a couple of times. We are no more than God's creatures. Once, twice, ten or twelve times in exceptional cases... But then we start to feel fed up and forgetful and we are reduced to those phrases which we cling to in justification. She doesn't write back because she isn't interested in the news he sends her; perhaps his news bores her silly even, who knows? Or: Maybe she's moved house again. Or even: Who knows, she might have got married again. The excuses we make for ourselves.

I can hardly still remember him. We are never able to recall a person or a landscape except perhaps on the first day we saw them. How ought I to see him again as he was then, I who am now thirty-six years old, an old thirty-six at that. An old woman, full of wrinkles, with white hair, who has ceased – how long ago? – to be a woman? I'm sure that Lucia's mother still goes to the hairdresser every fortnight, still has her nails done, still plucks her eyebrows with tweezers, still rubs in her anti-wrinkle cream at night. It's almost laughable… Lucia's mother does all this, while I…

How can I possibly remember Luís Gonzaga? I was twenty-eight in those days, about to get divorced, unhappy, but I was only twenty-eight. I still loved António, of course. I'm still fond of him today, knowing that I'm going to die. I suffered a great deal, to be sure, but now I don't think of it as suffering. It's funny, but as the years go by we recall past details with a precision that is almost photographic, we hear again a phrase in the voice that uttered it, but whatever we felt at a given time is stuck there firmly in the past; having had its moment it has died. But it was because I was suffering, because I was unhappy that I clung so strongly, almost desperately, to Luís Gonzaga. In his eyes there was a serenity which I needed. His calm voice and his gaze, too, which rested on people and then lingered on them, absorbed, brought with them a feeling of well-being which I had never encountered and which I never again found in anyone. Yet this calm did not allay the hint of anxiety which sometimes appeared in his gaze, but served only to mitigate it. He had never spoken to me again, nor to anyone, of the possibility that he was going to be a priest, but I knew from his silences, from the sentences begun and then broken off in the middle, that the matter would always be linked, though tenuously, with the church, the seminary, even with the Catholic church itself, that this idea was fixed in him. I knew by the very fact, which must seem incomprehensible to some people, that he had never tried to convert me.

We went out a lot. I had an almost physical need to get out, to see people, to go here and there, to see things as far away from me as I could, to get out of myself. In the end I got a job as a typist in a shipping company, but when I left work I always, provided he was free, met Luís Gonzaga; we went to exhibitions and matinées at the cinema, and on Sundays, for want of anything better to do, went to the zoo to see the animals. On the bad days I talked to him about António, about Estrela, about myself. He used to laugh and tell me that at twenty-eight I had much more than them to live for.

'You can still get married, you'll see,' he said one day.

He, too, had his bad days. He would seem preoccupied and spoke little. Once he told me that the seminary wasn't doing him any good. All the decisions had been taken for him and he didn't know how to get out of it.

'The signs can be seen all over you,' I said, 'they leap out at you. Just think, of the brothers it was you who was chosen by the family to be the priest. Don't you think it's rather a large coincidence that you have a religious vocation? Unless of course you believe that you are in a state of grace and thus your sin is pride.'

He smiled: 'We all sin through pride sixty times an hour, sometimes more. You, Mariana, saw the signs and you *know* you are right. I, I *know* that it is I who am right, although I don't know the reason why. So much pride…'

Estrela and António got married one morning in June; a religious marriage, naturally. I, as I said to Luís Gonzaga, had only had a civil ceremony. It was Alice Mendes, an old colleague of Maria Amália with whom I'd always kept in contact, who phoned me to say what had happened. Obviously it was only by chance that she did so. The thing came up in conversation through a mere association of ideas. What she said at least was 'What the hell!' Perhaps it was true. Among many bits of news – Alice always had lots of news though she never knew how to pick out the best bits – she spoke of an old fellow student of hers, not a very pleasant person, whom she had met a few days ago in Versailles. 'And what the hell, do you know who she's marrying today? Your husband, António.'

I would rather have heard the news the next day, or a week or a month later. But Alice couldn't resist. Poor thing, it was important not to hold it against her, that failing that she'd had since school. At bottom she wasn't malicious; just a victim – like all of us, isn't that the way of it? – of her genes. It's quite something to enjoy that kind of talk: to be a little bit unbalanced so that you don't know whether to say something or leave it out. And of course you can make other people really suffer.

That afternoon I went to get Luís. I couldn't stand to be alone with Estrela and António; they wouldn't leave me, I couldn't get them out of my head. I had phoned Lucia but she had gone to the cinema with her mother. I had been several times before to Luís Gonzaga's room, to pick up books or take something that I had promised him. It was a small room, on its own, extremely modest, in the Conde Arronde. It was the room of a single man, tidy and with no distinguishing features, which made it look uninhabited. The narrow iron bed had a crucifix over the head. When I left it was already night. Earlier he had told me, looking me straight in the face, that he could not marry me.

'I know,' I said.

'Because it's almost certain, virtually inevitable, that I'm going to be a priest.'

'It doesn't matter,' I replied.

Then on the way out, my hand already on the door knob, I asked him, I don't know why: 'You'll be going to confession early tomorrow morning, won't you Luís?'

'Why are you asking me this?'

'Yes, indeed, why?'

We met several times more and then one night he phoned me. He wanted to speak to me, it was urgent. I went to see him the following morning; I was tired, my lined features those of someone who had spent a sleepless night. Everything had been decided, finally. He had seen to everything and was leaving in two days.

I put my hand on my belly where my son had still not begun to move and then stretched out my hand to him. I spoke (though I don't know what I said) but I do remember that my gesture and my words had a false theatricality about them which I enacted to please myself with all the awareness and ardour of a bad actor.

'Goodbye, then,' I said at last. 'We'll never see each other again, will we?'

'We can always see each other again, Mariana. Haven't we been friends till now?'

'And we're friends no longer?' I replied.

'I didn't mean that, rather that we can still be friends as we were previously. If there's anything you need, whatever it is…'

'I'll go looking for you… What's the point of those words, Luís? Goodbye simply means goodbye, and no more.'

He hadn't brought my world down about my ears as had happened the last time when António looked deep into Estrela's eyes. This time it was as if a screw somewhere had worked loose or a beam had snapped and one or other of these things had been patched up. Nor did I feel alone because I had my son, a son who was mine alone.

As I went up to Luís Gonzaga I began to think, quite coldly, how, in that situation, a tear would make him happy; however I was in no way disposed to shed a tear for him. At first I had felt sad, disconsolate, but now I was beginning to feel a strange sensation of freedom, which was almost unsettling at that moment. Luís seemed to be waiting for me to say something, no matter what. I found myself saying to myself, silently, words like 'abandoned with a child in my arms' and 'what a mess I'm in' and even 'where will I get money to pay for the birth?' And these words that came to me suddenly made me want to laugh out loud.

'I can see you're suffering Mariana,' said Luís. 'Why, why? Cry if you feel like it.'

The vanity of men! Why should I cry, why should I want to cry now that I had my son? And he thought it was just because he was going away… The vanity of men, the incredible, ridiculous vanity of men…

I was at Lucia's house. She still hadn't returned and her mother, Dona Corina, was talking to me about her daughter's new young man, whom she found delightful. Her eyes sparkled; in her enthusiasm she had put her knitting down on her plump knees. She was a lady of a certain age (Lucia had been a late arrival) but she looked after herself very carefully. Her mouth, which was already ill-defined with its circles of wrinkles beneath smudges of lipstick, was like a faded flower.

'He's an excellent boy,' she said with conviction, 'an excellent boy.'

When Dona Corina spoke of a good boy, she was referring neither to his age nor his bearing, whether physical or mental; nor would I say she was concerned about his moral outlook. He would have though – and this was of the greatest importance – a salary of more than three thousand escudos. The category into which she had just put him gave me some idea then of the worth of Lucia's young man, whom of course I still did not know, but who must have been earning at least five thousand escudos.

'How old is he?' I asked, just for the sake of saying something. 'The same age as Lucia?'

Dona Corina took off her glasses: 'Forty-five, but, you know, he doesn't look it at all. You should see him. He doesn't look a day over thirty. He's crazy about Lucia, crazy, you can be sure. He wants to rent a house, get married this year…'

'And what does he do?' I asked.

'He's an engineer, don't you know. Yes, indeed. And he's very well thought of. He works in Tabor, you see… and he earns well, very well…'

With some effort I swallowed the 'how much?' which was on the tip of my tongue. It wasn't so much curiosity that made me want to ask – I've never suffered from that – but the desire to know just what were the very qualities which had earned him the epithet 'excellent'. But after all, what for? Dona Corina resumed her knitting and I switched on the wireless. In Lucia's house – Lucia, the friend I'd always had and always would have – I felt as though at home in my own house, the house I had no longer had. It was immeasurably better than the boarding house where I now lived. The music was abominable and I switched the radio off. Lucia was late and I began to think about how odd it was that she hadn't yet introduced me to the fiancé whom she was shortly to marry. For some reason she wasn't ready to, I was sure of that. What other reason could there have been?

Without putting down her work, Dona Corina returned to the subject which was preoccupying her: 'He's from a very good family, you know. You must surely know the name Vale de Pomar... you don't?'

She frowned in surprise; it was rather as if I had just confessed that I hadn't heard of the English royal family. Then she put down her work to go to the kitchen to see what the maid was doing: 'Nothing, isn't that typical. It's the way these days. You'll excuse me, Mariana, won't you. These maids, if you don't keep on top of them...'

Alone I waited for Lucia. I hadn't anything to say to her, I found myself thinking. So what was I doing there? What? Too lazy to move, I let myself stay. The chair was comfortable, and the picture of flowers hanging there in front of me was pleasant to look at. I felt my already heavy body becoming even more indolent. Lucia came back round about seven. She seemed very cheerful, prettier than usual, and asked me, with apparent indifference and without waiting for an answer, if I wanted to stay for dinner and what had I been doing recently. For half an hour or so we spoke about things perfunctorily. In the end I just had to laugh: so what was all the secrecy about? I had been expecting her at least to ask me to the wedding...

She laughed too, somewhat forcedly. Ah, so her mother had talked to me about it. She couldn't keep a secret, that one... No, she wasn't keeping any secrets, how could I think that; in truth nothing had yet been decided. Her mother was always one for thinking things could be done just like that. As if a person could get married at the drop of a hat...

'But you never even mentioned him to me!' I said.

Oh, was that so? I must certainly be mistaken…

I got up; I said I must be on my way. No, I didn't want dinner, someone was expecting me at my lodgings. I went to the window to see if it was raining. When I turned round I noticed that Lucia was staring at me, at a certain part of my body. The sharp questioning stare of someone who wanted to be sure of something.

I hoped with all my heart that I was mistaken and while hope persisted I didn't go back to Lucia's house. She knew where I lived, didn't she?

For months I had no news of her.

One day my boss sent for me. Usually he was an overbearing, unpleasant man, but on this occasion I felt sorry for him. He looked at me and didn't know where to begin. He coughed and shuffled his papers; he was very pale.

'Someone has had a word with Mr Bruno (the owner) and told him that you are, that you are going to…'

'Have a baby. As you can see that's quite correct. And it's equally evident that this person's labours were quite unnecessary. It only needed Senhor Bruno to look at me.'

'Senhor Bruno has requested me to ask you to leave the company before any further scandal is caused, because enough is enough. He has already twice suggested that I ask you… without further scandal, we've had enough already. That's all, Dona Mariana. I am very sorry. You can pick up your salary from the cash desk. I am so sorry, believe me.'

His hands shook above his desk. He wasn't a good man. No, he was coarse, unprincipled and overbearing. He was enjoying the chance to show himself in a good light for once. But I said nothing because I knew that he wouldn't understand me.

I had to get by with the meagre earnings I had until Fernandinho was born and I could get a new job. I began to live frugally so that I could pay for my stay in the maternity hospital.

One fine day I read in the paper the news of Lucia's wedding; it was in 'Society Echoes'. The ruined count was her godfather and her godmother was a family friend from a line of grocers, but of solid wealth for all that. The bridegroom's godfather was an engineer, Senhor João Frederico de Castro e Nunes Vale de Pomar, with other long names that I don't remember. I couldn't be angry with Lucia, poor thing. How on earth could she have introduced me to her new family?

'This is my friend, Mariana, who, as you can clearly see, is going to have a baby…'

'And what about your husband, how is he?' they would ask.

'My dear lady, I don't have a husband.'

'Well then, who is the baby's father?'

And then Lucia would say, matter-of-factly: 'Nobody really knows. Do you know, Mariana. Sometimes you know, don't you? It just happens…'

These kinds of conversations came into my head several times a day. But still I could bear no grudge against Lucia. the time which she, her fiancé and her mother must have spent trying to come to some solution! The suggestions they rejected and the ones they tolerated at least until they had to make the final choice. Should they have put it to me frankly? They wouldn't have the nerve. Introduce me in spite of everything? 'You're crazy, Lucia. Think of my family, all those Vale de Pomars?' Silence was the best bet, obviously. They had to make me see that I was not someone they could introduce. 'What does mother think?' And then Dona Corina, very firmly: 'It's important that a lady should know how to protect her good name.' I can just hear her. She must have taken off her glasses and put her everlasting knitting down on her knees. The hours they wasted on my behalf. Poor, poor Lucia.

That was yesterday. Today, poor me. I'm going to need pills before I can get to sleep.

The landlady woke up in a bad mod. She spent the morning berating the maid whose response was silence and much sighing. The burden of today's complaint was the girl had got up too late. In spite of the disorder and the lack of cleanliness which struck me from the first Dona Glória liked to think of herself as a good house-wife. Lucia's mother, too, used to say sometimes: 'I am a good housewife and the man who takes my daughter won't be doing too badly either. Lucia can do everything. It's vital for a woman: men like a well maintained house, clothes all done, meals on time. Me, I was always a slave to my home.'

I wonder what my mother was like. She died when I was only three and my father wept whenever he spoke about her. I wanted so much to know what this mother that I never knew was like but I never knew how to ask my father. At times I would spend hours looking at her picture above my father's dressing table. I gazed at it so much that I though that her eyelids moved and her mouth twitched in a smile.

No, she wasn't like that, she couldn't have been like that. She made the meals, washed our clothes (we didn't have a maid) but she was not a good housewife, not that.

I hate good housewives: if they are poor they wear themselves out working; if they are comfortably off or wealthy they get one or more people to wear themselves out on their behalf. In any case they are either slaves to work itself or to the business of keeping an eye on the other slaves under their control. Life goes on out there, husband and sons getting on with it too, busy living, while the housewives are scrubbing, scouring, polishing metal. Or keeping an eye on those who are doing these things. Look, you haven't shifted all the dust; look the tap isn't properly scoured. It can't go on like this, this has got to stop, Yes, indeed. Meanwhile life has passed them by and they haven't seen anything, they haven't even noticed. They are left alone without even realising it. Their husbands die without ever having been around, their sons leave home to marry other housewives who are somewhere to be found among all the other pretty, lively girls who might have fallen in love with them. And so life goes on. Look, this can't go on like this, this has got to stop, yes indeed. And the sons of those sons thinking of running away from it too and dreaming of other girls they might fall in love with…

And then I met Estrela in the Restauradores; Estrela or someone just like her, what does it matter? And Fernandinho went to his eternal rest, he and all the other brothers and sisters that might have been. He was a little boy, the nurse told me. As if I hadn't known. The nurse had seen him but I knew a great deal more about him than she did. I was sure that he would have light hair, big eyes, slightly slanting, and António's transparent hands… António's…?

'He was a beautiful baby, such a pity.' Professionally, the nurse shared my grief.

'Yes, he was,' I said.

And then I closed my eyes, making a great effort to staunch the flow of tears. The nurse sat next to me and ran her hand through my hair. I screamed at her to go away, I screamed so loudly that everybody in the other beds fell silent and for a long time the only sounds in the ward were my sobbing and the startled cries of the newly born.

I left the boarding house where I had been living for another, more economical, place, Dona Glória's house. She knows nothing, either of my life or of my dying; nothing, except that I have been divorced. Several times, especially over meals, she has tried to get me to confide in her in the same way that she has let me into her confi-

dence. She talked to me about her husband who died of an infection of the blood (unfortunately this was before penicillin, Dona
Mariana), about her younger sister who at seventeen ran away with
a lieutenant and was, poor thing, terribly unhappy. I have even seen
the photograph of her little sister, Ermelinda, a girl with excess flesh
and a vacant look. Little sister Ermelinda is already dead. At rest in
God, as Dona Glória always says reverently; that she must be dead is
clear from her picture, drawn in charcoal, without expression or hint
of a smile.

'What the poor thing had to go through, Dona Mariana. All kinds
of troubles, short of money, treated like dirt by her husband… the
lot. She was so pretty, don't you think so?'

'She had lovely eyes…' I say to make her feel better.

'Lovely.'

'The eyes, that's exactly it. There was nobody who didn't mention
her eyes, who didn't say that she and the rest of her family didn't have
lovely eyes. They run in the family. I had them too, that's what it was,
I had them too, lovely eyes. Just like your mother, my father used to
say dreamily, just like your mother's.' From time to time Dona Glória
sighs lightly. 'That's life, we all have our cross, as Dona Mariana
knows well enough.'

That's the excuse then. I smile, nod in agreement. I do know, say
my smile and my gestures. I offer her, though, an empty phrase: 'Is
there anyone who doesn't know, Dona Glória?'

'There are people, see, there are some people. Sometimes I get to
thinking…'

I never discover what it is that Dona Glória gets to thinking. She
falls silent, her gaze distant. When she speaks again it is of something
quite different: 'Now then, tell me what you want for dinner…
You've got so thin, you're not eating… Isn't there anything you
fancy? Really? I was wondering about some little fishcakes with rice
in tomato sauce…'

I say yes, I'd really like that, and Dona Glória is happy.

Dona Glória has pictures of her sister and her husband; I have
none, neither of my father nor of António. I left all my things in the
house on the Avenida de Berna, so hastily did I leave. I realise it now
because I had always kept beside me the photograph that António
took of me in Gouveia, the one where I'm leaning up against the
tree. It's the only one I have of him. He's there, reflected in my wide
open eyes.

I went back to work, this time as a secretary to a part-time writer who every day produced several sheets of paper typed by me in single spacing. (He thought to leave them to posterity, poor man.) The job took as long as was needed to commit to paper all the various doings of a wealthy family who lived in a manor house not far from Viseu, and then I was again unemployed, almost without money and without anything close enough to hang on to. But I felt almost happy.

Sometimes I lie down and spend hours just looking at the ceiling or at the wall next to the bed. The flowery wallpaper with its once white background, now yellowed by time, is full of musty stains where I can make out ridiculous little faces, which are occasionally terribly disquieting: in outline almost demonic, smiling oddly, silently; they are all the more perfect the more time I spend staring at them without blinking, as if, without being able to help itself, my gaze filled in the shape, quickening the features, giving them life, making them vivid. At other times the faces are horrible, moulded in the stucco of the ceiling or formed by the shadows which the furniture throws when I put on the light. At times one of the shapes becomes, little by little, Estrela's face, laughing that silent laugh of hers. I close my eyes but now I meet her inside my head. I take one, two, tablets, but often it is only after the fourth tablet that her face and her smile fade into a deep, heavy sleep.

One day while I was reading the newspaper I came across an interesting advertisement. An English couple with two children wanted a Portuguese governess to go abroad with them. I reckoned my English was good enough so I replied to the advertisement. They made an appointment in a hotel in the Baixa where I met a tall, thin woman, no longer young, with ruddy, freckled skin. Her husband was fat and powerfully built, his hair almost white, cut very short on top. The children, blond and graceless with the precocious, intense gaze of more mature children, shook my hand solemnly.

I couldn't complain about the terms. The Harpers wanted their children to learn Portuguese. They were going to spend some months in London, perhaps a year, and only then would they move to Portugal, in Oporto, where Mr Harper had business interests. On the way back they intended to spend some days in Paris. Ah, so I knew Paris? Well then, I was sure to enjoy seeing it again. Anyone who had been there even briefly dreamed of going back one day, wasn't that so? Mrs Harper smiled. Why should I say that it was in Paris…? Why should I say anything about that woman who meant nothing to me? She carried on talking. If at any time, for any reason

I should feel ill or dissatisfied or even simply homesick for my family (it would be quite natural) the Harpers would consider themselves relieved of any obligation to me, which didn't mean, she added, that they would be put out by any of the steps which I might possibly take to deal with the situation. It was agreed also that I would enjoy a degree of freedom. Her husband stayed largely out of it, emphasising only with smiles, and nods of his head, his wife's remarks. The house and the children were her domain; he got on with business. When I got up to go, having given the name of my long-winded writer and one or two other people I knew who might give some information about me, the two children came down with me to the door of the hotel.

Now there was a job I fancied but which I had never thought of before. I had often thought that I would have liked to be a nurse or a primary school teacher, but I wasn't qualified for either of these professions. My experience with the shipping company and in the writer's office had been a real nightmare. I couldn't face in cold blood the prospect of continuing to sit for weeks, months, years in succession, to the end of my days, before a desk, the typewriter at my fingertips, writing letters that held no interest for me, or putting onto paper those immensely fussy but empty novels. To grow old, to get fat (because I believe that being bored makes you fat), while you wallow endlessly in the same problems, those of other people. When he finished his novel 'in the usual way' the novelist offered to speak on my behalf to some under-secretary or other who at that time regularly had his face in the papers.

'You'll soon see; he'll fix you up with something… He's a very good friend of mine, he'll be delighted to do this favour for me. He's a first class chap; just as fine a man in private as in public… Why are you laughing?'

It was my abiding habit of laughing at things which others did not find funny… Public man… public woman… Was there not at bottom a certain kind of relation between the two? I banished the smile from my face and he continued with his praise of his friend and admirer.

'Just take him this letter of mine…'

I turned his offer down; in my purse I had, I think, a twenty escudo note. I had already asked him for an advance on my wages earlier in the month.

And now here was a job which really interested me. I began to live in hope once again; not much, but a glimmer of hope at least. It was a conscious hope, too, I would say. Who knows whether a change of scene, work which I enjoyed, the presence of those children, wouldn't bring me fresh inspiration and sweep away those worn-out notions which stopped me sleeping? I got myself a passport and dealt with the business of visas almost enthusiastically. My desire to get back to a life of normality was so strong that I even phoned two or three people I hardly knew, just to say goodbye. I think I needed to reassure myself that things were getting better and that the best way to be sure of this was to hear it confirmed by my own voice.

Then, on the day before the eve of leaving Mr Harper called me; he was very upset, getting his words all mixed up. His wife had just gone into a clinic to be operated on urgently. The doctors had told him it was rather serious and Mr Harper feared the worst. It was clear that for the time being he would have to abandon any plans for a trip. Even if everything went well Mrs Harper would still be extremely weak and so he had just phoned her sister in London to ask her to come and look after the children. He was expecting her by the first aeroplane tomorrow. Of course he insisted that I should let him know the expenses I had incurred.

Mrs Harper recovered, I learned later. One day I phoned the hotel just to know what had happened. Mrs Harper was convalescing they told me. She hadn't left and I was stuck fast in my old room, imprisoned forever within its walls.

'Well then, Dona Mariana, well then,' said my landlady. 'It would have been so hard to get to know another new face… God knows how hard it would have been. I even prayed to little St Teresa that you wouldn't go.'

The English woman had been spared and Dona Glória was happy. Little St Teresa had done everything for the best.

I began to feel more and more tired: tired of living but unable to die. Tired of being; of the ghosts that I still saw at all hours of the day and night swirling all around me, tired of everything that was close to me and of everything that was far from me. So thin did I become and so ill did I look that the landlady made me go to the doctor's.

'Have you thought that it could be tuberculosis, Dona Mariana?' she asked. 'Listen, that's extremely serious, it's contagious… I'm not saying this for my own sake, I've never been afraid of illness, but after all Augusta is just a little girl…'

I went to see my doctor. He looked at me carefully and then sent me for blood tests. It might not be anything, but in any case… I asked him if it might be contagious.

'No, not at all, the very idea...' and he laughed. I didn't see what was so funny; neither did he.

One afternoon I went into a cinema; I still don't know why I did so. How long had it been since I had been in one of those places? I was walking past the Tívoli, there were few people waiting at the door and I felt as though something was calling me. Why not? It was living, wasn't it? Formerly I used to love going to the cinema; then later just being there, being there when the lights went down and there was the dream before my very eyes. Formerly I used to love... perhaps I still did, who knows? So I went in, I remember now, just to see whether I was still able to enjoy something.

It was early and the cinema was almost empty. Beyond me two women, excuse me, two ladies were talking. Both of them had those kinds of piercing voices, contraltos, which carry and seem to belong only – I don't know why – to ladies who are 'well set up'.

'She's a very nice person, in fact; you're quite right. And so natural!'

'Didn't I tell you?'

'Absolutely. I was com-plete-ly bowl-ed ov-er. They seem to be very close, which these days is rare enough... and, you know, there's nothing cheap about them either. Pretty well-off, aren't they? and with a house like that... How long have they been married?'

'Four years, I think. They met in Paris, he got divorced, luckily he'd only been married in a registry office... It was apparently a case of love at first sight...'

'How unusual. But then I always thought Estrela was something special... not as a sculptor I have to say by the way. That "Bather Seated" that she showed at the Salon... well, my dear! No, I mean special as a person. So attractive, pretty, a real woman.'

'And a decent girl, too, a fine girl. You know, she always speaks well of António's first wife. That speaks volumes doesn't it? Some crazy woman who just a few months after her divorce was going round the Baixa, her belly sticking out like... well, you know what I'm saying...'

'I didn't know. Did she have a lover, a married man or what? Who was she anyway?'

'Nobody knew who she was. People only talked about her a lot because she happens to be the ex-wife of Estrela's husband. And you know Estrela always speaks up for her. Of course she has to agree that she chose a bad time to do such a stupid thing, it could hardly have been worse, but nevertheless, under the circumstances... A decent girl, when all's said and done. A good wife, a good mother... When the oldest boy had that problem with a throat infection, what was he, two, you know...'

'I didn't know they had children...'

'Yes, two. Now the oldest, Fernando...'

The lights went down. I got up and stepped over various people who complained. The usherette said something too which I didn't understand but which I remember hearing. In the street I breathed again and set off down the avenue without noticing where I was going. I realised at one point that I was by the river. At the same time I saw some people looking at me; some of them were laughing. Two little boys stopped in front of me and then ran away quickly. I put my hands to my face and when I took them away they were wet with tears.

On that day, yes, I did think of killing myself. I was still thinking of it the following morning when Dona Glória and her maid set off for the market. I closed the window and the kitchen door tight and then turned on the gas and sat down to wait. I did it without thinking, without wanting to think. The air was becoming heavy and just at that moment somebody rang the bell. I turned off the gas, slowly opened the kitchen door and then the front door. It was the postman with a card from Luís Gonzaga.

Life went on after that. Can I call it life?

Why don't you go out for a while? Try another doctor, Dona Mariana, everybody speaks well of Cardénio Santos... My sister, God rest her soul... We all have our cross... There are people, though, there are people... A rabbit stew, Dona Mariana? What do you say to a rabbit stew?

'I'd love a rabbit stew, Dona Glória. I'm dying for a rabbit stew.'

In the end I went to Professor Cardénio, one of those characters who never, ever, make a mistake in their diagnoses. Only because I wanted to know for sure; and now I know and I'm waiting. I don't have to have any more tests or go again to a doctor. So what if I die in a month or two months? I know that I can expect nothing from life and so I want just to be calm. I really want to... it's my end, my only one. I can't choose any other, there isn't any other. For the first time someone is coming for me, someone is coming looking for me. So why shouldn't I be happy, I, the chosen one?

But I can't. I feel like a virgin who has been raped: I'm full of things but completely empty. Empty because even hope has gone.

Hope but not my will to live. Even in this room with the foul smell that I no longer even notice, even with António far from me and little Fernandinho in the arms of a mother who isn't me, even so I want to live. In the way I know; in the way I know how to. And my life seeps away, day by day, seeps away without my ever having lived.

I can no longer get up; I don't have the strength any more. Dona Glória came in today and set herself down on the old chair and chattered away for half an hour. I don't know what she said because all her words slipped by without making any impression on me.

'Don't you think so, Dona Mariana? Don't you think it would be much better?'

I didn't know what she was talking about but still I nodded agreement. She was perfectly satisfied.

'Of course it's better, Dona Mariana, much better. You'll want for nothing there. And don't worry about a thing, I've already spoken to Dona Manuela who's a nurse in Santa Marta hospital. She's a wonderful woman, an absolute treasure, to say the least. She offered the moment I spoke to her, the moment I asked.'

What would be the point of refusing? The woman was in her house, her castle so to speak. Lucia was right. How could I…? So I just said without opening my eyes: 'Won't little St Teresa be a bit put out, Dona Glória? Don't you remember how you asked her to make me stay…'

'But it's for your own good, Dona Mariana, it's for your own good…'

'Ah well, if that's the way it is…'

I'm going to the hospital today. I thought that I would die in this room but no, not yet. I put the picture in my suitcase; perhaps they'll let me look at it, I don't know. Dona Glória dressed me as if I was already dead. On my head she put the hat with the feather, wrapped me in my coat, gave me a pair of her stockings because I didn't have any that weren't full of holes. We are both waiting for the taxi which Augusta has ordered. Dona Glória is coming along with me. It's as if we were both going to my funeral.

David Mourão-Ferreira

AND SHE SAID NOTHING

translated by Patricia Odber

It wasn't even midnight and Lieutenant Sanches was already snoring. Behind the door he had left half open, you could only just make out the other bed where only around five o'clock in the morning I might be allowed to rest a little. A crafty old devil, Lieutenant Sanches had thrown all the bothersome details of night duty on to my inexperienced shoulders: supervising the soldiers' return from leave, the watches, filling in endless papers.

It was one of my first nights on duty in the unit. At that time (I don't know if things are still the same today), we militia men could only carry out the duties of 'prevention officer': the 'officer of the day' had to be someone from the permanent roster. And who should I land up with but Lieutenant Sanches! An officer who had risen from the ranks, suspicious and thoroughly idle, they told the most appalling stories about him. They even said that he'd been vaguely involved in some crime or other and because of that he had been overlooked for promotion and would die a lieutenant.

I must confess, however, that the vague awareness at the time of being exploited was somehow offset by a certain feeling of pride, of power, of responsibility. In my care, under my protection, were hundreds of bodies and souls, starting with the body and soul of Lieutenant Sanches himself, who was snoring enough for the whole regiment on the other side of the partition. All this, even with the sleepless nights, was tremendously exciting for a lad of twenty-two. And times were bad: almost all of Europe was at war, almost the whole world was at war. Of my comrades from the COM, most had been detached for duty in the Azores; some others to gloomy frontier units. Thanks perhaps to my father's connections, I was one of the lucky few to be privileged with a posting to a Lisbon garrison.

On the left sleeve of my jacket was the red arm-band of the prevention officer. I looked at it with delight and, delighted, was just about to touch it when the telephone suddenly rang. It was one of those old-fashioned models, boxy and very slim. I instinctively jumped up from my chair and must have gone pale (pale, but cocky) at the unknown appeal of that miniature gallows. A pause. My God, what was going on? But then, shriller and more insistent, the bell rang once again. And Lieutenant Sanches hadn't even stirred! Another pause. I closed my eyes (Right! A leap in the dark...) and seized the receiver. A female voice then reached my ear quite clearly. (A telephone operator?) Perhaps it was a call from outside. My God, what could be happening in the provinces?

'How's that? What?'

To begin with, I didn't understand. Drawling, almost languorous, the voice asked whether this was the Rex Coffee House.

'No, madam!' And, heavily, with a sigh (relief? disappointment?) I sat down again in the revolving chair. The Rex Coffee House indeed! 'No, madam. You've dialled a wrong number.' And I hung up.

Next came a faint noise behind the partition. Then Lieutenant Sanches summoned me with his nasal, deliberate voice:

'Hey cadet! Cadet! Didn't the phone just ring?'

'Yes it did, Lieutenant.'

'Anything new?'

'No, Lieutenant. It was a wrong number.'

I got up and went over to the half open door. As befitted an officer of the watch, Lieutenant Sanches hadn't undressed: he'd just taken off his jacket and jackboots, loosened his belt and stretched out like that on top of the bed. Now he was sitting up and scratching one of his legs, just below the knee, between his sock and the bottom of his riding breeches.

'A wrong number? Some tart, was it?' Then he cursed: 'Damn these bedbugs! So it was a tart, then? Damn it! This is sheer torture!' (He was referring to the bedbugs again). 'Ah, you still don't know what it costs to run this place!' (Was he alluding to the bedbugs or the telephone calls?) 'There's hardly a night goes by when some tart doesn't call here... You're young men. You're the lucky ones... We know what they're after! Sometimes it's just a chat... Other times...' And he said no more. He lay back down and dismissed me with a gesture.

In fact, Lieutenant Rebordão and second Lieutenant Simões had already told me about that kind of thing. Simões, who was very vulgar, had even remarked:

'There are some women who do their own recruiting every year...'

But when I answered the phone, this hadn't even occurred to me.

Perhaps that business of the Rex Coffee House had only been an excuse… I had a bright idea: I looked out the telephone directory and hastily leafed through it. There was no coffee house with that name in the directory.

I lit a cigarette and went out on to the veranda that encircled the duty officer's quarters. It was a sultry night, a night at the beginning of summer. There was no moon and there were very few stars. And yet you couldn't say it was a dark night. Beyond the flat, open space of the parade ground, beyond the barracks yard, floated, hesitant and diffuse, the reflection of the lights of Lisbon. You couldn't see the city from there but the presence of that hidden amphitheatre was no less overpowering, almost suffocating, for all that. The city! Just how many passions were seething down there! Yet no matter how I tried to imagine the most diverse dramas and events, all I could imagine here and there were faceless women. And what would they be like? Old? Young? Single or married? Divorced? Widowed? On their own, certainly, sending out random appeals by telephone, searching for… Searching for what? Entertainment? A romantic idyll? A casual fling?

Just then the phone began to ring again. Ah, but this time I was ready! Very sure of myself, I went back into the office and lifted the receiver. Just as I expected, a woman's voice:

'Hello? Who's speaking?' she asked.

And I, with sublime insolence:'Hello, madam. This is not the Rex Coffee House.

'What?'

'And I might as well inform you that there is no such coffee house with that name. Not in the directory, at least…'

But I couldn't continue: from the other end, vastly amused, pealed a gurgle of laughter. And she exclaimed: 'What on earth are you talking about?'

I was confused. 'It's just that…'

'I just wanted to speak to…', and she reeled off a number which was really very similar to the telephone for the barracks. 'I don't see what that has to do with the Rex Coffee House…'

This last sentence was pronounced in a drawling, almost languorous tone, which awakened new doubts in me.

'But wasn't it you…?' And I told her the brief story of my mistake… if it really was a mistake. I left this suspicion hanging in the air, hoping to catch her out. But she assured me that she certainly hadn't tried to speak to any coffee house…

'A coffee house that doesn't exist, into the bargain…'

She broke into a mocking little laugh. Without a doubt she was very vivacious and even seemed to have forgotten the "other" telephone call which she said she had intended to make. I made the most of the opportunity. (After all, what did it matter to me if she was or wasn't the same woman who had telephoned a short while before?). I tried to retain her, entertain her. She seemed very surprised when I told her that she'd called a barracks. She wanted to know my rank.

'Cadet…'

'Militia? Or from the Academy?'

'Militia,' I replied, a little amused by the military 'expertise' she was displaying. But, as if to allay any unflattering suspicion, she immediately told me that she had once gone out with a lad from the Military Academy. He was still a cadet…

'We were engaged…'

'Then what happened?'

Ah! It was a very sad story. She sighed. Such a stupid business! He died. He died in an accident.

'In an accident?'

'Yes.' She hesitated for a moment. 'In a shooting accident.'

'Oh!' I exclaimed foolishly, in the voice of someone offering their condolences. 'Was this a long time ago?'

'Four years.'

I quickly did the sums in my mind: if that were true, she must still be young. And what would she look like? In the meantime, almost as a matter of etiquette, a brief, respectful silence had fallen. She broke it, giving a shocked little cry: after all, there she was confiding in… a total stranger.

A stranger? What about that then? We weren't strangers, not any more we weren't. And – I don't know how this lasted – I went babbling on like an idiot. The more I spoke, the more she backed off. In her voice I heard first the cool disdain of a very experienced woman followed immediately by the endearing evasiveness of an innocent young girl. Suddenly I decided to change my tactics. Abandoning my argument half way through, I let fly: 'I have to be with you, Maria da Luz!' (Almost inadvertently she had let slip a little while before that she was called Maria da Luz). 'I really must be with you!'

That did the trick. With a kind of groan, she retorted: 'Oh! Henrique…' (I had told her, shortly before, that I was called Henrique). 'How foolish for us to be talking like this!'

Foolish? Why foolish? And, impassioned, vehement, confused, I told her of the loneliness in which I lived, I told her of the loneliness I had sensed in her voice. With my hand cupped around the mouthpiece, I could almost feel in my own fingers the rising heat of my honeyed words. Maria da Luz was completely bowled over by that new tone: within minutes she had agreed to meet me the following day. She'd stopped considering all that 'foolish'; now all she said was the occasional 'What madness! This is all madness!' But despite her pessimistic words, she did get round to arranging a time and place for us to meet. We would have no difficulty in recognising each other, nothing could be easier. She would wear a suit, with a white linen skirt and jacket, I… I would go in uniform.

As soon as I'd hung up, I went back out on to the veranda. A soldier came running across the parade ground. He came from the sergeant of the guard: the 'sarge' wanted to know if they could open the gate and whether I wanted to watch the last enlisted men reporting back from leave. What? One o'clock already? At one the gate was opened for the last time.

I went there. The men came in, one by one, striking the corner of their caps in a sleepy salute. Automatically they handed their late passes over to the sergeant of the guard. Then they dispersed about the parade ground only to join up further ahead in groups of three, four, five, on their way to the huts. They had come back up from the city, from the maelstrom of the streets of Lisbon; but almost all of them had come back dejected, either dejected or weary.

The gate was bolted at last. At the other end of the barracks the voice of a sentry rang out and the watchword went rolling from sentry post to sentry post, monotonous, automatic, sullen. Shortly after, I had to take a turn around the huts. The parade ground was completely deserted again. My boots echoed almost gloomily on the crushed gravel.

At midday, huh? At midday. During the morning she would need to go to the dressmaker's. And near the dressmaker's house there was a very discreet little coffee house. For my part, I came off duty at ten o'clock in the morning when the guard changed in the barracks. However, I still had plenty of time to get ready. I'd be there at midday on the dot.

But who was to say that it wasn't just a hoax, I thought, already very sceptical, and kicking distractedly at one loose stone after another. Yes, who could give me any guarantee? That Maria da Luz could easily be someone who had decided to have a laugh at my expense – and who on the following day would merely stand and observe from afar the asinine expectancy of a credulous militia cadet all dressed up in his dress uniform… Oh no. It wasn't a good idea to lay myself open so unwisely! Deep in my heart of hearts, another fear gnawed away at me. Maria da Luz! The name, wrapped up in the clothing she had described, the white linen suit! – suggested a the picture of innocence. But what if she were ugly? If she were really, really ugly? The best thing, then, would be to prepare in advance a graceful strategic retreat.

By the time I left the barracks next day I had already decided not to go in uniform. If she appeared, if I recognised her, all well and good; if she were worth the bother I would introduce myself, giving her any old excuse.

I went home, shaved, took a shower and dressed with care, having first pinched from my grandmother's room some drops of the excellent eau-de-cologne that my father used to bring back from Paris in the pre-war years. At that time my father was consul in a Scandinavian city; and both I and my younger sister (who was still unmarried) lived in Lisbon with our grandmother, whose house was fairly close to the barracks. But from there to the neighbourhood where my mystery caller had arranged the rendezvous was a long haul: to get there before twelve noon, I had to go by trolley to the Baixa and then take a taxi. I had no trouble finding the coffee house. It was more than discreet: it was almost in isolation. It stood a little below street level and at the entrance you went down four steps. On the one side, in a murky gloom, the counter occupied pride of place, beside it, at an oblique angle, was a glass-fronted display case with cakes, flies and chocolates. Over on the other side, in the semi-circle created where the walls of the building met to form a corner, fanned out five or six tables. Two of them were occupied; at each one a solitary customer. Excellent! I would simply be just another 'regular'. For this very reason I sat down, choosing one of the tables closest to the front. Opposite but higher up was a narrow vent that acted as a shop window. No sooner had I sat down than I saw a white figure go past on the other side of the shop window, on the outside, up above. Moments later, the figure appeared at the top of the stairs.

Then something almost inexplicable happened. Perhaps she saw me make a gesture, give a start. Certainly from the top of the stairs, for a second at most, her enquiring, half-closed eyes looked into mine: she was short-sighted. Afterwards, with extraordinary assurance she descended and made her way over to meet me. Meanwhile,

I was irresistably drawn to my feet. She was already standing before me when she exclaimed: 'So you didn't come in uniform after all.'

It wasn't a question or a criticism. A complaint, perhaps. Whatever it was, I felt no need to explain or even defend myself and merely pulled out a chair so that she could sit down.

She was, in fact, ugly. Nor did she seem all that young. But I would have noticed her absolutely anywhere! To the great horror of my sisters, I had always been attracted to a particular kind of woman. The kind they clearly considered beyond the pale, whose features were usually, if not coarse, then at least irregular. Irregular and impudent. My grandmother, who understood even less of these matters, used to say that ever since I was little I had always had a common streak, which didn't really explain anything at all since I have found these same features in all social classes. Maria da Luz, now, she largely matched that kind of piquant and perturbing ugliness. Of course I would have preferred her with a neater nose, not so snub, less thick. But her eyes, her eyes were almost admirable, slantingly greenish, her cheekbones very prominent, and her mouth very wide as well; and the flaring nostrils themselves seemed to exude a sharp mixture of mystery, stupidity and malice. She wore her hair which was very dark and long caught up on top of her head, 'refugee style' they used to call it.

In our first exchange she now corrected a previous misunderstanding and told me her name was Lucília. Lucília, not Maria da Luz. She'd said Maria da Luz the night before, but it had been a joke. And she laughed. From time to time, her eyes fixed on me with the insolent attentiveness of short-sighted women. And I talked and talked and talked, skilfully mixing utter drivel with clever comments. At the same time, I was testing her responses to see which would produce the best results. But her reactions were contradictory.

We drank something then left. Outside it was warm; it was dusty; and there was that calm that you find in disreputable neighbourhoods during the lunch hour. The sun, high overhead, slid down the façades: some of them were tiled. In the road we walked along only the first floor balconies cast a trace of shadow on to the walls.

Further along, we cut along a street that was being dug up. The central lane, completely gutted, showed some repulsive entrails of pipes and debris. At certain points the pavement itself was blocked and then we had totter across some very narrow, awkward walkways. At this point I would lead the way and help her across; I took her by the hand, the wrist, at other times by her arm.

'This way, Maria da Luz.' Then I corrected myself: 'This way, Lucília.'

Trusting, she leant on me, and placed her feet wherever I told her to. She had delicate ankles, but they seemed firm; and whenever she took a longer stride, her skirt – fashionably short – revealed round knees and the fine hem of a light blue slip. Not fat, almost elegant, she had one of those unmistakably Portuguese bodies that seem to attract attention because of the accentuated outline of certain specific zones. You could even check them off – 'Here are the legs, here are the hips; there are the buttocks; the breasts further up' – before taking a complete picture of the whole.

There was a gas leak in the street, but mixed in with that stench was the aroma of grilled sardines. Lucílias's hand was damp, damp and warm with sweat; the contact with her arm – hard, hot and dry – was more agreeable. Even after we'd crossed that site with holes, girders, pipes and piles of earth, I continued to guide her, to keep my hand under her arm, around her wrist. She didn't object or try to break free. And that was how we went into the Anjos Garden.

It is a sad garden, as everyone knows, with little shade, and that boulder-like church there in the middle. But at the back, behind the church, some peaceful benches sit dozing in provincial tranquility. They were all empty; almost all in the sun; only one was favoured by the sickly shade of a nearby tree. The choice was not difficult. And as it was only fair that we should share that scanty shade, we sat together at one end, very close to one another. I put my arm round her back; with the pressure of my fingers on her shoulder the Maria da Luz of the previous evening's telephone call reappeared.

'Oh! Henrique…Oh…Henrique. This is complete madness…'

But only her lips avoided the kisses that I wanted to give her: on the other hand, she stretched out her neck like a seagull, as if to yield to me, there, a much wider surface. And I kissed her neck, and kissed her nape, and the more she stretched her neck to the front, the more her nape contracted. Sometimes it seemed to me that my lips remained there, sucked in by this unexpected whirlpool. From time to time, I was forced to take a brief pause – mainly because a lock of her hair which had worked loose was tickling my nose. Then I took advantage to have a discreet scratch. It was on one of these occasions that she grasped my face with her two hands and pulled it violently towards her. It was one kiss, just one, but so long, so soft, and so wet that I had the feeling that everything in me and around me was being engulfed, spinning, disintegrating: the bench, the grounds, the Anjos garden.

Afterwards she broke free – or let me go – and standing before me, adjusted her clothes.

'Is this any way to behave?' she asked. Then with a mocking smile, in a throaty voice, her lower lip caught between her teeth, her eyes narrowed and black behind her thick lashes, she hissed with evident enjoyment: 'You savage!'

Such generosity! Half grateful, half afraid, I realised that she had decided to take command. But, magnanimous in her victory, she was allowing me the illusion of mastery.

'Oh my God! So late!' she exclaimed, glancing quickly at her wristwatch.

How could it possibly be so late? With a start she changed completely. She permitted me to accompany her to the trolley stop and no further. She told me that her father was an awful bully. If he saw her with a man, there'd be trouble! There'd be terrible trouble! She wouldn't give me her address or telephone number. She would phone me at the barracks whenever she could.

'At least give me your telephone number!' I begged, grovelling ignominiously.

No, certainly not. There was no point in insisting. And then, with a brusqueness tempered with tantalising hints: 'If you want it that way… all right… If you don't…'

She stepped up on to the trolley and off she went, waving to me from the platform.

On the next day she proved that she was a woman of her word. The bugle for the first break in morning training had just sounded when they called me to the telephone: "It's me, Lucília." Luckily for me she had telephoned during the break, for they certainly wouldn't have called me during a training session. But when I heard her voice, I got so excited and big-headed that I forgot to warn her about this important detail. I don't believe I ever did get round to it, I never needed to. With astounding prescience Lucília always telephoned me at break time. And during the week our contact was restricted to those brief distant conversations. Brief but very frequent: there were sometimes four, sometimes five telephone calls a day. But a date, a new date, the new date for which I kept begging her – there was no way to make it happen.

But it wasn't her fault. Honestly, it wasn't her fault! On certain occasions, she told me this with tears in her voice. And then came the litany of complaints against her father (sometimes she said 'Papa'), that rigorous and austere 'Papa' who seemed to be keeping her prisoner. Was it fair? Was there any justice in a thing like that? She wasn't a child any more! (She was – so she said – twenty-six years old).

One day, in the middle of such weeping and wailing, she let slip a phrase, which her tone of voice endowed with a very dubious meaning: 'As if I were still a girl!' She expelled the word 'still' with a sneering challenge and she pronounced 'girl' in a tone of mock innocence.

This phrase nearly drove me wild. Because of it, I redoubled my pleas. But I could see perfectly well that it wasn't up to Lucília to decide. At the end of the day we just had to bide our time. Her father –so she had told me – was a bank clerk. The hours when he was at work coincided with those I spent in the barracks, and these were precisely the hours which Lucília had free. Nothing doing there, then. But –and here more the outlook grew more cheerful – he did have to carry out occasional inspections on the outskirts of Lisbon and usually had to spend a night away from home. This happened about every ten days, maybe three times a month. So it was a question of waiting patiently for one of these opportunities.

'And where shall we go?' I would ask, already very eager.

But from her side, her voice would shy away: 'Well now! Wherever you want. A cinema, a theatre…'

I pretended to make do with the answer: it was better not to rush matters. But was it certain, would we definitely be able to meet? Certainly, she promised me. She was relying for this purpose on her mother's complicity – her mother was much more understanding – that of her mother and her sister. (She had a younger sister.) And Lucília's words led me to suppose that they too longed for those short-lived breaks from the petty domestic tyrant.

Meanwhile, my life was nervously divided between the barracks and my home. If Lucília's constant telephone calls kept me on permanent alert in the barracks, there was an equally enervating atmosphere of expectancy at home where my older sister awaited an imminent 'visit from the stork'. My grandmother had insisted that she stay with us so that when her time came she could get to a clinic where a doctor relative of ours had his practice. My brother-in-law had stayed on in the Alentejo where, after a misspent youth, he appeared to be administering his father's estates with great zeal.

But occasionally he would set off in an old Reo car, to which he had fitted a gas-producing trammel, and burst into the house laden with bonhomie, fruit and sausages, talking about the harvests and his future heir, slapping everyone on the back, and dragging me off at night to the Arcádia, 'just to satisfy our longings, Henrique, just to satisfy our longings'.

Off we'd go. And in the middle of those obliging Spanish women, (my brother-in-law still knew most of them) I suddenly felt very sure of myself: my experience with women was proceeding apace and I would be able to subdue all the Lucílias who appeared before me. But on the following day, as soon as she telephoned me, I would plunge into the most demeaning trepidation. There was no doubt: Lucília had 'taken charge of operations'. I was a mere underling: it was up to me to wait for the order to attack to be given – and, meanwhile, to maintain good discipline over my insubordinate feelings. And of course there were still benefits in those expeditions to the Arcádia; they were more than a spur, they were training, a military exercise. After all, everyone knows that no shooting range, no matter how well equipped, can satisfy the appetite for a real battle.

And then, at last, the occasion was announced! It was to be a Saturday. Did it suit me? Did it suit me! I would be on duty on Friday. I had all of Saturday afternoon to rest and, at night, I wouldn't be worried about the next day, since the next day was a Sunday. Of course it suited me.

We ironed out all the details three days in advance. This time we would meet in another coffee house, near Restauradores Square: I would buy tickets beforehand for some show or other. The show would be my choice, it would be a surprise...

Of course, this all concealed a very sordid little plan. In my youthful cunning – a real smart aleck – I had already decided not to buy any tickets at all but drag her off to some beach on the Cascais coast. I even went so far as to look up a diary which listed the phases of the moon: on Sunday, the crescent moon. It might not be completely dark but at least it would do.

On Friday I happened to have Lieutenant Rebordão as my 'officer of the day'. Lieutenant Rebordão was a good comrade. He'd spent some years overseas and considered himself the most 'laid back' officer in the regiment. He wasn't even thirty. He drank a bit.

'Hey, Andrade!' he began by saying to me. 'I'm not going to pull rank. We split the jobs between us – that's how I've always worked.

All that stuff about doing the rounds is for the sergeants: if anything crops up, they'll whistle.'

After a lavish dinner, generously washed down in an atmosphere of manly fellowship, amid recollections of Africa and obscene jokes, Lieutenant Rebordão called the batman:

'Hey, Faísca! Have you brought the cough mixture?'

'Yes, Lieutenant.' And Faísca quickly pulled a bottle of Spanish cognac out of a wicker basket.

We went to the officers' mess to drink and listen to the wireless. There was a programme of dance music. Then came more jokes. By eleven o'clock, we were both dropping with exhaustion.

'Right, Andrade! It's time we were off to bed. Tomorrow morning we'll fill out those 'pamphlets.' In Lieutenant Rebordão's colourful lingo, all papers were pamphlets.

Lucília had already warned me that she wouldn't call me that night. So I went calmly to bed. What a beautiful thing, life! What a beautiful thing, a world where there were girls, passionate and a little crazy, and where there was cognac and dance music, and comrades who were good, decent chaps!...

On the following day we quickly made out and agreed on the report, the schedule of late passes, the meals bulletin and God knows what else. Before ten o'clock, Lieutenant Sanches and the other cadet who were going to take over from us turned up in the office. I had missed by one day another night on duty with Lieutenant Sanches! Once that ridiculous hand-over of power had been carried out, Lieutenant Rebordão stood us a round of cherry brandy which he had ordered from the mess. Only Lieutenant Sanches refused: 'You must be mad, man! What about my liver? And my colic? Well I am surprised...' With a very liverish smile, he cautiously raised a hand to his side.

Then off he went, already wearing his sword and armlet, on his way to the changing of the guard.

I stayed on in the office, pretending to do various little jobs. The truth is I was waiting for a phone call from Lucília. A little while later the telephone actually rang. Everything was confirmed: her father would leave that afternoon for Setúbal where he would have to spend the night. We would meet at a quarter past nine ('Don't be late, will you?').

I spent all day in a great tizzy, restless as a soldier moments before the battle; superstitious as an actor in the hours that precede an opening night. I was completely unsure of Lucília and about what might happen. A fight? A farce? Victory? Success? Or a complete fiasco? I didn't know. Before then I had had some *affaires*, but on the threshold of each one, I would always find myself unprepared, baffled, and so avidly impatient that I could easily ruin everything at the last minute.

I spent part of the afternoon in my room. Elsewhere, at the back of another building, someone (it had to be a maidservant) was humming the theme from *Balalaika* as if her life depended on it. How exasperating!

Before dinner my younger sister Rita knocked at my door.

'Henrique! Mariana doesn't feel well…'

'What?'

'Come quickly!'

In grandmother's room, my older sister was sitting in an armchair, with an uncomfortable but extremely serene expression.

'What's going on?' I asked.

'Come on now, what do you think?' retorted my younger sister, very curtly, with a gaudy pile of tiny clothes in her arms. On top of the bed lay an open suitcase which grandmother was filling with that profusion of silks and knitwear, bows and ribbons…

'But… are you having pains?' I asked, still very incredulous. I'd always heard of those 'pains' which came in advance, heralding such events.

No, she wasn't experiencing pains. And Mariana shook her head, ashamed not to be having pains.

'Well?' I crossed my arms in a gesture of consternation. I still couldn't understand why they had gone and bothered me.

Rita exploded again, looking daggers at me: 'Oh, what a fool you are! Her waters have broken, don't you understand?'

Grandmother called her to order: 'Young lady!' And very gently, she told me to telephone Manuel my brother-in-law and call a taxi.

I still didn't catch on. Until then, I only knew about 'pains'. But Rita's catastrophic words made me feel very sorry for Mariana, who was always my favourite sister, so off I went to request a long-distance call to the Alentejo and to summon a taxi.

By the time I returned grandmother had fled to the room with the oratory. A maid had already put the suitcase in the corridor. Mariana was still sitting in the armchair, tense, almost smiling, her eyes wide open. Rita, bossy as always, called me to one side: 'You go with her. Keep her spirits up, ok? I'll stay with grandmother. And telephone as soon as something happens.'

Leaning on my arm, Mariana descended the stairs. And because of the way she went down, because of that mixture of caution and dainty sureness, I suddenly understood the great miracle that was beginning to unfold inside her. And it was my sister, my older sister, it was the first child whom I had encountered in this world.

In the taxi she was the one who seemed to be giving me courage in the end. I felt moved, confused, crushed. We went along holding hands. We crossed a garden.

'Do you remember?'

I remembered. We'd been there once before, almost at dawn. We were returning from a dance to which I had escorted her. I was seventeen then, she was twenty. As if I could forget! I had just spent two months in Paris with father (at the time of the International Exhibition) and I had returned very grown up, very worldly wise, blasé. And after that ball, where we'd both been moderately bored we'd stopped off in that garden: I told her all about my stay in Paris, I told her my plans for the future – just like my father, just like my grandfather before me I would have a career in the diplomatic service – and my riotous decision to live life to the full.

Mariana interrupted me: 'But there's more to life than that, Henrique. Life…' And she fell silent. After all, she didn't know what life should be either. She was very sensible but never known for her intelligence in the family, our Mariana. With tears in her eyes, she even said to me: 'I really don't like to hear you talk this way.' It was perhaps the first time I had let her down.

I glanced surreptitiously at my watch: it was ten past eight. I had to find some excuse to get away as soon as I had left Mariana at the nursing home. And how would the meeting with Lucília go? Suddenly I felt guilty for having dreamed up that mean little trick… But wasn't that just what she wanted? At the same time, I almost felt moved by the artlessness of that plan, the haste with which I had rushed to look up the phases of the moon in that diary! In certain respects, I felt younger and more ingenuous at twenty-two than I had been at seventeen. I must confess, this touched me and excused my behaviour in my own eyes.

We reached the nursing home. Mariana went straight into the observation room. I remained in a musty waiting room: in the centre on a table were piled up reviews and picture magazines of the war, in a curious promiscuity with pharmaceutical advertising brochures. Then I went out into the corridor. It was a labyrinth with white walls, with luminous signs shouting 'Silence'. The observation room was down at the end.

Suddenly came a muffled eddy, a swirling of air, a smell of chloroform, the sound of footsteps. They'd opened out a screen. Gloomily, a maid came to inform me that they were now preparing a room for my sister. Meanwhile I could keep her company. I went to meet Mariana in the matron's office; she was in very good spirits. And her pains had begun.

'Ah! This will all go very well: round about midnight you'll have a nephew,' declared the matron, wreathed in smiles.

Mariana asked me to make a number of telephone calls: we had to inform that doctor relative of ours, reassure grandmother and find out whether Manuel was already on his way. Of course I couldn't get away. And it was five to nine already.

It couldn't have been worse. The telephone calls took far longer than expected. Rita had already spoken to Manuel and he must already be on his way but grandmother asked me to remain there until he arrived.

'Oh, but Rita…'

'Don't be selfish, send out for sandwiches. Make do with sandwiches for today,' she countered. And she hung up. As if my problem was just missing dinner!

I could not possibly disobey a request from grandmother. By the time I got back to Mariana she was already in the room they had prepared for her, completely transfigured, racked by some atrocious contractions. I felt that even without that request I couldn't bring myself to desert her. Next came a lull. I assumed it would only take a moment. But no: it was several minutes. Mariana regained her serenity in full. As those minutes ticked by, a certain bitterness overtook me: the image of Lucília, of a Lucília who would still be waiting for me (it was half past nine) rose up to clash with my better feelings of brotherly solicitude. Mariana smiled, she felt better; and for some unknown reason that smile infuriated me. Only then did I come up with a solution that should have occurred to me long before: to telephone Lucília at the coffee house where she was waiting for me, call her to the telephone and explain what was happening. But just as I saw this way out, my sister stiffened once again in longer, more violent contractions. I rang the bell to call the nurse, absolutely convinced that the child would be born at any moment. The woman was vastly amused at my distress:

'Now, now… This won't be as fast as you imagine…'

But I had been thrown off balance, and once the crisis was over,

I couldn't remember what it was I had decided to do, although I had a vague notion that some solution or other had occurred to me. But it returned clearly enough when a maid came to fetch me to the telephone.

I went; and when I recognised Lucília's voice, I thought it was a hallucination. But nothing could have been simpler: when she realised that I wasn't going to turn up, she'd telephoned the barracks to ask for my home number (which I had never given her, under the pretext of getting my own back); then she'd phoned my house and found out where I was and what had happened. Hadn't she been clever! Well? There was a childish note of triumph in her voice. Indeed, her voice had never sounded so sympathetic. And she expressed the wish that everything would go well, that my sister would be very happy, that she would have 'a good delivery'. She would call back next day, first thing in the morning.

'Thank you, Lucília, thank you.' I felt almost moved. 'But I'm so sorry that we can't get together this evening!'

'Don't worry… It'll keep for another time.'

It was only after I'd hung up I was overtaken by misgivings: how would Lucília make the most of her night of freedom?

Meanwhile, the pains racked Mariana in an increasingly rapid rhythm. The pauses, short as they were, didn't even leave time for the cold sweat to dry. My anxieties seemed to describe an ellipse: one of the foci was Mariana, the other Lucília. When the pains slackened off, my sister ceased to exist. And a vision of Lucília would appear before my eyes, alone, at that time of night, sufficiently weak, passionate or flighty (I couldn't fathom out which) to give in to the temptations that might beset her — if she herself didn't provoke them!

Around midnight they took my sister to the delivery room. I went in a trice to eat something in a nearby coffee house. Shortly afterwards my brother-in-law turned up: they'd lent him a Buick ('Wonderful, old chap! I'd never have got here in the gas-powered model'); he'd averaged almost 80 kilometres per hour. The excitement of the feat he had performed gradually gave way to a more frantic and sombre anxiety. I had slumped, suddenly worn out. But he dragged me along the corridor; without a word, he looked pleadingly, questioningly at the nurses and the maids who came out of the delivery room. At one point he seized my arm: 'Oh, Henrique! What if…' But he didn't finish.

He rummaged in his pockets and asked me for a cigarette.

Just after one o'clock the matron came to tell him he now had a son. And was he perfect? Was he perfect? The fit of anxiety with which he asked that! The nurse burst out laughing: 'Absolutely perfect! And he looks just like you!'

Shortly afterwards we went to see him. It was indeed quite astonishing how a newly born baby, swollen, purplish, with his eyelids closed and puffy could look just like Manuel on his way back from the Arcádia, with five or six whiskies under his belt!

Only then did we remember to enquire after Mariana. She was fine. Everything had gone extremely well.

'Who was that girl who telephoned?' Rita asked me next day at breakfast. 'She rang here yesterday… What a common voice.'

I smiled. And shrugged my shoulders, without explaining anything. It was true, she did have a common voice. And on our telephone at home, this was more obvious and more striking than on the barracks telephone. It was, however, the same voice that had gripped my attention the night before. Ah, but at night (and on *that* night!) things always take on special proportions. How everything changes in the morning, after a cold shower!

The birth of my nephew seemed to heighten our feelings of family unity. Since the weather had begun to warm up, for some weeks before, Rita and I had been taking advantage of Sunday mornings to go to the beach or to play tennis: on that Sunday we went with grandmother to mass at St Mamede's.

The week following this Sunday was marked by deafening exercises in a tiny shooting range at the barracks and by continuous scares at home: the child was losing weight from one day to the next. Although the doctors assured us that this weight loss was perfectly normal, we all disagreed: at heart, we all wanted little Manuel to be the exception to the rule, naturally. Meanwhile Lucília continued to telephone me with her usual frequency. Half way through the week, she found a way for us to meet one day at lunchtime, very quickly, in Edward VII Park.

At that time the Park was like a foreign garden, a refugee camp, an international zone. The very trees, the grass, the bordered paths, seemed to absorb exotic suggestions from the pages of the foreign newspapers that elderly gentlemen with semitic profiles unfolded and read on the green benches. The place where we arranged to meet was a nook in the *Parc Montsouris*. Lucília turned up looking so very Portuguese, so very Lisbonese. Not from the more or less typical Lisbon, the more or less conventional Lisbon, the Lisbon of the theatrical revues and popular dances. She belonged to the Lisbon of the neighbourhoods with no history, the Lisbon that was beginning at that time to acquire wirelesses and debts, the Lisbon that listened to the BBC at night and argued in the rations queue in the morning, to an ignominious Lisbon, shadowy, fatigued and indolent, with half-price *matinées* in the cinemas that specialised in re-runs, to the Lisbon that wore lipstick and rouge to conceal the pallor of its very modest vices, and to suggest perhaps a longing for other, more daring ones… On that morning, Lucília struck me as a heart-rending, striking symbol of all this. Doubtless because she even spoke about it all.

Thanks to the pretext that she had been held up in a ration queue, she was able to arrange that rendezvous with me. She spoke to me about a film running in the Lis, with Robert Taylor. And a radio programme which she couldn't always listen to because her father preferred the BBC… Despite the rouge and despite the lipstick, her appearance offered a painful contrast with that of the foreign women who we could see in the vicinity, all of them very suntanned already. It was obvious that she still hadn't been to the beach. This detail, which had escaped me in the Anjos garden where it was completely meaningless, now took on an unexpected significance. Besides, Lucília's body wasn't one of those you would want to see in a bathing costume. One suspected a pale, domestic flesh, like that of a chicken: it surely wasn't a body to be displayed on the beach. But for all that, one still wanted to feel it completely naked. I should say so! We strolled along arm in arm; because she was considerably shorter than me, the dragging and the rhythmic pressure of her hip against the top of my thigh promised hidden harmonies, ripening, a deeper understanding. From time to time, in the corner of a path, abetted by the shade, we would kiss. Then we would continue on our way. To one rather crude question I asked her, she answered yes, there had already been a man in her life.

'… The cadet?'

'No, no,' she exclaimed, with a start. 'Another man.'

A sense of peace, the heightened peace that comes from being quite sure, then took hold of me, mixed with a sudden smell of eucalyptus. Delighted, I breathed them both in. It was the high point of our assignation.

Towards the end of the week, my nephew began to put on weight. Within three days Mariana would be pronounced fit and well. And

Lucília informed me that on the following Tuesday that her father would have to go to Santarém. He'd spend the night there, of course. This time there was no mention of buying tickets for any show.

But on Tuesday there was a surprise in the 'Order of the Day': one of the cadets had been taken ill and on the following day I was the one to go on duty. When she heard the news, Lucília was desolate: it almost seemed as if that rendezvous of ours was jinxed! For my part, I again felt apprehensive: wouldn't she enjoy yet another night of freedom without me? And I couldn't refrain from telling her so. She shrieked with indignation; she really had a rather pathetic shriek: well couldn't I see, well couldn't I see how much she liked me? She couldn't believe it! Just who did I think she was? I had no alternative but to back down, making all the excuses under the sun. At last Lucília was appeased; and finally she said to me: 'You're very naughty, you know? You don't deserve anything at all. But just so that you don't have these ideas, tomorrow I'll spend all night telephoning you… do you hear?'

That was exactly what I wanted: I already knew I'd be awake until five in the morning. (To make matters worse, that damned alteration to the roster even made me land up on duty with Lieutenant Sanches!) At least such a promise brought the hope that the night wouldn't pass so badly.

On the following day, just after dinner, the telephone rang. But it was a false alarm: no one answered. Lieutenant Sanches, still up, was the one to answer, and in his nasal voice, he kept on exclaiming, in vain:

'Hello? Hello? Hello?' (He came from a generation that still said 'Hello?') Only after eleven o'clock, when Lieutenant Sanches was already snoring and I'd begun to despair, did the telephone ring again. This time it was Lucília. The maid had gone out, her mother and sister had gone to the cinema: she was alone in the house.

'And do you know what I've done?'

I didn't know. What she had done was, after all, very simple: she'd already undressed, and since the telephone was in her parents' room, that's where she was speaking from.

'I don't know what I must look like, here all alone, in this enormous bed!'

All this was said in a thrilling tone. What is certain is that the thrill communicated itself to me. This was the first time that the word 'bed' had been spoken out loud in our conversations. And it suddenly seemed to me that we were alone in the middle of the world; and that in the middle of the world one single object ruled supreme, around which we had been playing hide-and-seek. It was a combination of catafalque and campaign tent, but only now had Lucília's words had torn back the curtains: it was a bed! The obsession was revealed. The magic word had been uttered. That was the night when we began to use the intimate form of address.

From then on we tried even harder for that rendezvous which, in her words, seemed fated never to take place. I even contemplated going sick: that way I'd have a few free afternoons to meet Lucília. But Captain Lobo, my company commander, was not a man to trifle with: if any officer went absent on sick leave he immediately sent the unit doctor round to his house. And we had also begun manoeuvres and were going up to the Monsanto Hills every afternoon.

I must add that to a certain extent, those war games were my safety valve. Given the state of my nerves, such tactical feats came as a welcome relief, and I took part in them with an eagerness, a passion, a boldness which amazed me.

One of those afternoons we had to 'imagine' ('imagination' played an crucial part in all of this) that a company of riflemen had come within assault range. My platoon and second Lieutenant Simões' formed the attack column. We had previously advanced in speedy bursts, without firing (indeed, we only had blanks). We took full advantage of the 'imaginary' neutralising effects of the 'imaginary' artillery, of the non-existent aeroplanes and of the equally imaginary firing base. On top of a hillock stood Lieutenant Sanches (as the oldest officer, he always stayed 'on the defensive'), accompanied by three sergeants and two dozen recruits; they constituted the 'primary target' (as well as the only one). I ordered the manoeuvre, relaying the position back to the command post, as the rule book advised. After the imaginary raising of the imaginary artillery fire, there I went, dragging my unit along in a quick march, no halts, at a truly heroic pace. Once we had come within close combat range, to make things more exciting, more realistic, my men fired the agreed volley in the air. But in the middle of the tumultuous confusion of victory came a piercing yell. And, on top of the hillock, a figure twisted and writhed, his hands clutching his belly: it was Lieutenant Sanches. I was terrified! What a ghastly sight! One of those animals had probably got his hands on a round of live ammunition – and landed me right in it! And it was all my fault! Like a madman I ran up to Lieutenant Sanches. Two sergeants had by now taken hold of him and dragged him, painfully, downhill.

'Lieutenant! Lieutenant! What's wrong?'

But Lieutenant Sanches couldn't answer me: he just shot me a glassy look, and his greying head drooped, bloodless, on his shoulder. Puffing and panting, one of the sergeants explained: 'It's the colic!'

The other sergeant repeated, in a funereal echo: 'It's the colic!'

Some of the corporals explained: 'The colic!' And the word spread among the soldiers, as terrifying as the rumour of an epidemic.

Straddling his fat horse, Captain Lobo rode up: somehow the news had already reached him, goodness knows how. He gave orders for Lieutenant Sanches to be driven home at once and still mounted on his horse, he remarked to the officers on foot surrounding him:

'One of these days that man will die! These things can finish you off. And all out of bloody-mindedness. He has a gall stone this big! This big!' And he showed his thick gloved hand, which at the same time was squeezing the bunch of reins. 'But no! He doesn't want to have an operation...He doesn't realise that in a case like this...'

The horse grew restless. Cautious, we all stepped back in a circle. And so that we could hear him, Captain Lobo continued almost in a shout, from up in his saddle:

'Yes, in one of these cases... it would be a question of duty...a question of duty... to let them operate on him! Even Lyautey said...'

But the horse reared right up, and Captain Lobo had to dig in his spurs and move off at a trot to calm him down, without telling us what Lyautey said.

Captain Lobo had also spent some years in the colonies when he was a junior officer. But he was in all respects the exact opposite of Lieutenant Rebordão: in his habits, a Spartan; in his actions, voice and well-groomed moustache, a thundering empire-builder. I had occasion to appreciate his qualities more fully some six days after Lieutenant's Sanches' colic. We were on duty together, in very special circumstances. Almost all the barracks were deserted: the conscripts, a large number of the 'other ranks', and the majority of the officers had gone off to camp somewhere on the outskirts of Lisbon, on exercises with live ammunition. Only we two officers remained in the unit, along with a lieutenant and another cadet who would take over from us on the following day. A few enlisted men had stayed as well, among them the batmen who would 'hold the fort' during these two days. There were also half a dozen sergeants, clerical staff, some cooks, a couple of military policemen, one or other sick person. At most, there would be a hundred of us. Anyway, there wasn't much work.

Nevertheless, Captain Lobo, active and busy as always, found tasks for all of us. I myself spent the morning checking supplies of toilet paper. But after lunch we stayed behind for a few minutes in the officers' mess enjoying a pleasant chat. Tactical matters, it goes without saying. And since we were talking about the German advances on the Eastern front, Captain Lobo sent to the regimental classrooms for a map of Europe; then, with some pins and pieces of paper (he was very nimble-fingered) he improvised some little flags: and standing, legs apart, his body slightly bent over the huge table, there and then he decided the destinies of the world. Did the destinies of the world turn out differently? Not through any lack of competence or good will on Captain Lobo's part. He was in constant need of maps, graphs, models. He was just getting ready to trace on to some paper the ground plan of the zone where our unit's live firearms exercises would be taking place when they called me to the telephone.

It was Lucília. She'd spoken to me less often in recent days. And usually in great haste, usually from public call boxes. Her father was at home almost every day now, drawing up a report or something of the sort. But he was probably going to spend some days in the North inspecting the Oporto branch. He would be away for at least a week. The matter was confirmed: he would leave on the following day, on the 8.40 express. We could meet as early as that afternoon. But the afternoon didn't suit me: it was my nephew's christening. Well, in that case... in that case our meeting would have to keep until evening.

I spent the whole day brooding over where to take her. But in fact I still had plenty of time ahead and could ask my brother-in-law to give me some suggestions on the following day. Since his marriage, Manuel considered himself 'retired' from the fray, but still took considerable pleasure in sponsoring other people's adventures. In principle, Lucília and I had arranged to meet in that same coffee-house where we had seen one another for the first time. That way, so her intuitions told her, everything was bound to work out well.

My spell of duty in the unit seemed to me even longer than usual. At the end of the afternoon, there was an unpleasant incident: Faísca, Lieutenant Rebordão's batman, who was on sentry duty at the powder magazine, was caught napping. Woken up, he began to quarrel with the corporal of the guard. He was absolutely sozzled.

We found out later that he had pinched a bottle of brandy from his boss.

'The parental home is the child's first learning ground,' Captain Lobo remarked discreetly. But you could see he was looking for a more fitting axiom; at last he found one: 'The example comes down from on high…'

And he ordered that Faísca be put in the gaol. Faísca was the most popular batman in the whole regiment; and his shouts and the tears he shed and the loud cries of repentance upset us all. But Captain Lobo was inflexible: standing on the landing of the officers' mess, with his hand stuck napoleonically between two of his jacket buttons, he watched, unmoved, the sad spectacle afforded by Faísca as a corporal and two soldiers dragged him off to the calaboose.

At dinner time, Captain Lobo informed me that it was my job to record the incident. Nothing could be easier, he added. And he indicated to me which witnesses I should hear and the precise terms in which the case should be drawn up, insisting particularly on the application of the set formula, 'When asked the usual questions, he said nothing', with which the identification of each witness should be completed. And he thought it advisable to explain to me the meaning of that notarial formula:

'"When asked the usual questions" means: when you are asked if you have any family relationship with the accused, if you are his friend or his enemy, etc. Do you understand?' He repeated again, almost voluptuously: 'When asked the usual questions, he said nothing.' And to conclude, he mimed the gesture of someone writing a full stop.

Along with his love of maps, schemes, graphs and models, Captain Lobo was very fond of maxims, aphorisms and adages. And the excessive use that he made of these sometimes gave rise to misunderstandings. That same night, while we were doing the rounds, he suddenly said these words to me:

'Do you know that I've thrown a lance in Africa?'

At that moment we were crossing the artillery park. I was tired, and in the middle of that warlike atmosphere and since he had been in Africa, I actually believed that the 'lance' was not metaphorical. But it was.

'You know, I've persuaded Sanches to have the operation…'

'Oh really, Captain?'

'You'd better believe it. Right now he's in the Estrela Hospital. And tomorrow morning… slash! he goes under the knife… There was nothing else for it! It was something that had to be done.'

Then he recounted the hideous tale of Sanches' colics – which represented, quite apart from anything else, a dereliction of duty. Every so often, an attack of colic. And then he had to stay at home for days on end, undergoing treatment that didn't cure a thing.

'Yes, because the stone' – and he held up a clenched fist in the air – 'the stone was still there!'

Still, you could see that he was a trifle uncomfortable about the responsibility he had taken on, persuading Lieutenant Sanches to undergo surgery. One thing is for sure, on the following day before we went off duty, he telephoned the Estrela Hospital twice. But at ten o'clock they still did not know how the operation had turned out.

Then Captain Lobo suggested to me, as well as to the lieutenant and the cadet who were replacing us, that we should telephone the hospital in the afternoon (he would do likewise), so that we could find out how things had gone. As most of the officers were away at the firearms practice, it would be nice if all of us who had remained in Lisbon could demonstrate our concern. I said yes, 'Have no fear, captain!' then promptly forgot all about it.

In any case, I had a tremendously busy day. The christening party was quite simple; even so, thirty or more people had gathered at grandmother's house. Mariana showed the various cousins and other ladies little Manuel's layette, little Manuel's perambulator, little Manuel's cradle and little Manuel himself. And little Manuel went from lap to lap, and he got his own back, wetting the *moiré* dress of Madam Sofia, who had been my sister's piano teacher. Madam Sofia did not conceal her irritation, because she had to go on to a wake.

Before the buffet was served, I escaped to one of the bathrooms. I have always loved the peace and safety of bathrooms in the midst of the hubbub of such bourgeois festivities. I had a tepid shower. Afterwards, I took care not to drink too much, despite Manuel's insistent challenges. Very casually, I filled him in on what was happening and asked for his advice. Manuel preened visibly at this sign of trust and told me about a house – very discreet, very well-appointed – that would suit me down to the ground.

At the end of the afternoon they set up two games tables: bridge for the men, mah-jong for the ladies. I took advantage of the opportunity to make my escape.

But it was still very early. So I walked down the Avenue to the Baixa. The sea breeze that had blown up from the Tagus and come frolicking ashore, down there in Black Horse Square, to conquer the city by night, penetrated deep into the geometric streets with muffled whistles, finding there, on a level with the branches of the trees, hot air rising from the cobblestones on to which the shadows had already fallen… The marriage between the two was so discreet, celebrated so vaguely, that I was left feeling a nostalgia, a yearning, quite sure of the coldness to come. I wanted – without even knowing why – to delay, to prolong that walk… It was in that state of mind that I crossed Restauradores Square and made my way towards the southern tip of the Rossio, where you used to take the trolley for Graça.

By nine forty I was already in the coffee-house. Five minutes later – we'd made our date for nine forty-five – the telephone rang; and here was the waiter enquiring, in a low voice, whether there was a Mr Andrade, they were calling Cadet Andrade to the telephone. It was for me, of course. To begin with, it didn't seem like Lucília's voice. Then I thought she might have a cold or a sore throat. But no, she was simply speaking quietly. Surprisingly she told me we could meet at home, at her home. And… wasn't that dangerous? No, not in the least. Was there no danger of her father appearing from one moment to the next? I imagined a false departure, a sudden return – goodness knows what! She calmed me down.

'There's no danger at all. Don't worry.'

And she gave me the address. It was a street that I only knew by name; I had a vague suspicion that it was over by Penha da França. I took a taxi. The building was old (perhaps dating from the end of last century), big and greyish. I went in through the door, which was still open, after checking that the bell wasn't working. The stairway, narrow and with an iron banister, received a dim light from the lamp placed above: the light on the third floor, which was the one Lucília had indicated to me, to be precise. This thoughtful gesture touched me. I imagined her alone, bustling around, perhaps a little nervous, putting the finishing touches to everything in order to receive me.

I rapped on the door with my knuckles. But it was a dishevelled-looking maid who came and opened up to me.

'Ah! Pardon me.' I feared I'd made a mistake. 'Does…Miss Lucília live here?'

'Ah!' The mop of hair quivered beneath a smile of foolish complicity. 'Miss Maria da Luz. She does indeed. Please come in.' And she almost pulled me down a very dark corridor where two men were talking quietly beside a coat and umbrella stand. But a screen then opened and Lucília (Lucília? Lucília or Maria da Luz?) appeared.

'Ah! You got here very quickly...'

Without any further explanations, she seized me by the arm and dragged me to the other side of the screen; along there, as far as I could see, the corridor continued into darkness. Through a chink in a door emerged a faint light, but Lucília, who was walking ahead of me, did not stop and opened yet another door a little further along. I saw at a glance it was a bedroom; and sitting on the bed with his back to the door was a figure. No, in fact, there were two figures: the one with his back turned – a man, still young – turned his head; and, at the same time, from behind his shoulder emerged another head, this one a girl's, peeping out at us. It looked to me as if she was sitting on his lap, or kneeling lower down. With a gesture, Lucília left me standing in the corridor and went into the bedroom, pushing the door. Once inside, I could hear her exclaim: 'You might at least have locked yourselves in!'

Then came voices, muffled laughter, the sound of footsteps. When the door opened again, the players had changed position: the boy was standing by the window with his back to us; and the girl, also standing up, but close to the bed, sketched me a greeting.

'She's my sister,' murmured Lucília by way of an introduction. Then she pulled the door open again, and added: 'My sister and her boyfriend.'

After this, already in the corridor, she threw herself into my arms, making herself very tiny, encircling my waist.

'Oh! Darling... I was beginning to think that it wouldn't be today either!...'

Following this, she took me by the hand and led me to another chamber, which was in darkness. She switched on the light: it was a drawing room.

'Darling! Wait here a moment, will you? I'll be back in a minute. Then I'll explain.'

Intrigued by such mysteries, I stood for a moment without knowing whether I should rush after her – or get out of there as quickly as possible!'

And the two men beside the coat stand? And what about the sister? The sister and her boyfriend...And Lucília? Lucília or Maria da Luz? I had expected to meet her alone and found myself in a house full of people! It all struck me as dreadfully wrong.

I got as far as turning the doorknob. But a sudden noise, a dull sound, right there inside the drawing room, halted me in my tracks. With a start, I turned back. It had to be my imagination. The 'drawing room' – a sofa, half a dozen chairs, a piano set at an angle – was in the best order. At the corners of the window which was completely covered by a filet lace curtain, stood two columns; and, on top of each one of them, balanced a fat *cache-pot* with artificial begonias. On one of the walls there were lithographs representing the Good Jesus of Braga, the Bay of Naples with Vesuvius, and the Rossio, still with cobblestones in the central carriage way; on another, beside the piano, a bas-relief framed in mahogany with a little frieze of childish faces with very chubby cheeks, symbolising the seven musical notes. But from beside the piano, I could hear, quite clearly, a buzzing of soft things. I approached, I peeped: behind the piano were two hens and a nest of chickens, sitting drowsily on some bundles of straw. At that moment Lucília came back in.

'Oh!' she exclaimed, a little flustered. 'You were looking at the "live-stock"? That's Mummy's business… Because of the shortages, we've been rearing poultry here at home. But since they don't all fit on the balcony… And since this room is almost always closed…'

'Oh yes, of course…' That was the last thing I was bothered about. And I moved towards her, my arms extended the length of my body, the palms of my hands opened outwards, my chin raised:

'Come on now, just what is your name?'

'You don't know, then?' she rejoined, very sly, her hands behind her back.

No, I didn't know. But I wanted to.

'Are you called Lucília or are you called Maria da Luz?'

'Darling! Why are we bothering with such things right now? I'm called Maria da Luz. All right? Are you happy now?' And without giving me time to reply, she then changed her tone:

'Look, darling, take that tie off. I have another one here for you.'

I was going to protest (mainly out of vanity), when she took her hands from behind her back, displaying a black tie. Only then did I notice that she too was wearing black.

'Something really stupid has happened, you know? Papa has died.'

'What?'

'He was taken ill in the station, we brought him home and… well, he died of a fit. He's in there. We have to go and keep vigil over him. For a little while, at least. You do see, I just couldn't leave the house in these circumstances.'

And she said this as if she were reciting a lesson, with her eyes cast down, shrugging her shoulders from time to time; and she rolled and unrolled the tie. Then she threw her arms around my nape, almost hanging from my neck: 'Darling! Don't be nasty… Don't look at me like that! You know perfectly well that Papa…Oh all right then! Poor thing… now there's no point in our complaining any more. But you know perfectly well: Papa…'

And, as she tried to kiss me, I noticed that she smelled of alcohol.

'Lucília.' And I immediately corrected – 'Maria da Luz! You've been drinking:'

Yes, she'd drunk a tiny little drop of Madeira.

'Imagine! My father, he even kept the Madeira under lock and key! But now' (and she kissed me, impishly, beside my ear) 'now I have a bottle there, in my room… for the two of us!' Then, releasing me: 'But before that you must express your condolences to Mummy. Come on, get a move on! Put the tie on.'

I obeyed almost automatically. There was a promise, shameful, but extremely persuasive, a devilish suggestion in the way she had said 'in my room'! Shortly afterwards she led me once more along the corridor to the room with the chink of light under the door. The dead man was lying in a wide double bed, and the hem of the sheet covered his face, leaving no more than a handful of greying hair in view. On one side of the bed, a very fat lady was waving a handkerchief at the flies that were buzzing round the pillow. When she noticed us coming in, she raised the hankie to her eyes and sighed – very lightly.

'Look, Mother, Henrique,' murmured Maria da Luz, clearing a way for me between two chairs occupied by a little woman with a shawl (I found out later that she was the *concièrge* of the building) and by another woman whose identity I never learned. The slovenly maid was on the other side of the bed. I drew near, feeling myself the cynosure of all eyes; and, with a slight bow, I sketched a kiss above the old lady's hand.

'Oh dear, Mr Henrique! Who could have told us? Only yesterday, so hale and hearty…'

I saw that the lady had been coached. And that, before those people, I would be an intimate friend, perhaps even Maria da Luz's '*fiancé*'! This gave me an uneasy feeling, softened by the realisation that no one had liked the dead man, that no one was making the least effort to pretend a grief that did not exist. Which was quite reassuring. In the meantime, Maria da Luz's sister entered, followed by the boyfriend, and re-enacted more or less the same scene that had taken place with me. As the room was not very spacious I had to move over to beside the door in order to let them through. And, beside the door, Maria da Luz took me by the hand: furtively, we stole out of the bedroom. Once again, we went down the corridor, but now even further along, down to the end where her room was.

Judging by what I had already observed, this had to be the most stylish, the most elegant part of the whole house; the furniture, light and varnished, had a much newer look than the junk in the other rooms. The bed was very wide. On top of one of the bedside tables stood the portrait of a middle-aged gentlemean in a bronze frame.

'Do you know who this is?' Maria da Luz asked me.

'Your father?' I rejoined, unconvinced.

She shook her head, and declared, very confidently:

'You'll never guess!'

'Your…' The wide bed had roused my suspicions.

'It's my husband.'

'Then you…' And, puzzled, I immediately wanted to establish an association of ideas. 'Don't tell me that… in there…'

Heavens! No, nothing of the sort: the husband was the one in the picture. And the other, the one who was inside, well, the dead man, that was her father.

'But what about him…' I murmured, pointing to the photograph.

'Oh! He won't show up!' She sighed. 'He's very far away:' Picking up the frame, she held the photograph before my eyes. 'But do you really think he looks as if he could be my father?'

It was the voice of someone who wanted me not to think that at all; so, generous to a fault, I didn't. Then, with great care, she put the frame back on the table, modestly turning the portrait to the wall. And she remarked:

'It's all a very long story.'

Next, she switched on a bedside lamp, turned off the ceiling light, checked that she had already locked the door.

'Well, at last, my darling!' And she threw herself into my arms.

I felt again the disintegration I had felt in the Anjos Garden, the tremendous peace of the Edward VII Park, and at the same time, the excitement, the fever, the unhealthiness of certain telephone calls! While we kissed, I dragged her over to the bed. We both collapsed on top of it. But suddenly she broke free, and in a very calm voice, exclaimed: 'Don't you think there's too much light?' She got up and looked out a flowery handkerchief from a dressing table drawer; with great skill, she wrapped it around the lampshade.

'Why don't you get undressed, darling?'

With an abrupt gesture, she herself pulled off her dress and slip. Then she turned down the bedspread, pulled back the sheet and blanket. And all this, the skill and confidence which she did all this, the ease with which she gave herself to me, the throaty cries, the gesture, at the very last moment, of digging her nails into the pillow – all this gave me the almost repulsive sensation that I was dealing with a professional. At the very least, she made a very convincing tart. But when I opened my eyes and saw the expression in her eyes, the face which had suddenly become much younger, that blissful glow – I felt I was being unjust, I felt how unfair it is for us to condemn any one, no matter who. She looked about seventeen years old. Her coiffure had collapsed; her hair had fallen across her forehead and on to her shoulder. And she was having difficulty in opening her eyes. But she was smiling.

Afterwards, she covered herself with the sheet and asked me to look in the wardrobe for the bottle of Madeira and two glasses: they were hidden in the corner, on the left hand side. With her elbow propped up on the pillow, she filled up the glasses; and in that brief and happy gurgling, I seemed to hear a laugh of mockery for the miserliness of the dead man. What the devil, the dead man! But the Madeira wasn't at all bad. We made a toast. and remained lying side by side, momentarily calm, savouring the wine in little sips.

'But your husband, after all…'

Ah! It was a very long story…

'Just imagine! I was only seventeen…'

'And him?'

'Him? Thirty-eight. Or thirty-nine. It was a marriage "arranged" by my father. My father owed him a lot of favours. But he was an agreeable man, what do you think? He was really a perfect man!'

She showed me the photograph again:

'It was taken three years after we got married…'

I have never fully grasped the notion that certain women have of 'a perfect man'. That one had a face that was almost round, little eyes, thin lips and, above all, an air of stupid seriousness.

'But where is he?'

'He's in Africa. In Angola.'

Then, looking up at the ceiling and exhaling a sigh in which there sounded a certain thrill of pride: 'He ruined his life for me!' And in another tone, almost furious: 'I have never forgiven my father!'

'What? For the marriage?'

'No! The rest…'

And she fell silent. I understood that the time had not come for her to tell me 'the rest'. And I thought it wise not to rush matters. I looked at the photograph again. The scene was simultaneously comic and grotesque: we were each holding an end of the frame; and we were naked, beneath the sheet; a few feet away lay the very corpse that was making this intimacy possible for us. But there one could feel completely safe and secure. The third side of the classical 'triangle' appeared merely in effigy. There was even the reassuring certainty that he could only appear in effigy. Suddenly, almost solemnly, this foolish remark escaped me:

'You can see he must have been a very austere person.'

'Oh! As for that…' she let out a malicious gurgle of laughter. 'That depended on the occasion.'

Then, proud and with a gratified smile, almost nostalgic, she recounted her memories one by one: some coarse, others so idiotic as to be almost innocent. Some, especially the latter, she whispered in my ear, otherwise she would feel ashamed. Again she replaced the frame on the bedside table. And again, we found ourselves in each other's arms. By the end, she was seventeen years old again. She belonged to that breed of women to whom lovemaking restores the age of one's first raptures. It was a fact: she had, beyond any doubt, liked her husband.

We remained, afterwards, for I don't know how many minutes, in a strange, blissful torpor – a torpor that would have lasted much longer and perhaps even turned into sleep if Maria da Luz had not been overcome by a sudden panic:

'Henrique! We must go in! Just for a little while. Then we can come back. It's because of Mummy… It looks so bad!'

We hastily tidied ourselves up. We found far more people in the room in which the vigil was being held: besides the widow, the maid and the two little women, there were an old couple (they were neighbours, I gathered) as well as the two men I had seen beside the coat stand. The door on to the corridor was now standing wide open. Maria da Luz's sister and the boyfriend also reappeared soon afterwards. Minutes later, we heard some one knocking at the stair door and Maria da Luz went to see who it was. She came back looking quite dismayed and murmuring: 'It's Aunt Ester.'

Maria da Luz's sister hissed to her boyfriend, with a spiteful but slightly scared voice: '…My hysterical aunt!'

And there she came bursting in – tall, thin, grubby, with equine features and grandiose gestures. She didn't speak to anyone.

'Where's my brother?' she bellowed. 'Oh, my dear brother! Oh, they've killed you!'

The widow, terrified, made an effort to rise from her chair. But Aunt Ester had already fallen to her knees at the bedside.

'Oh, my dearest brother! No one ever understood you! Oh, you were always an unhappy soul! Ah, I was the only person you could confide in!'

With trembling hand, she groped at the inert body, smoothed the material of the coverlet.

'Oh, my sweet brother! Oh, how I want to see you again!'

And her hand reached the top of the sheet, and was preparing to uncover the dead man's face when an indignant Maria da Luz dragged me out of the room.

After that everything seemed like a hallucination. Maria da Luz's sister and her boyfriend came out after us and disappeared into the bedroom. Aunt Ester's shouting followed them out into the corridor.

'That really is too much, isn't it? That really is too much!' exclaimed Maria da Luz, pulling me along pell-mell. We didn't stop until we got into her room.

She slammed the door loudly, made a big thing of turning the key. With a jerk, she wrenched off her dress. It was a gesture that made a complete mess of her hair-do. And she began to pace up and down, in her silk-speckle slip, shaking the dress as if it were a limp wand:

'That really is too much, huh? She's been on bad terms with us for absolutely ages then she turns up here at the house just to cause a scene like this! My father was the only person she got on with. And she was always pestering him with stories about us. Ah! If I were in my mother's place! I'd grab her by the arm, and I'd turn her out in a jiffy!'

She hurled the dress over the bed. It was as if she'd been deprived of her weapon. Her arms dangled, lifeless, beside her body. Thoroughly disheartened, she leaned against the wardrobe. 'But poor Mummy is weak. And the two of us take after her. We've never been up to coping with these matters.'

Her eyes were lost in a sudden reverie then found the ceiling light on. With a gesture she asked me to turn the switch. And, in the dark, she slid over beside the bed and once more switched on the bedside lamp, the shade still covered in the floral hankie. For a moment, she remained kneeling on top of the bed, with her hands in front, resting on the dishevelled sheets. Her eyes, green, short sighted, slanting, were glinting. She was a cat. Then, with a whirling movement of her front paw, she seized the dress. And, contrary to what I expected, standing up, in silence, she began to put it on again. While she was smoothing it around her hips, she murmured, eyes cast down, in a colourless voice: 'When it comes down to it, she was the one who killed him.'

'Your father?'

'No.' She hesitated for a moment. Then, sitting down on the edge of the bed: 'That boy whom I told you about… the cadet.'

'Oh.'

She leapt to her feet again and pleading, threw herself towards me, seizing me by the elbows: 'But on my word of honour, there wasn't anything going on. Do you hear me? My word of honour! We were like two sweethearts… At the beginning he didn't even know I was married. He was such a good boy. You can't imagine. We got on so well together. And don't forget, I was fond of my husband. Really fond of him. But what can you expect? I'd never had a boyfriend…' And she said this with tremendous naturalness, placing the palms of her hands together and lowering her head at an angle, with her eyes wide open, as if it that business of having a boyfriend was not only inevitable but somehow indispensable.

In the meantime, she had released my arms and went over to the table with the bottle, filled a glass and downed it in one gulp.

'How old was he?' I asked.

'Who? David? Nineteen.'

'And you?'

She set down the glass. She spun on her heel, turning back towards me: 'Twenty-one. Twenty-one or twenty-two.' And, beseeching, she made yet another appeal to my credulity: 'I swear to you…on my word of honour. On my husband's health, there was nothing going on.'

Distressed, she began to pace up and down again.

'But then… your husband… he eventually found out?'

She came to a halt. And, looking me right in the eyes, with the stare of a madwoman, she stretched out her arm towards the dead man's room:

'It was my aunt. It was that aunt of mine. My wonderful aunt Ester!' The words came out in a crescendo of indignation. Then she took a deep breath and, sitting down on the bed, her back to me, continued: 'She saw me with him on two occasions and rushed off to tell my father all about it. And my father went and told my husband. My husband kept very quiet, but then he took to spying on me, to watching what I did. This was around Easter time: David was on holiday, we used to meet nearly every afternoon. Little did we know!' She sighed. 'And some time later my husband asked my father for a gun. Now my father must have known what he wanted the gun for. But he still lent him it. He lent him a gun, do you hear me? And one afternoon I was coming back with David from a *matinée* and we went into… into a stairway. It was just so we could kiss. I swear to you, it was only so we could kiss each other. But my husband came in after us. I managed to escape up the stairs. And then he shot him twice.'

I had lit a cigarette and remained standing, leaning against the wall. Still sitting with her back to me, she began to take off her dress again; but when the waistband was up around her shoulders, she pulled it back down. And I asked: 'What happened next? Did the other chap die?'

'Yes he did. On the following day.'

'What about your husband?'

'He was put on trial. But they proved that we had been… that we had almost been caught in the act.' She stood up. She took some steps forward. She rested her hand on the handle of the wardrobe; and her thumb slid along the edge of the mirror, as if she were rubbing out some stain. 'Imagine… imagine, in that building (but honestly, we didn't know!) there was a house that rented rooms by the hour. The lawyers really went to town on that! On the one hand… do you see? Just as well! It was better that way…'

And she sat down again on the edge of the bed.

'Some coincidence,' I thought. Moreover, there were details in that story which I refused to believe. And yet… 'There is nothing more unlikely than the truth,' a diplomat friend of my father's used to say. On the other hand, the vehemence of Maria da Luz's words (in which, however, there was already quite a measure of alcohol) prevented me from interrupting her. Nor was it worth the effort! I merely added fuel to the flames: 'And your husband? Was he sentenced to a term of imprisonment?'

'Yes, for around two years. But his life was ruined. He went to

Africa. And he didn't even want to see me before he left…'

She got up from the bed. With a sudden movement, once more she tore off her dress. The business of taking her clothes off seemed more than a habit, it seemed to be a nervous tic, an obsession. And, in her slip, she came to me humbly and snuggled up to my chest. I felt sorry for her. You could say that she was trying to solve everything with that wild gesture of undressing. And she began again, in an almost wheedling tone: 'My father… My father is the one I can never forgive!' But then her voice took on a note of rancour; and, at the same time, she unbuttoned my shirt and groped at my chest: 'Afterwards, I had to come back home. You can't imagine what hell it was! He kept me here like a prisoner. And he begrudged me every mouthful I ate! My husband… My husband only left me this furniture. But every month he sent money for my keep, what do you think? My father, my father was convinced I knew nothing about it. And he insulted me! Oh! But I took an oath. I swore that I would have my revenge. And that I would hoodwink him, right under his very nose!'

'What?'

'Nothing.' She breathed deeply. 'Pour me another glass.'

Had I been used as an instrument of revenge? But, as if to allay any such unflattering suspicions, draining the glass, Maria da Luz threw herself at me, moaning, yearning, and she was shameless, she grovelled, she was reptilian. At times, she pretended to be an eagle, and that I was the reptile. She was very drunk.

It was well after midnight. In a petulant voice, Maria da Luz would ask me from time to time: 'Go and have a look. Go and see if aunt Ester is still there… And then come back and tell me, ok?' She had absolutely no desire to come face to face with her again.

At last, I began to get dressed. My head was swimming. And I felt dirty. But I couldn't bring myself to ask her where the bathroom was.

'Come back here and tell me, ok?'

I tucked the bedclothes around her neck: within seconds she would be asleep.

I went, almost stumbling, down the corridor. It felt as if the muscles of my legs had been ripped out. And my brains had been squeezed then dragged apart: they were two lumps of lead on my temples. In the middle of my head there was nothing.

As I drew near to the dead man's room, I thought I heard a familiar voice. It was, in fact, an extremely familiar voice. It was saying:

'...It was only then I found out you had already brought him home.'

I reached the door post. There he was, there was no doubt about it! It was Captain Lobo. Impeccable in his uniform, he was talking to the widow. On the bed lay the dead man, his face uncovered now: it was Lieutenant Sanches.

I leaned against the door post so as not to fall over. Captain Lobo turned round and caught sight of me.

'Ah, it's you. Excuse me, madam.' He sketched a bow, came over to greet me. 'What kind of face is that, man? Do you feel ill?'

I shook my head. In the meantime, Captain Lobo supported me, took me by the arm, led me out of there into the corridor.

'What a calamity, eh? What a thing to happen! To die like that, during an operation!' Then, in another tone of voice, slapping me on the shoulder: 'Yes, sir, I can see that you have done your duty. Because this is all part of your duty! Lyautey used to say...'

But it wasn't on this occasion that he would reveal what Lyautey used to say. Stepping back a little, he looked me up and down, and tut-tutting. commented:

'What a pity! What a pity you didn't come in uniform.'

Herberto Helder

THE POLICE

translated by Patricia Odber

Little Monsieur Leclair had let me down once again. On that rainy December day, I had gone to Communist Party Headquarters, recommended by Mr Maurice Leclair, and had received a letter for the forges of Clabeck. In Brussels my jobs were few and far between. It was only by chance I got hold of any money. I did a bit of everything: I chopped up vegetables in the *Sobela*, packed shreds of paper in the *Nouvelle Maison Vermeiren* or helped out at *Chez Lemaire*, a frying joint. My papers weren't in order. No one would give me regular, long-term work. Maurice wanted to put me in Clabeck, in the forges (hard labour), and hoped through this means to have a work permit requested at the Ministry. He was relying on the influence of someone in the Communist Party. I was particularly amused when I thought that Monsieur Maurice was a former collaborator and therefore did not enjoy civil and political rights. Belgium was a funny, mixed-up sort of country. For example: my mentor's best friend, a Fleming who loved strong beer, had been a member of the Resistance. I wanted work, that was all. And a bit of warmth too. I thought about girls I could sleep with or go with to the bars on the Chausée d'Anvers on a Saturday night. I had a sad room, with no heating. One of the windows overlooked the church and bourgeois cemetery of Laeken. The other looked out on to some distant lights. Goods trains passed over a nearby bridge. Sometimes I made up carefree, innocent poems with these foreign elements. And I also felt moved by solitude. I found myself outside the cadres, wandered about the city. I was already dangerously well known *Au Nord*, near the station, where the police informers and whores were legion. From time to time I'd while away a whole afternoon there, I'd scrape together the money for a beer and a packet of chips.

On that rainy December morning (later I'd talk to Annemarie about the slow, long downpour), Monsieur Maurice began to have doubts about his influence and the influence of the Communist Party. He told me he could no longer do anything for me. I'd be better off going to Germany or France, or even finding a berth in a boat leaving Antwerp. I mulled over my friend's words while I drank beer in a bar close to the station. In the heat of the bar my clothes gave off steam. Drops of water around. Calm solitude without pain. There was music. God! My soul knew its ways. The world was big, perhaps it was endless. Whatever I did, everything that happened to me, would not make me greater or lesser than faith or desperation. Because the desperation was old: a fine, extremely tenacious root. It was an experience, a thought, a destiny... something that I accepted, a means whereby I might perhaps come to love life. I was alone in the middle of the tranquil rain. We can always drink a beer as if it were the last one. At each moment the world can still manage to be complete: it is the only one, and that very fact makes it new again.

Annemarie sat down at my table. I saw straight away that she couldn't be alone any more. She was the most lonely creature on earth. And her story emerged – simple, gloomy – between our two beers. I wasn't moved. If I were going to be moved it would be by the world, myself, the rain over the city. There would be merely an ironic allegory in the two of us sitting in front of two beautiful glasses of cold beer, both understanding so easily what was happening to us and what would happen, for we were in no hurry. We could die there and then. We were waiting.

Annemarie was French, from Lyons. She'd abandoned her two-year-old son. Her husband was fighting in Algeria, perhaps he was dead. (She said she loved him – and why not? Love and desperation and disorder – all these are part of the world.) Annemarie didn't want to go back to France. But she was living in Belgium without papers. She'd already been put across the border twice: she'd come back, she'd always come back. What can a person do but come back, stand outside, be completely foreign, have no papers? The earth is enormous. We stop in one place. And now we're sitting here and we seek with our simple and desperate story, to attract care, other people's fervour. That's how it is. We renew the endless wait; the miracle where there are no miracles; the light at the end, always at the end. We are illegals on earth, each day we create a rapid, very brief surprising beauty in the face of terror.

Monsieur Maurice had lost his last hope of saving me. The Communist Party, the return train journey to Clabeck, the rain, an impossible salvation (what salvation?) – wrapped up inside me, and I felt drunk, happy, irresponsible: I felt close to death.

Now a woman was drinking beer in my solitude, talking about the child she'd left behind, of the husband who'd gone to war. (She pronounced her words slowly, she wrenched them inexorably from that vocabulary of fear and indebtedness, always alive and always secret.) She said she was lost, smiling. She liked Belgian beer, found Brussels insupportable. Yes, she wanted to die. She wanted to die anonymously, at the end of the world. I understood.

The police were there, sniffing around the *Gare du Nord*, they sniffed at us all, whores, pimps, marginals, people without papers, illegals. They knew she had come back: she would be put across the border once again. And she would come back. Or would she be arrested? She had already had been several times: that wasn't the worse. It could even be the only way now possible to think about things, to weigh up the world. But the game ended there. You couldn't say: I'm free. You couldn't risk your freedom (And ask: what freedom?)

I too could be arrested, repatriated: afterwards I would go round Lisbon sleeping in friends' rooms, in doss-houses. Scrounging a lunch, a bowl of soup, a glass of milk. All places are in a foreign land. And I would walk along by the river, looking at the pale, rough mass of water, the other bank with the red smoke of the refineries, blotting out the white light up and down. I was already imagining the prison in Brussels. I had to deceive the police. Fall apart with hunger, yes, like a foreigner, but never lose my freedom (And the question: what freedom?)

Annemarie had the gift of subversive poetry. She subverted everything. At her side I felt that my life mattered. I might risk it, time and time again, I might lose it, but I would never yield up any part of my inner self. The love of danger was intoxicating me.

Then we took on the police of the whole world. When night fell, we left the bar and walked, watchful, protected, to my room in Laeken. We skirted around anything that struck us as suspicious: a stationary car, a slow-moving shape, shadows, voices. We even had to sneak up the stairs of the building, for the landlady had already sent me thrown me out, firstly because I didn't pay her the rent, secondly she didn't want problems with the police. But then the room was ours. Annemarie got undressed and lay down naked on the bedspread while I tried to heat up a little water. We spoke at length of the rain, of love and the laws.

At two o'clock in the morning we went to the window and watched two policemen go down the street. They seemed to be observing our window. Complicity and ardour, the sharing of mutual vulnerability, the courage to face everything with so little:

those were our weapons. And we could call on the best talents of lustfulness. Annemarie pulled me inside, and we loved one another on top of the bedspread until morning, until we drowned in the cold light of day.

It kept on raining. We felt the rain on the whole earth. We were invincible. Let it be said there are many things that you, of this nation, do not know. Perhaps God will not grant you inspiration.

Mário de Carvalho

PROFESSOR PFIGLZZ AND
HIS STRANGE COMPANION

translated by John Byrne

When I was very young, I was purser on board a large mixed cargo ship, the *Fernão Ferro*, which plied lazily between Leixões, Hadlleh and Carvangel, calling at various minor ports. The captain was an ill-bred scoundrel, a tight-fisted drunkard called Anselmo, or Telmo, or Teles – I can't quite recall – who exuded, from a great distance, an unmistakable odour of gin. It was said that he had already sunk three ships in heavy seas through navigational error.

The crew feared and avoided him. For my part, preserving a suitable reserve, I had no real cause for complaint. The trip had been going well, 'favourable' as the captain would say, and with no significant setbacks.

One day, when we were taking on new passengers in some obscure place, Professor Pfiglzz came on board; a very stout, short, stiff man in a coconut palm hat, which was uncommon in those parts and times, and wearing a crumpled, light-coloured suit in Prince of Wales check.

I would not have even noticed Professor Pfiglzz, the passengers generally being so diverse and so uninteresting, had it not been for a curious feature which distinguished him, at first sight, from all other men.

Floating just above the ground and clinging to Pfiglzz's back, with its blond head raised and a vague air of boredom, its distinctive wings clothed in light blue down, there followed, clearly visible, his guardian angel.

From what the captain told me, this peculiarity of Professor Pfiglzz owed itself to a night of gambling, perhaps the only one of his life, since he was a man of prudence, always well-versed in his business affairs and in Commercial Law which he taught at Kvellah University.

It happened that, one already frenzied night among cronies and colleagues, having thrown away many thousands of silver thalers at poker, and aware that substantial inroads had been made into his fortune through the luck of the cards, Pfiglzz, sprawled in abandon on the sofa with his waistcoat unbuttoned and his head already dizzy with so many drinks, had exclaimed, 'Ah, if only my guardian angel were here!'

And before the astonished eyes of the whole company, and with a great start from Pfiglzz himself – who heard a low voice whispering in his ear, with great sweetness, half ironical and half in sad resignation, 'Here I am' – there materialised in that room a beautiful guardian angel, solemn and dignified with its large wings spread protectively over the professor's bulky shoulders.

All present at that time affected not to attach great importance to the apparition, confident that it would melt away with the last of the alcoholic vapours, or even that it was a personal hallucination to which they dared not own up, since certain kinds of impetuosity do not go down well in those circles.

And all the rest of the night was spent with an enormous, elegant guardian angel, its arms crossed discreetly, following the conversation of those gentlemen, who affected not to notice it. And not even the steward of that exclusive club, when he came in to collect the empty glasses, appeared to be put out by the unexpected presence, limiting himself to a phlegmatic and neutral 'excuse me' when the tray he was carrying grazed against the angel's wings and a few delicate tufts of feather fell into the empty glasses.

Fitting the guardian angel into Professor Pfiglzz's car was a serious business, accommodating the colossal wings in the narrow space of the back seat. The astonished driver, not knowing what to think, came to help, and from that point it began to dawn on Pfiglzz, his head resting on a soft downy wing, that this was no passing affair.

From that night on life became a constant ordeal for the Professor. The angel tried hard to be discreet, not to cause trouble, it spoke rarely, tried to be inconspicuous, but it did not neglect its custodial mission and held itself always to attention, sometimes beside, sometimes behind the fortunate Professor.

Whether or not he should receive clients, or instruct his book-keeper or even receive the eloquent workers' delegations from behind his vast guaiacum desk, in the presence of that blond, distinguished, impressive figure, was the question. In dealings with the workers in his businesses it was even an advantage, since the angel succeeded in intimidating even the most stubborn and cantankerous deputation.

It was now totally impractical to try to teach in the Business Faculty, beneath a vigilant azuline figure, with the tip of its wing brushing his shoulder and, what was worse, hiding from time to time a discreet yawn with the palm of its beautiful hand. A restless murmuring would ripple around the lecture rooms, breaking out from time to time in sudden outbursts of laughter. It was becoming extremely difficult to discuss grave concepts of Commercial Law beneath the sheltering wings of a resplendent angel.

The rector of the University himself elegantly called Pfiglzz's attention to the matter and invited him to rid himself of the angel, or to render it invisible again like everyone else's guardian angel. And saying this in his courteous and wise tone of voice, he looked sideways at the angel which was following him and Pfiglzz on their walk, now behind, now in front, along the corridors of the Faculty. And it was the angel itself who disabused the rector with a polite gesture of its delicate forefinger, while Pfiglzz merely spread his arms out wide, palms up in a gesture of despair.

And thus Dr Pfiglzz's career as a teacher of Commercial Law came to an end; business man, respected entrepreneur, holder of a University chair, now pensioned off, to his great displeasure, because teaching was what he most enjoyed in life.

Little by little the whole city became used to seeing that solemn gentleman walking along its avenues, surmounted by a graceful figure, observing everything alertly, hovering a handspan above Professor Pfiglzz's coconut palm hat. Demonstrations of astonishment as he passed by in the street or in public places (since nobody wanted to make a fuss anyway) were daily becoming rarer. And whenever strangers displayed any amazement the inhabitants of the city would turn round and say: 'What's the matter with you? That's Dr Pfiglzz's angel…' with no little pride as they shrugged their shoulders in disapproval.

Nor was the presence of the angel truly much of an impediment in business. At first it is true that the levels of profit, of orders in all his undertakings, fell dangerously. It was no picnic doing business with a man who always came armed with a guardian angel. A sense of gravity, a resistance to the unusual, all characteristics of the market, gave rise to moments of profound unease and the withdrawal of funds. But it is true too that the situation soon re-established itself, all the more because of Professor's sagacity found a way of turning to advantage the presence of his exotic companion. For, from a given moment the angel henceforth appeared as the symbol of his commercial interests. His commercial stationery bore the impression of two huge wings, in bright blue ink. His visiting cards now showed in the top left-hand corner the delicate outline of an angel, drawn by one of the best graphic designers in the city.

The angel also served as a bookplate. When he published his monumental treatise, his life's work, *On the Breach of Contract of (the Condition) of Tacit Resolution*, Pfiglzz had drawn on the cover of this austere volume the graceful figure of his protecting angel, with its wings spreading over the gold letters of the frontispiece. It was a great hit in all the bookshops and the treatise was soon sold out, being seen even in the salons and drawing rooms of those who were normally somewhat backward in the juridical mysteries. And in this way not even Professor Pfiglzz had any good or objective reason for complaint against his angel.

It was in matters of the heart that Pfiglzz was hopelessly distressed. The doctor was a bachelor and would discreetly put an end to those amorous episodes which flared up suddenly with ladies of doubtful virtue, and which of course high society bore with equanimity; since he compensated them regally with various gifts, this was perfectly acceptable in the circles in which he moved since his discretion ensured that the relationships were decorous and unspoken.

Now, however free or even lascivious were these friendships with women, the fact is that in every case intimacy became increasingly difficult; this was not simply because of the usual problems to which Pfiglzz, hardly adept in matters of love, was prone but above all because of the disruptive presence of the angelic figure, hovering perpetually above the bedhead, observing reproachfully.

Whether it was because they anticipated the inhibiting disapproval of the angel, or whether it was because they were beset by improper thoughts, one or other of these ladies were unable to stop themselves thinking how much more agreeable it might be to stroke those soft feathery wings or those handsome, unclouded cheeks rather than the flaccid, wrinkled, sweaty, heaving flesh of Professor Pfiglzz; in any case the fact is that Pfiglzz's love life moved from merely relative to complete disaster. And it was no use either to try to separate himself somehow from the angel, or make his room darker because the angel glowed all the more in the dark and the effect was a thousand times more inhibiting. After three or four disastrous attempts Professor Pfiglzz dedicated himself to chastity but reserved for the angel a deep-rooted resentment which derived from these experiences. To speak frankly, it was a mortal hatred; but how does one kill a guardian angel? *Dicant Paduani*, as the Professor would say with his legalistic penchant for the Latin tag.

It is true also that at this time, when his business suffered a sharp drop in orders and sales as the market shrank, that Pfiglzz needed all his skill to convince the angel that his role as protector went far beyond the mere prevention of common physical mishaps and should embrace also the economic well-being of the professor's companies. In this way the angel was put on its mettle and became interested in the way business was done; and so great profit accrued to Pfiglzz from the acute and lengthy scrutiny which the angel began to devote to his books, from the analysis of his accounts, and from the advice and suggestions it whispered in his ear. The angel was indeed exceptionally intelligent.

But even a man like Pfiglzz, gifted with the outstanding practical sense we have already mentioned, needed his little bit of intimacy, of time to himself, just to be alone sometimes. And despite the various advantages which his keen astuteness had managed to garner from the continuing presence at his side the fact is that he began to feel an ever increasing hatred for the angelic personage, a hatred so deep that it overtook his customary self-control and made it snap.

It was not just a matter of knowing that there was someone behind him, watching him, looking over his shoulder and reading his newspapers, breathing hot or cold down his neck, in summer or winter; it was basically the feeling that he was cut off from a basic right of all men, a right that even dogs have, the right of even the most miserable beggar, the right to be alone.

So much so that the graceful, diaphanous, angelic presence weighed like lead on poor Pfiglzz...

Whoever visited him thought it was charming that he should have such distinguished, reserved company, better, graver even than the best trained butler, although of course it did not supply the little services common to the latter. It was said that in many good families in the city they murmured in low voices, secretly, sometimes amid scenes of sorcery and the fumes of burning incense, with the blinds down and candles lit, the invocation of Pfiglzz from which had arisen that apparition and presence: 'Ah, if only I had a guardian angel with me!' But these envious ones were disappointed: nobody else might have his guardian angel made visible, at his disposal.

For his part and before he lost all hope, Pfiglzz did all he could to ensure that the angel was once again transported to the realms of invisibility.

There came to his house numerous men and women of great virtue, together with their acolytes, to sprinkle the air with myrrh and other exotic, overpowering perfumes, uttering great incantations of cabalistic import, spending hours in great ceremonies of benediction, staged with extraordinary ostentation by the light of strange smelling candles; all the while the guardian angel sat meekly by the side of Pfiglzz, smiling distantly, while the tip of its wing gently rubbed the shoulder of the one he was protecting.

The unofficial cabalists – the ones the dupes always swear by – having proved ineffective, there then came the official cabalists to try their luck. Priests and priestesses of all the acknowledged religions – Catholic fathers, pastors, rabbis, Koranic doctors, all of them – came in their multitudes – and were paid by the book – to pronounce benedictions, to burn exotic substances in an effort to exorcise the angel. The latter seemed to find the performance of these rites interesting and diverting but showed not the slightest desire to move or leave Professor Pfiglzz alone, not even when there came into the house the stout Archbishop of Cantuária, accompanied by an ample retinue in full fig, and who was reputed to be, at that time, the great master of the translation of creatures from the higher spheres to the lower, and vice versa.

Months passed in this fashion, a great deal of money wasted and Dr Pfiglzz was disabused of the idea that he might ever be free of his enforced companion through the ministrations of these practitioners. He began to think that he might have to have that sweet, watchful figure by his side for the rest of his life. And that would have meant great bitterness, or it might even be said great unhappiness, had Pfiglzz not been a man so short on feeling.

By this time relations between Pfiglzz and the angel had reached a stage which was more than critical.

Pfiglzz began to hurl things at it: books, paperweights, cigarette lighters, snuffers, anything that happened to be to hand. The angel plucked the things from the air and, with great patience, set about restoring them to their places. He tried to hit the angel with heavy objects so as to bruise or even wound it, but it dodged them effortlessly, appearing suddenly in the opposite direction from the lethal trajectory of Pfiglzz's improvised weaponry.

At one point Pfiglzz bought a fine revolver, made of nickel and with an inlaid silver handle. At first he waved it sardonically before the angel's beautiful blue eyes. Then he began to point the barrel of the gun at the angel's body, lingeringly, moving it menacingly over the most vulnerable areas of a human body. The eyes, the nape of the neck, the heart, the genitals... And the angel did not even bat an eyelid, impassive in its infinite sweetness.

One day Pfiglzz by now at the end of his tether in the face of such angelic serenity and the sweet reproaches with which he had to put up, squeezed the trigger; his eyes were closed, his teeth clenched, even as his aim rested on a point between the two beautiful slanting eyes of the angel. There was a loud bang and the noise of shattering glass as a valuable picture crashed down from the wall. Opening his eyes slowly, hopeful of seeing the body of the angel stretched out at his feet and with its tunic all rucked up around it, Pfiglzz met only the wide smile, magnanimous even, though tinged perhaps with irony, of the angel, who a hand's breadth in front of his nose had demonstrated yet again its most essential attribute: its invulnerability.

For a long time the revolver remained tucked away in a handsome chest of drawers.

So now Pfiglzz set himself to humiliate the angel; in private to begin with. He would ask it, with a roguish air, what sex it really was, and put his hands under its tunic, trying to touch it in its most intimate parts, while making repeated indecent suggestions, to which the angel did not respond, maintaining a great dignity all the while.

In public, too, he never lost a chance to annoy his companion. He would call him names, referring to him in conversation as 'this wretched shackle which I can't get rid of' and suggested selling him to a band of gypsies in the gloomy bars he was by now frequenting. The guardian angel bore everything with an ineffable smile, never protesting unless it was with the sweetest reproach, a gentle reminder of a more dignified way of doing things; but it never crossed its mind to abandon its mission, nor would it have known how had the temptation somehow overtaken it.

In despair, from that moment on Pfiglzz began to put the protective devotion of his guardian angel to the test. He threw himself head-first down the steps of great warehouses, whereupon the winged figure, with great patience, would pick him up by the belt and deposit him smoothly on the ground floor landing. He threw himself from bridges, from the highest arches, into the swiftly flowing river and the angel was obliged to glide rapidly and surely over the waters and snatch him up into its arms, even from the foul spume.

He would run carelessly along the avenues among the moving traffic, the angel opening a way for him, holding back the cars, protecting him from the impact of the huge lorries, whisking him under its arms up over the busy flow of vehicles.

Hardly a day passed without the important papers carrying a story of one of Pfiglzz's stunts and the corresponding prowess of the beneficent angel in saving him. Readers were already satiated with such news, so monotonous and old hat were they by now, and passed on to other matters. And the worst thing for Pfiglzz was that his fund of respectability began rapidly to run out, evaporating like ether in the sun.

In the end the city became tired of its Pfiglzz and his guardian angel. It was a peace-loving city, respectable, of orderly habits which did not welcome anything out of the ordinary, disorderly or protractedly scandalous.

One fine day, in the evening, after Pfiglzz had plunged the whole city into alarm and darkness by hanging from a high tension cable, a delegation of bigwigs came to his house: councillors from the Town Hall, the President of the Court of Appeal, Pflost the wealthy banker, the Marquesa of Cadernalt and Colonel Pflizzard of the Lancers.

These exchanges were painful for the doctor and extremely uncomfortable for the onlookers, embarrassed as they were by the azuline presence of the angel who gazed at them, respectfully, and with a profound expression of understanding. Pfiglzz in turn ranted, claimed certain rights, appealed to old friendships, invoked his huge fortune, tried to bribe them, was insolent and threw himself on the floor in supplication. The good gentlemen were unmoved. They dictated, in elegant phrases, the terms of Pfiglzz's exile. Either their friend Pfiglzz retired to his farm in Ermangel, on the shores of the Copper Sea, and stayed there 'as long as certain circumstances obtained', or he would have to face the wrath of a city which refused en masse to feed him, dress him or transport him. It was in short ostracism. He could either have the city in revolt against him or spend the rest of his days in Ermangel, in the sad apathy of its sweltering climate; Pfiglzz, subdued and dejected, opted for the second solution, meanwhile looking at the angel from out of the corner of his eye, weighed down with resentment.

And so it was, accompanied to the quayside by a large delegation of self-satisfied, relieved citizens, to the sound of shawms and fanfares, that Pfiglzz boarded a gig to take him to my ship, on which he embarked with his strange companion.

It did not take long for those of us on board to get used to that odd couple taking a stroll on the deck. Pfiglzz at first kept his distance, mistrustful of everyone, making friends only with the captain, who listened to his remarks with something approaching servility and pretended not even to notice the guardian angel, notwithstanding that he had insisted, in an exchange of telegrams with the port, that the latter also pay for its ticket.

As for the angel, it passed lightly in its posture of serene resignation, paying attention throughout to the steps of the gangway and the mass of the bulkheads as it followed in the footsteps of Pfiglzz.

Soon I began to wonder who this interesting angel person was, who seemed to be so much more worthwhile than his fat, sullen companion. And with me it was the opposite of what happened with the captain: I addressed my words to the angel and pretended that I hadn't seen Pfiglzz.

After long days of banal exchanges about the weather, the crystalline waters, the over-seasoning of the food on board and other small talk, and raising my voice each time Pfiglzz tried to interrupt us or mock us with his snort of derision, I began to find confirmation that, as I had suspected, the angel too had its own personality.

I lent it a novel, filched from the ship's bookshop. It gave me great pleasure to see it, nestling above Pfiglzz's shoulder, absorbed in reading, one eye on the book, the other on the perambulations of his rotund charge.

Little by little the angel began to detach itself from Pfiglzz although it never lost sight of him. It hovered in the air, reading, halfway between the decks, while Pfiglzz did the rounds, or sat above the air vents, coming closer when the doctor seemed as if he was going to slip on the narrow steps, and came to his aid when Pfiglzz deliberately became mixed up in some complication, as for example the time when he got himself tangled up in the ropes of the capstan and would have been crushed to death had it not been for the prompt and expected intervention of the angel.

This physical detachment from the doctor's person gave me the opportunity to strike up a conversation with it, free from that uncomfortable, worthless presence, the fount of triviality. The angel was grateful to me for the novel; it talked to me about the plot with much discrimination and some enthusiasm. Within a few days the barrier of its angelic frostiness was broken and the angel began to confide in me.

It had been just as uncomfortable and startling for it as for ordinary mortals to have to pass at lightning speed from the sweet ethereal regions, where it had been charged to watch Pfiglzz from afar, without any show of devotion or excessive attention, down to this shabby, opaque world of gross matter wherein it now floated.

It felt disturbed by the stares and by the allusions cast in its direction. At first it had had the illusion that since it made so little noise, gliding lightly by, nobody would take any notice of it. It was soon disabused. It became one of the most notable and popular figures in the city. As luck would have it some kind of religious feeling in the air, some residual fear of the supernatural, prevented this popularity from giving rise to vulgar excesses or bedlam among the young blades. People would see it, remark on the fact, smile at it, point at it with their finger, the papers would speculate about its origins, theologians would try to work out its name, among the lists of legions of archangels, angels and cherubims, the philosophers would strain to show that it did not exist, but all this never rose above a murmur, like the low, awed whispering in the nave when St Philomena rolled her eyes.

It was just that all this attention taken together increased the strain of the responsibility for Pfiglzz's physical well-being to the highest point. Previously, floating among the bright stars, it had merely cast the odd glance at its charge, or intervened now and then with a gentle hand, and deemed himself well satisfied with this discreet and relaxed vigilance, which is of course the way of all the other guardian angels.

But now it felt that everyone was observing it critically – and perhaps would go so far as to stone it – should the lightest scratch come to blemish the wrinkled body of Pfiglzz. And so they were days of tremendous anxiety in this ceaseless vigil, because of public opinion, so attentive to his art, so ferocious should it have the opportunity to censure.

One reason above all became pressing, a reason that the angel would not reveal but which I guessed at through its words. If anything should happen to Pfiglzz what would become of it, the angel? It would not be able to lend his services to another because this would mean competing with another hidden guardian angel and violating in the most reprehensible fashion the ethics of that body. Nor could it seek to influence the flow of events, doing good by chance here and there, completely overturning the laws of physics, the thrust of history or even the fate of all of us. This was all completely out of the question for it, and in its inmost being it felt the strongest inhibitions and constraints against such behaviour. So that all that remained to the angel in its opinion, should Pfiglzz die, was to stay there, fluttering back and forth over the strange city, closer to the seagulls and the sparrows on the rooftops than to men.

While it was talking to me it did not let Pfiglzz out of its sight as he strolled along the deck. From time to time it stopped talking, pricked up its ears, raised its head attentively lest Pfiglzz should find himself in some mischief and the angel be taken unawares... For Pfiglzz was exceedingly jealous of his guardian angel, and looked at me with loathing, searching for any excuse to send me packing.

In one conversation which ranged freely over many different subjects from the morning onwards, the angel hesitated at length, its eyes fixed on the horizon, then confessed to me, not without a struggle, that it cordially detested Pfiglzz, and that what caused it the most unhappiness, and was the most damnable of all the punishments, was to have to watch over that filthy rich scoundrel, obese and obtuse as he was, to have to put up with his presence, his feeble thoughts, his fits of humour, his whims and fancies, his half-baked legal savvy, his stock of specious wisdom and nice distinctions, his colossal egoism, his all too evident contempt for others and his flaunting of his wealth.

I let some days pass before I ventured a suggestion which made it rigid with horror. It discontinued its conversations with me, on various ingenious pretexts – an angel's pretexts – and began to hover over the deck, always a foot above the planks, going here and there, in the opposite direction to Pfiglzz, at whom on his perambulations it cast piercing glances.

At this time Pfiglzz had fallen in with a group of wealthy travellers, with whom he strolled around the boat, amidst much merry-making and outbursts of laughter. They were an ungracious gang of bullfighters, bankers, petty aristocracy and Anglo-Saxon millionaires. Pfiglzz enjoyed himself hugely showing off his guardian angel. He would go up to the gunwales and hurl himself from the highest side; he would be snatched from the very surface of the waters by the lightning swoop of the angel to the accompaniment of the loud cries of rejoicing from those idle ne'er-do-wells. At other times he would pass a long rope around his neck, tie it in a slip knot and jump from the highest bridge. Then would come the angel swiftly, holding him with one hand and untying the knot with the other.

Pfiglzz's party trick, the one which really dazzled his faint-hearted companions, was the one with the revolver. Pfiglzz put the loaded revolver against his temple, laughed mockingly and pulled the trigger. There was a huge bang, the flash of an azuline figure, and then an angelic hand which held between its thumb and forefinger the glowing, singed bullet from the explosion; Pfiglzz roared with laughter at the astonishment of the spectators, his cheek covered in black spots of gunpowder, showing off the bullet to the circle around him. An explosion of raucous laughter. Relief. And the angel, dignified, its arms crossed, nearby, alert, an expression of reproof and pity on its face.

At a point in the voyage, calling in at another port, yet more councillors, commanders and duchesses embarked and thus was the circle of Pfiglzz's admirers enlarged.

At the end of one afternoon this worthy decided, amidst much laughter and feeble jesting, to repeat his party piece yet again. The captain was there, leaning against the bow, puffing away at his pipe; I, too, having been dragged along by him. The guardian angel hovered over Pfiglzz, with a terribly sad expression on its face.

The Professor fished out from his pocket the fine nickel plated revolver, opened the lock, and passed it around so that everybody could see the barrel, loaded with new cartridges. The gun was passed from hand to hand, with cries from the duchesses who begged to be excused and indulgent nods of approval from the commanders. The captain and I indicated that we did not need to see it and the gun returned to the hands of Pfiglzz.

The latter cast a glance at the angel who was watching with great disdain from above. Pfiglzz rotated the barrel, smiling, with one eye on the weapon the other on his protector. I noticed that the face of the angel was hard, tense, and that the shadow of a strange foreboding seemed to pass over Pfiglzz's eyes. But he continued to laugh, a forced laugh, and the rotating barrel in his hands made a harsh noise like a roulette wheel going round. Around us everybody fell silent and held their breath in apprehension. The angel's expression gave a clue to the tremendous interior conflict which it was going through. Pfiglzz carried on with the game, pressing the revolver to his temple. He stopped laughing, screwed up his eyes; the gesture was too much for him and he gasped for breath. The angel's expression was stiff, set in stone, his unblinking gaze firmly on Pfiglzz. He hesitated, looked around him, saw the expectant faces, open mouths and narrowed eyes. And now he smiled crookedly, unconvincingly, his hand shook and his finger played unsteadily with the trigger.

Bang.

The bullet shattered the panel of the deck, taking with it a tangle of hair. Before Pfiglzz collapsed on the floor, like a stringless puppet, a stream of black blood spurted from his left temple. Bits of fatty matter were spattered all over the partition wall. The clamour of Pfiglzz's fall was accompanied by the shrieks of woe from the women and men. A large puddle of blood gathered there on the deck, with rivulets of blood running in all directions. A disorderly panic arose around the ridiculous mass of Pfiglzz, curled up on the floor, his head smashed to bits and flat on the deck, while his fat backside stuck up in the air supported by his heels and his arms bent up on either side.

The guardian angel in the midst of all the commotion remained calm, rigid, its hands resting on the rail of the bridge, its eyes averted from the turmoil below.

I saw that from one moment to the next its features and the corners of its mouth became wrinkled and that its hair, instead of its usual light blond, began to take on little by little a coppery hue.

Its wings were very slowly dissolving into the air and turning into an insubstantial, shadowy trace which was barely picked out by the indistinct, fluid lines which were rapidly melting into the same tints as the sky.

Its tunic lost its satiny sheen and hung down, floating limply in the breeze.

Its bare feet settled on the planks of the bridge with a soft thud, heavily, and the angel took its first steps half supporting itself on the bulkhead.

The tumult suddenly stopped and, rooted to the spot, everybody stared at it, their mouths open, the corpse of the fallen Pfiglzz forgotten for the moment, while it descended the ladder from the bridge, step by step.

Its heavy footsteps made the thin metal rattle.

Already on the deck the angel, by now very close to us, paused a while, staring at us blindly.

Then it made its way, still staggering, for the head of the gangway and disappeared from our sight, while the wooden steps reverberated against the hull in the laboured rhythm of its descent.

When the noises suddenly stopped we all rushed to the side of the boat.

There was nobody on the gangway. The sea was still and calm. Only the last plank was vibrating, almost imperceptibly.

Then the sun seemed to vanish at a stroke behind a cloud, so that it blended with the faintly red colour of the waters, which were turning almost carmine on top of the waves.

People shouted out loud, screamed and shivered…

It often happens on these stops,' observed the captain, putting out his pipe. 'They say it's the refraction of the air.'

On the following day the body of Pfiglzz was consigned to the sea, from a gangplank, with all due honour. Suitably dressed, and after the orchestra had played a military march with funeral harmonies, the captain gave a brief peroration, humdrum, as the occasion required, before the gangplank was tilted towards the sea. There were prayers, and other business…

When it was all finished I talked to the captain about what had happened. He said to me: 'So many suicides among these big shots; there's no doubt that money doesn't buy happiness…'

'And the angel, what do you say about the angel?' I asked him.

'What angel? What's all this nonsense about the angel? I know nothing of any angel,' he replied.

And he headed off, the happy sound of his steps on the deck drowning out my bewilderment.